STRIKE ZONE

A STANDALONE, ENEMIES-TO-LOVERS, SPORT
ROMANTIC COMEDY.

EVA HAINING

COPYRIGHT

ALSO BY EVA HAINING

MANHATTAN KNIGHTS SERIES

FLAWLESS

RELENTLESS

ENDLESS

COMPLETE MANHATTAN KNIGHTS SERIES BOX SET

MUSTANG RANCH SERIES

MUSTANG DADDY

MUSTANG BUCK

MUSTANG HOLLYWOOD

MUSTANG RANCH BOOKS 1-3 BOX SET

MUSTANG CHRISTMAS

MUSTANG BELLE

MUSTANG PLAYER

HALL OF FAME SERIES

FUMBLE

A VERY FUMBLING MERRY CHRISTMAS

INTERCEPTION

SCREWBALL

STRIKE ZONE

STANDALONES

WILD RUGGED DADDY

A CHRISTMAS TO REMEMBER

THE CARDINAL BROTHERHOOD (EVA HAINING WRITING AS E.L.HAINING)

THE CARDINAL BROTHERHOOD BOOKS 1&2 BOX SET

LUXURE

KADEDUS

GIER

CRAOS

ABOUT THE AUTHOR

I'm happiest when wandering through the uncharted territory of my imagination. You'll find me curled up with my laptop, browsing the books at the local library or enjoying the smell of a new book, taking great delight in cracking the spine and writing in the margins!

I'm a native Scot but live in Texas with my husband, two kids, and a whizzy little fur baby with the most ridiculous ears. I first fell in love with British literature while majoring in Linguistics, 17th Century Poetry, and Shakespeare at University. I'm an avid reader and life-long notebook hoarder. In 2014, I finally put my extensive collection to good use and started writing my first novel. Previously traditionally published under a pen name, I decided to branch out on my own and lend my name to my full back catalogue!

I write contemporary romance with all the feels, sports rom-coms and paranormal romance, and I am currently working on some other exciting new projects.

SOCIAL MEDIA

www.instagram.com/evahainingauthor
www.facebook.com/evahainingauthor
www.twitter.com/evahaining
www.amazon.com/author/evahaining
www.bookbub.com/profile/eva-haining
https://www.goodreads.com/author/show/20271110.Eva_Haining
https://tiktok.com/@evahainingauthor
http://www.evahaining.com/newsletter
www.evahaining.com

ONE YEAR AGO

WEDDINGS ARE the perfect place to find a one-night stand brides-maid, and tonight I have my sights on someone specific—Diana Lexington—sister of the bride and raven-haired bombshell. I've been hounding my now-married best friend to give me her number for months.

She looks incredible in a figure-hugging, floor-length lavender dress. The only distasteful accessory she's sporting is on her arm—some douchebag date with shifty eyes. He looks like he's waiting for the FBI to crash the reception and cart him off to the slammer. He can't be her type. Diana is the reigning women's UFC champion with a body that could make a grown man beg—*this* grown man, to be specific. She's stunning, and my cock is twitching at the sight of her. Unfortunately, she's letting herself be corralled around the room by some schmuck who doesn't deserve her. Not that I do either, but watching the way she moves, I know we'd have insanely hot sex.

"You're drooling, bro." Anders, my best friend and groom, slings his arm over my shoulder with a smug grin on his face. "She has a date. Don't make me have to back you up in a fight with that guy. It would be sad how quickly you knock him out."

A wry grin tugs at the corner of my lips at the thought of it, and a chuckle escapes my chest. "Right? Who the fuck is he anyway?"

"I think his name is Anthony. She's pretty cloak-and-dagger about the whole thing."

"He looks like a total douche nozzle. What does she see in him?"

"Maybe he's rocking some major hardware."

"I just threw up in my own mouth. Thanks for that."

Anders slaps me on the back. "Consider it a wedding gift... on my wedding day. Now, for the love of God, go and chat up one of the single ladies here tonight. Dee is off limits."

"Why would you say that to me? Now, I want her more. Look at her, she's hotter than a blow job in a sauna."

"I'm leaving now. My new wife is ready to be swept off her feet and out of that dress. It's going to look so much better on the floor of our suite."

"I hate you." I pull him in for a bro hug. "I also love you, Anders. I can't believe you've got a ball and chain. Fuck me. Never thought I'd see the day."

"Me either, but when the right woman finds you, it's not a choice. It's a compulsion." He stares off into the distance, and I follow his gaze to where his new wife, Brooke, is laughing and joking with her sister—the southpaw spitfire. "I'd crawl through broken glass to the ends of the earth for that woman."

"No woman is that good a lay, but I wouldn't mind being proven wrong by your new sister-in-law. She's a goddess."

"Keep it in your pants, Linc."

"Yes, sir." As I watch Diana laughing with her sister, I can't help wondering why she came here with a date. I would've blown her fucking mind tonight—still would if she gave me half a chance.

CHAPTER ONE
LINC

PRESENT DAY

"NO PRESSURE, Linc, but if you don't hit this, we're not going to win the World Series." Why do people start a sentence with the phrase, 'no pressure?' It has the opposite effect. They may as well say, 'just to heap the pressure on... blah-fucking-blah.'

"And here I thought I could phone it in at this point."

"You've got this, bro." My best friend and teammate, Anders Verbeck, was the one under pressure this time last year when his pitching was the difference between a World Series win and a crushing defeat. Tonight, it's my turn.

The bases are loaded, and I'm the last up to bat. The smell of freshly cut grass is sorely lacking as I step up to the plate.

Astroturf isn't great for bringing back fond childhood memories. I'm slightly disturbed by the scents that comfort me in these major moments. Countless months of sweaty funk in my helmet and the dirt that's accumulated on the grip of my bat—it's nasty—like a jock-strap with toe-jam mixed in. It's the smell of success.

I really wish my jockstrap hadn't just come to mind. I need to be laser-focused for the team, but now all I can think of is how sweaty my balls feel at this historical moment in my career. I'll be sure to leave this out when I write my memoirs years from now.

"Swing and a miss. Feeling the pressure, Nash?" The Red Sox catcher has a shit-eating grin on his face through that grill of his.

"Just warming up. I'd hate to just rip victory straight out of your hand. It'll be better with some dramatic effect."

"Striking out and losing will definitely be dramatic, pretty boy."

Shit. The second pitch flies past me as my bat connects with nothing but air. I can't be the guy who loses the World Series. For starters, Anders will never let me live it down. He was the man who rose to the occasion last year and laughed in the face of pressure.

I adjust my grip and stance, readying myself for the final pitch. It's now or never, at least for this season. Everything slows down—the roar of the crowd and the ball as it leaves the pitcher's hand. I can see it hurtling toward me at close to a hundred miles an hour, but I know exactly where to position my bat.

The ball connects... CRACK! Disappointment ripples through the crowd and is reflected in the dugout, but it's not the faces of my teammates because I just hit a motherfucking home run! Anders comes barreling toward me, full tilt, knocking me on my ass before I get a chance to run the bases.

"You fucking did it, bro."

"Not yet, I haven't. I still need to take my lap of victory."

"Shit!" He rolls off me, laughing his ass off as the rest of the team bounces on the sidelines, welcoming our teammates to home plate as they complete their runs. Before I begin mine, I take great pleasure in turning to the catcher as he squats on the ground with his head in his hands.

"Tough break... pretty boy. Make sure to watch my home run, just so it really sinks in that you lost."

"Fuck off, Nash."

"Parting is such sweet sorrow. Kiss goodbye to the World Series trophy and pucker up for my winning ass." I give him a shit-eating grin and take off at a jog as the crowd goes wild. My heart is pounding so hard I'm a little concerned it might burst right out of my chest before I slide into home plate. I didn't think anything could top winning last year, but this moment right here is the single greatest of my life. One swing of my bat stood between us and victory. Me. *Lincoln-fucking-Nash.*

I take it slow, throwing my hands in the air as I jog the bases. I can't hear myself think over the roar of the Yankees fans celebrating. Tens of thousands of New Yorkers cheering for us—for me. We made this season work, but in the end, it came down to me. One fucking hit of the ball. Talk about pressure. I drop my head back, staring up to the heavens as I round third base.

"If you're up there, Pops, I know that was all you on the last hit. Thanks." My grandfather was the only father figure I had growing up and a baseball nut. He'd have loved seeing me make the major leagues.

The entire team is waiting for me at home plate in a collective huddle of sheer joy, bouncing so high it seems superhuman somehow. Chanting my name, they welcome me with open arms, shouting obscenities as words of congratulations.

"Fucking legend!"

"You are the shit, my friend."

"Swing that dick, brother. You fucking did it!"

"Lincoln-fucking-Nash."

"World Series-winning motherfucker."

"I'd drop to my knees and blow you right now, bro." That one catches me off guard as I run into the arms of my teammates.

"Easy, Aymes, I'll have plenty of women lining up to do that tonight... because we just won the World Series!"

The tension that was coiled in every muscle of my body releases, replaced by a wave of elation and unadulterated delight. There was a moment there after the second strike when I thought I was going to lose it. Then I remembered I'm not a loser and knocked it out of the park—literally.

Anders finds his way to me, pulling me into a heartfelt embrace, slapping me on the back. "Way to go, bro. You didn't fuck it up."

"Is that your way of saying I'm a legend?"

He gives a hearty laugh. "If you need to label it. That was one hell of a hit."

"Damn straight."

Brooke comes running onto the field with all the other wives and girlfriends, and just for a second, a teeny, tiny part of me wishes I had someone to share this moment with. It didn't bother me last year when we won because I was swept up in a collective win. Today is personal, and for one dumbass second, I think it might be nice to have a hot girlfriend climb me like a jungle gym and throw her arms around my neck in congratulations.

It's short-lived.

I lose track of time as we lift the trophy, fireworks going off and music blaring through the speakers. The Red Sox and their fans are long gone, but the Yankees will be reveling long into the night. By the time we finally wander down the tunnel toward the locker room, I'm in a daze. Everyone slaps me on the back as they pass by, and for the first time in my career—heck, in my life—I feel worthy of the accolades I've accumulated over the years. I've been number one for a long time, but in the back of my mind, I've always questioned it, hearing my mom telling me I'd never amount to anything. Today, her voice has been overwhelmingly deadened. Snuffed out with certainty. Knocked out of the park with that final crack of my bat.

Gripping my bat tight, I let it swing back and forth at my side. I'll be framing it tomorrow. This is it. The highlight of my career—of my life. Parties galore, endorsements left and right, interviews with all the major networks are just a few of the perks coming my way over the next few weeks and months.

"Ready to celebrate?" Anders' voice cuts through my daydreaming as we enter the locker rooms, and I nestle my bat snug in my locker before stripping out of my ash-stained uniform and grabbing a towel for the showers.

"Where are you thinking?"

"Already got a message from Carter. VIP lounge at Viper is the team's if we want it."

"Fuck, yeah. I might invite a few friends to join us." As I step under the steaming hot flow of water, it soothes every aching muscle I didn't know I had until now.

Anders slams on the showerhead next to mine. "Would they be friends of the female persuasion?"

"Yeah. I plan on celebrating, bro."

"And one woman won't suffice?"

"I don't have a ball and chain. Why settle for one woman when many will be desperate to ride me like a bucking bronco after that last swing of the bat?"

"Thanks for the mental picture, or should I say, nightmare. You're not wrong about that hit. As a pitcher, I've no fucking idea how you got wood on that ball."

"Because I'm me."

"Fuck, your ego is never going to be the same again."

"Don't give me your shit, Anders. You upped your ballcap size after last year's winning pitch. If anything, you just have to point me to the right size in Lids now."

"Touché." He laughs as he reaches for his towel.

"I'm assuming your bride will be celebrating with us tonight?"

"Of course."

"I don't suppose she wants to invite that delectable sister of hers?"

"Dee would snap you like a twig, bro."

"But what a way to go." Just the thought of her makes my cock twitch. "Fine. What about her teammates?"

"Now, that I can probably swing. I'll ask Brooke to make a few calls."

"Sweet. I'm going to stop by my place and get changed. I'll meet you at Viper in an hour."

"Sounds good."

I slam my hand against the wall, restarting the shower. As everyone else filters out, I take a few moments to let the gravity of it all sink in before heading home. So many ridiculous thoughts flash through my mind—childhood moments, conversations with my grandfather, fights with my mom, the ever-present lack of a father, and the many teammates and coaches who've been there for me on this journey.

Tears well in my eyes, and I'm glad that I have water raining down on my face because even though no one is around to see it, I feel like a total pussy for crying. I allow myself ten seconds to be a pathetic idiot and feel the sadness that threatens to creep in on this amazing high. Then, I stomp it down like I always have and get ready for a night of celebration and debauchery.

I head back to my place for four things—a sharp suit, my World Series ring from last year—I didn't want to bring it today and jinx the game—cash, and condoms. Everything you need for a killer night, Nash style.

THE VIP LOUNGE at Viper doesn't disappoint, and neither does Anders' wife, Brooke. She delivers her entire women's baseball team, all hot and ready to party. The drinks are flowing, and it seems like every single twenty-something female in Manhattan wants to beg, borrow, and steal her way into this party.

I'm good with the ratio of men to women, the women having us outnumbered three to one, and when you take into consideration the guys like Anders who are married, then it changes dramatically. All the more for me.

Our friend, and the owner, Carter, congratulates me with a glass of my favorite whiskey and a clap on the back when I arrive.

"You won me a lot of money tonight, Linc. Killer hit, but did you have to wait till the last second?"

"I wanted it to be memorable. Edge-of-the-seat kind of stuff."

"Then you succeeded. Everything is on the house tonight, my friend. Enjoy. You deserve it. Just make sure you glove up."

"Yes, dad."

"Hey, I've seen and made too many questionable decisions over the years, and this place is packed with women who want to fuck you tonight."

"Yes, it is, and I plan to get names and numbers. You know me, man, I'm a people pleaser at heart."

He throws his head back in laughter. "Truly selfless, Linc. Just make sure your dick doesn't fall off, okay?"

"No such thing as overuse, Carter. I've got the stamina of a porn star."

"On that note, I'm going to go find a sharp implement to pierce my own eardrums. Enjoy the festivities, brother. Come visit Addi and me soon. Bring Anders and Brooke."

"Will do."

With an endless flow of drinks in hand, I find my way to the center of Brooke's teammates.

"Any of you ladies want to dance with me?" My ego is growing by the second as they swarm me, moving in one, gyrating, fluid collective of bodies. It's a twelve-year-old's wet dream. The bass is so loud it vibrates in my chest as I move to the music, closing my eyes and letting loose after a stressful season.

Arms, legs, breasts, and perfectly plump asses brush against me to the rhythm of the music. I have no idea who's at my back. Hell, I have no idea who most of these women are at this point in the evening, but I'm having a good time, and so are they.

Anders drags me aside at some point with Brooke tight at his side. "I'm out, bro. I'm drunk, and my wife's horny."

"Sure. Sure. Have fun."

"Dinner, Sunday? Our place."

"I'll be there."

He pats my jacket pocket where he knows I stash my condoms. "Just checking."

He disappears through the crowd with Brooke, and I'm left wondering why everyone is so concerned with my cock clothing tonight. I've never—and I mean never—fucked a woman without one. I have no intention of becoming a father by some random chick or catching anything that'll make my cock crusty.

As the hours pass and my teammates leave with their wives or girlfriends, the rest of us keep drinking. There are a few of Brooke's teammates who have real moves on the dance floor, and I'm a sucker for when they start dancing with each other, grinding and sliding their hands down each other's sides. Tonight might have to be a two-for-one kind of deal.

I sling back a few more drinks and have some laughs with them before I go in for the kill. With my best panty-melting smile, I lean in, brushing my lips against the leggy brunette's cheek. "Why don't the three of us take this party back to my place?"

She erupts into a full-on belly laugh, holding her stomach for a good thirty seconds before relaying my seemingly hilarious proposal to her friend. I watch the same reaction play out in stereo. I just won the World Series, and I'm easy on the eye, so is this really such a crazy idea? I've had threesomes before, and no one was laughing. I've never had a woman, let alone *two*, laugh in my face at the idea of sleeping with me. Eventually, they realize my balls have retreated inside my body cavity and may never return.

"I'm sorry. It's not funny, and it isn't you."

"Shit. You aren't using the it's-not-you-it's-me line, really?"

"In this case, it's the truth. You don't have the necessary equipment for us."

"What? You don't like a massive cock, great abs, and a tongue that never gets tired?"

"Cock is a big no. The tongue is enticing, but you're missing two major assets up top." She reaches over and grabs her friend's tits. "Sorry, Linc."

After a few too many whiskeys, I misread the signs, and the girl-on-girl action had zero interest in any involvement from me. They aren't friends, they're lovers. "Fuck me."

"No, thanks. That's kind of the point."

I can't help but laugh. "Bad word choice there. I must be really drunk. How did I miss that you two are a couple?"

"Maybe because you just won the World Series and are celebrating with a few... dozen drinks. And rightly so."

"You two are really fucking hot. Not going to lie, though, wish I'd set my sights on some of your less-hot friends now."

"Usually, I'd find a reason to call you a pig for reducing women to looks alone, but let's face it, my girlfriend is gorgeous." She turns and stares at her, all doe-eyed and adoring.

"Yes, she is, and so are you. God, happy couples make me sick."

"O-kay."

"I like being single. Is that so bad? I like the rush of meeting someone new, falling into bed together, and having wild, uninhibited, uncomplicated sex."

"Don't you ever want more?"

"Occasionally, and then I remember I'm young, hot, and not tied down to one woman."

"That's great until you meet the right woman. Then you'll want to be tied down." Her girlfriend has fire in her eyes that could melt the glass in my hand.

"You're making my cock twitch."

"On that note, I'm going to take my girlfriend home and do all the things you wish you could watch."

I physically have to adjust myself. "Not fair."

"Something tells me you'll be just fine without us. Congrats on the win. It was truly amazing."

"Thanks. I'm sure we'll see each other around. Have a good night knowing I'm so jealous my balls just turned green with envy."

"Never say that to a woman you want to sleep with. Just a friendly word of advice."

"You know, I thought that the second it came out of my mouth. Duly noted on my list of phrases never to pass my lips again."

As they walk out hand in hand, I can't help that small pang of longing I felt earlier when everyone was celebrating with their loved ones. Three eager women are quick to take their place next to me, but to be honest, I'm sort of over it for the night. I hate to admit that I'd like to celebrate with someone who knows and understands what this achievement means to me. This calls for some no strings, no feelings but familiar fucking. One of my regular drunk dials. I know just who to call. Candy.

A quick text, and she's on her way to my place.

I quickly down the rest of my drink, say goodnight to the women who are actually disappointed I don't want to take them home, and head outside to grab a cab back to my place. When the concierge calls to tell me my friend has arrived, I'm a block away and give him the green light to send her up to my place with the spare key.

She doesn't wait for me to make herself at home. By the time I get up to my penthouse and see her pouring two glasses of wine, she's a sight for sore eyes. Six-inch heels shape her already incredibly long legs that disappear beneath the hem of her coat. "Hey, Linc. I'm glad you called. I was watching the game."

"I'm going to stop you there. We can talk about my Hall of Fame worthy win later. Right now, you're going to lose your clothes, and I'll do what I do best."

"And what would that be?" she asks with a knowing grin.

"Playing your body like a fiddle. I have some of that manuka honey you like for a sore throat in the bathroom cabinet because I plan on making you scream till you're hoarse."

She unbuttons her coat and lets it drop off her shoulders, puddling on the floor at her feet. She's wearing nothing but lingerie, and even that's minimal—my favorite kind.

"Am I overdressed?" Running her hand down her stomach, her eyes find mine, full of dark desire.

"Definitely. Come over here, so I can take those panties off... with my teeth." And just like that, everything else is forgotten, at least for the next few hours.

"JESUS CHRIST, now I have to scrub my eyes with bleach."

My brain has a heartbeat of its own this morning. Is it even morning? "Anders? What are you doing here?"

"Can you pull up the sheets, bro? You're showing your brain." It takes me a few seconds to realize what he's talking about. My morning wood is on display. He's seen it all before, but I grab the sheets so he doesn't feel inadequate in the presence of my super-human cock.

"What's up? I thought you'd be nursing a hangover with your lady love this weekend."

"I would be, but you didn't answer your fucking phone yesterday, and then you didn't show up for dinner tonight. Brooke being the caring woman she is, wouldn't give me a fucking break until I came over to check you hadn't sexed yourself to death or died in a pool of your own vomit from alcohol poisoning. Mission accomplished."

"Your wife is one of the good ones. You did the right thing marrying her."

"Yeah, and she made you a kickass dinner that's now in the trash, and I'm over here instead of inside her because you can't get your act together. I'm going to get you one of those emergency buttons that old people who live alone have. Then if you're choking on your own vomit, you can yank it, and I'll try to get over before you croak."

"You're a heartless motherfucker sometimes."

"What am I being heartless about? You've been partying for days. Am I wrong? Do I even want to know who you've been fucking?"

"Legs eleven. Candy. God, she's got a mouth on her like a vacuum cleaner. She can suck like..."

"Please, for the love of God, stop talking. And for Christ's sake, pull the fucking sheet up more. You're still showing your one-eyed rooster." I fumble around for my sweats on the floor.

"And Candy, really? She's a bunny boiler in the making."

"No, she's not. She detests the idea of commitment. She's the perfect lay."

"If you believe that for a second, you're a bigger idiot than I know you to be. I'm telling you, you're going to pull back the shower curtain one day, and she's going to go all *Psycho* on you with the knife."

"But the sex, bro. The sex." I shrug into my sweats and go in search of a hoodie in my closet. He said I missed dinner.

"I'm not going home empty-handed. You're coming over, if only to show Brooke that you're alive and well, even if you've lost your mind. Then you can drink and fuck all night long, having satisfied my wife's requirements."

"Oh, I didn't realize that's what you meant. If Brooke wants to drink and fuck me..."

"Finish that sentence, and you die."

"I'm just messing with you, bro."

"Yeah, and if you finish that sentence... You. Die."

"Geez. You used to have more of a sense of humor about women."

"None of them were my wife. Brooke is a no-go when it comes to any form of jokes or jibes or info on our sex life."

"Buzzkill."

"Just grab your keys."

"What day is it?"

"Are you serious?"

"Yes. And when did we arrange dinner? I thought it was morning. Fuck. What time is it?"

"Jesus, you've completely lost the plot. It's Sunday. It's nine o'clock. When I left the club after we won, I told you to come for dinner tonight. I texted you yesterday to come over at six. Have you seriously been with Candy all that time?"

"What better way to celebrate?"

"I don't know, maybe with your teammates and friends."

"You're just jealous that your meaningless sex days are behind you."

"Hell, no. I'm done and happy about it."

"Fine, then mind your business and let me enjoy a few days of fucking Candy."

"Why her? You had the entire women's baseball team eating out the palm of your hand, grinding on your junk, and you went home with her. I didn't even think she was there."

"She wasn't. It's a story."

"What the fuck, bro? You couldn't seal the deal? One-hit wonder that day." He amuses himself, and as much as I want to keep it to myself, knowing he'll give me shit for it, I tell him about my drunken radar misfiring, leaving me with the only women in the room who didn't want to sleep with me.

"*Holy shit!* That's priceless." He can't contain his side-splitting hysterics. "How drunk were you? Lincoln Nash managed to hit on the only women who don't enjoy a stable diet of cock. Fucking brilliant."

"Laugh it up, Chuckles. It was totally worth it. I couldn't be assed picking up someone new, and when I got home, Candy was here, ready and waiting in her lingerie."

"She came over in her underwear?"

"Yep. Coat, heels, and some sexy almost non-existent lingerie. She might be the mad hatter, but, fuck, does she look good in black-lace panties."

"Nice."

"Yeah. Who's crazy now?" I grab my keys, satisfied by the dumb-struck expression on Anders' face. He may have the perfect wife, but I've got close to naked hookups on speed dial. That's pretty great.

Right?

CHAPTER TWO
DIANA

TRAIN. Sleep. Train. Sleep. It's all I do in the months leading up to a fight. I live and breathe the cage. I can love it and hate it in equal measure on any given day. Today is tipping the scale on the why-do-I-do-this-to-myself career crisis. Not because I'm subpar, in fact, it's the opposite. I'm the reigning UFC bantamweight champion and most decorated female fighter of all time. What's the saying? Heavy is the head that wears the crown. For me, heavy is the waist that wears the belt.

My mom had dreams of watching me dance in *Swan Lake* or *The Nutcracker* when I was five. I had balance and could move around the floor with ease, but grace was something that eluded me.

I realized in the schoolyard that I was a fighter. If someone was being picked on—even if I didn't know them from Adam—I stepped in to fight in their corner. I was good at it. Great, actually. From then on, I knew I was destined for a sweaty old gym. No frills or pretty pink tutus for me—I wanted punchbags and a gumshield. I originally thought boxing was the way to go, but it didn't quite sate my hunger, so I started to look at other fighting styles. Karate was too rigid, but I explored all different kinds of martial arts and started using the pieces I liked, creating a Frankenstein style that worked for me.

When I found my stride and a coach who believed in my talent, MMA came knocking, and I gladly opened the door, much to my mother's distaste. My father, however, felt like I transformed into the son he never had. I'm not super feminine, so I guess it didn't bother me that much when he started calling me Dee instead of Diana. I still like guys, and I don't have junk in my pants, but I could take on an average dude in a bar and win a fight.

Over time, everyone started calling me Dee, and when I was a kid, I thought nothing of it, but looking back now, it's as if my femininity was taken away that day. That sounds dumb, which is why I answer to anything, but over the years, I guess I've started to see myself the way others perceive me. Harsh. Tough. A bitch on wheels. It matches my chosen profession, and I've just leaned into the stereotype.

In truth, my mom didn't luck out with either of her daughters. Brooke is a professional baseball player, not exactly a prima ballerina. She's more girly than me and already married. I don't think Mom is holding out much hope for me. After every fight, she'll come see me when my face is swollen and I'm covered in bruises. She'll do the same thing every time—sigh and dab salve on my wounds before telling me I'm too pretty to mess up my face like this. Then she'll ask me about my sex life during recuperation and recommend the best vibrators on the market. Every time, I explain that she already sent me the best seller and it still works just fine—better than fine.

I love my mom, but she's wildly inappropriate. Where Brooke gets uncomfortable, I've learned to embrace the weird. Pee into the wind. Give as good as I get. If Mom tells me some scarring detail about her and my dad, I'll counter with a detail about the last guy I dated. Something about his ginormous cock or how he cried during sex, and it just totally put me off. Or that he wanted me to bitch-slap him as he came. Thank God that has never happened, but it makes her laugh, and heads her off at the pass. It's fucked-up, but this family dynamic works for us.

Today, if my life were a movie, it would be time for a *Rocky* montage. I'm feeling downtrodden like I don't have the grit to dig deep and find the strength I need to win this thing. Some inspirational eighties power ballads, a crop-top, and sweat bands are required. I need to find a log to push in the snow, but it's not snowing in New York, and I live in an apartment, so a random log might be difficult to find. A run in Central Park before working out in a gym that's way too nice for a montage moment, but it will have to do. I also have zero bruises right now, and my hair looks oddly amazing this morning. As I stare at myself in the mirror while I brush my teeth, I look nothing like an MMA fighter. There's something unsettling about that for me. I appear—feminine.

There's a hollowness to my stare. Last night, I found out that my 'boyfriend'—in the very loosest sense of the word—is *not* single. He's now my *ex*-whatever-he-was. I'm not into serious relationships, but I hate to admit that I let my guard down a little with him. He seemed like one of the good guys, and we'd been together quietly for almost a year. I thought he wanted to keep our relationship out of the limelight, but he was just trying to cover his ass. Clearly, my judgment leaves a lot to be desired. If it weren't for an aptly timed phone call while he was in the shower, I'd be none the wiser.

The screen lit up with her picture—the two of them on their wedding day. I didn't answer. She deserves to know what a scumbag he is, but I'm not going to be the one to explode their marriage. He'll do it in the end. Guys like him always do. He'll get caught with some other unsuspecting woman. One thing's for sure, I'm not the first, and I won't be the last of his secret flings.

I kicked him out with his clothes in hand and his naked ass on display for my neighbors, should they have been unfortunate enough to be in the hallway at the time.

He tried to placate me with 'I love you,' 'I'm going to leave her,' and 'I was going to tell you.' I've always prided myself on the fact that I'd *never* sleep with a married man. There's nothing magical about my vagina. I'm the first to admit it isn't worth ruining a marriage over, and I hate that he's made me feel dirty. So, today I find myself staring at my reflection in the mirror and wondering who the unfamiliar woman is staring back at me.

When I'm done gawking at myself in the mirror like a vain Valley girl, I slip on my running shoes, put in my AirPods, and set up my music for a five-mile run that will end at the gym. The temperature is beginning to drop in Manhattan—crisp and perfect for running. The concrete jungle is buzzing with suits swarming as they make their way to the boxes they spend their days in, chasing dollars. I don't know how they do it. I honestly think I'd lose my mind if I had to sit behind a desk day in and day out all week.

I bob and weave through the crowd, pounding the pavement, warming my muscles, hitting my stride just as I hit the entrance to the park. That's the amazing thing about Manhattan, one minute you're in a bustling metropolis of skyscrapers, and the next, you're transported into Narnia—a wondrous forest of stunning green and tranquil vistas with much to explore and enjoy.

This is where I do my best thinking when I run, focusing on the beat of the music and my heart. It's amazing what a lungful of oxygen can do to clear your head and let your mind work without being clouded by menial tasks that don't matter.

By the time I've finished my run and made my way to the gym on the Upper East Side, I've stomped down the guilt my ex left me with, and my coach is waiting, ready to ride my ass.

"Hey, Graham."

"Sorry, sweetie, the Miss America contest is down the street. This is a gym for serious people to do serious shit like fight in Vegas."

"I just ran five miles."

"With your crown on? Quite an achievement, I'm sure." His gravelly, sarcastic tone is particularly annoying today. Mostly because I knew I looked different this morning, like finding out Anthony was married fundamentally changed something about me. There was a shift in the universe, and now I look different. My edge is gone, and I'm nothing but a little girl left wondering what went so wrong.

"Shut the fuck up, Gray. I get it. I look weird today. I'm all fresh-faced and shit. I wasn't trying to look half-decent for a change, I just sort of woke up this way."

"Oh, how hard it must be to be you, princess. Wait while I grab a handkerchief and dab my tears for your anguish."

"Do you have to be such an asshole?"

"Are you here to train or be like every other woman on the planet?"

"You know the answer to that. I'm the least looks-obsessed woman you'll ever meet. Just give me a few rounds with a sparring partner, and it'll knock the glow right out of me."

"Damn right it will."

"Brenda! Get over here and warm up for a workout with Dee." Of course, he shouts for the only woman who outweighs me in the gym. I can still kick her ass, but she packs one hell of a punch. Her hands are huge, making her fist almost the size of my face. It's also a little disconcerting that her voice is a good octave below mine and possibly lower than Gray's.

I strap on my favorite martial arts gloves. They're less restrictive than boxing gloves but give enough protection during training so I don't go into a fight with open wounds or a black eye. Brenda works me hard, but she's too slow to really tax me. She has some powerful hits, but I can dodge ninety percent of them.

With only two weeks until my next fight in Vegas, I'm amped up and hyperaware of every little thing. If a muscle, a punch, or a kick is ever so slightly off, I feel it in every fiber of my being.

Gray spends most of today's session riding me about every move. It would seem I can't do anything right. I knew there was something off this morning. How could there not be after last night's epic fuck-fest of a breakup? As a fighter, you get a feeling—something you can't quite put your finger on or explain—when you're off your game. It could be anything. Balance isn't quite right. Spatial awareness is out by a fraction of an inch. Timing is out by half a second. Any one of these things could end with you hugging the mat with your opponent's sweaty foot on your mouth. It's disgusting and humiliating.

"You're fighting like a princess today. It's embarrassing to watch, Dee. I think we should just call it a day and start over tomorrow."

"I can work on the speed bag for a while. I've only got two weeks before Vegas, I don't have time to waste."

He wraps his arm around my shoulder, pulling me tight to his side. "It's safer that you don't..." he says in his thick New Jersey brogue, "... for all of us. We've all got a lot riding on this fight, and if you knock yourself out with a speed bag, we'll never live it down." A playful smirk tugs at the corner of his lips.

"I hate you right now. Mostly because you're right." He responds with a hearty laugh.

"Everyone has off days. Go home, relax, and we'll pick it up in the morning."

"Sure."

I grab a bottle of water and walk home, beating myself up for letting that lying, cheating son of a bitch get in my head today. I don't want to give him one more second of space or energy in my life. Tomorrow is another day, and all I can do is not let myself get worked up and thrown off by an asshole like Anthony. That motherfucker will not drag me under. I have a title to defend.

When I get home and wash off the stink of the gym, I curl up on the couch with reruns of *Friends* and call my sister, Brooke.

"Hey, sis. How's married life?"

"Great."

"How's the house now that there's three of you living there?"

"What are you talking about?"

"You, Anders, and his newly inflated ego. Him and that friend of his lifting the trophy for the second year in a row. As a Yankees fan, I was jumping for joy, but we're never going to hear the end of this at

Thanksgiving dinner. And, that muppet of a best friend of his must be drowning in pussy right now. That home run was impressive as hell, but I'm so glad we didn't make the beast with two backs at your wedding."

"First off, eww. Second, if he's so *impressive*, why are you glad you didn't sleep with him? And three, why do you care if he's drowning in pussy?"

"I don't. You're hearing hooves and thinking zebras rather than horses."

"What?"

"You're reading too much into it. He's hot, but he is a jackass."

"You don't even know him. He's a good guy. We've all had our slutty moments, you and I included. You seem to have some preconceived ideas about Linc, and I'd think you more than most would understand how wrong people can be when they assume stuff about you."

"Oh, yeah, because I'm the crazy fighter chick, so I must understand his pathological need to fuck everything that moves. You're clutching at straws, Brooke."

"Did you wake up on the wrong side of the bed today or something? You're in such a bad mood."

"What tipped you off? My sarcasm dripping through the phone or the disdain I have for all men?"

"Whoa, that just took a turn. Talk." I dug a hole for myself by running my mouth.

"Bad week. Ex-whatever the hell the guy I was seeing could be called. And, I'm two weeks away from my next fight, and training today was like a teenage growth spurt. You know what I mean? When you grew an inch and had to figure out your center of gravity and spatial awareness all over again. It was embarrassing. Gray sent me home early."

"We'll come back to the ex-guy later. Whoever he is, he's a dipshit if he let you go, and we don't need to waste any time on him before a big fight. Now, talk to me about the training issues. Are you PMSing?"

"No."

"Fuck. Are you pregnant by the ex?"

"Seriously? Yes, I'm with child, Brooke. That's exactly what's wrong. I went to training pregnant and let myself get my ass kicked, including my tiny peanut of a fetus being beat black and blue. What's wrong with you? No, I'm not pregnant."

"You're cranky as hell. It's definitely a hormonal issue." She's probably right. Sometimes my period goes a little haywire when I'm training heavily in the lead-up to a fight. This is the ugly side of women's UFC that men don't have to deal with. But I'm also just fucking angry—at the world, at men, at Anthony, and most of all, at myself.

"With you guys doing a victory tour as the World Series champions, will you still be able to fly out to Vegas for my fight? After today, I could use some friendly faces in the crowd. I'm getting too into my own head."

"Of course. Anders and I have been planning on coming for months, regardless of whether they won or lost. Can I invite Linc too? I know you seem to really dislike him, but he loves UFC. He's actually a huge fan of yours. His love of Dee Lex predates me stumbling into Anders' life."

"Why would you tell me that?"

"What?"

"That he's a total fanboy."

"I thought it might soften you a little toward him. He's going to be around. I'm married to his best friend. I want you two to get along."

"Fine, but you have to promise you won't let me sleep with him."

"What? You said you were happy you didn't sleep with him at my wedding, and two minutes ago you called him a jackass."

"Yeah, but let's face it, he's stupid hot. It's not even funny how hot that man is. The only reason I avoided the horizontal mambo with him at your wedding was because I had a date. A sexy date who still wasn't even half as hot as Lincoln Nash. One smile from him and the right number of shots after a win in the cage, and I'd lose my panties quicker than a whore in the back seat of a Mercedes Benz."

"Nice, sis. He's easy on the eye, but if you don't like his personality, isn't that a turn-off?"

"Just promise me. It'll be your fault if I get naked with him. If I lose, I might succumb to commiserating with him, specifically *because* I don't like his personality. And if I win, I'll want to jump him now that I know he's a fanboy. Do you have any idea how hot the sex with him would be with the upper hand like that? I could ride his face all night long."

"I'm ignoring that last part because it's so disturbing... I just can't even. There will be no succumbing. You won't lose. One off day of training isn't the harbinger of doom. Don't be a drama llama."

"Brenda straight up kicked my ass. That never happens. I'm not going to lie, it rattled me."

"Well, stop letting it. Do you want me to come and train with you tomorrow? We can go for a run, and then I'll just be ringside for moral support."

"You mean you don't want to spar with me?"

"Fuck, no! I love you, but I don't have a death wish. Unless I'm allowed to bring my bat in the ring, I'm staying firmly on the outside of the ropes."

"One round. I'll give you a thousand bucks to go one round with me." I'm grinning ear to ear, unable to mask the laughter in my voice.

"I wouldn't do it for a million. I'm too pretty to take a fist to the face."

"God, you're such a princess."

"I don't care!"

"Fine."

"Is that Anders I hear in the background?"

"Yeah."

"Can you put him on? I want to say congrats." The phone

exchanges hands and Anders' low tones replace my sister on the other end.

"Hey, girl."

"Hey, bro. Congratulations on the World Series win. What a game. You guys had to keep us on the edge of our seats until the very last hit."

"We got there in the end. I'm looking forward to getting a break in Vegas, and I'll be putting my money on you for the win, so don't let me down."

"No pressure then. Thanks, brother."

"You thrive under pressure. And FYI, I'm bringing Linc... you know you want him. I'll just keep him on a leash until you realize it for yourself."

"You baseball boys are so sure of yourselves."

"With good reason. Just ask your sister. She has no complaints."

"Can you put her back on the phone, please?"

"Sure, but seriously Dee, don't sweat a bad training session. We all have them. It's not the end of the world. You're an amazing MMA fighter at the top of your game."

"Tomorrow is another day. I'll figure it out. Thanks for the vote of confidence."

"No problem." He hands the phone back to Brooke who's so loved-up and happy it makes me want to vomit. I actually feel a little seedy.

"Isn't he just the best?"

"Yep. You're a lucky bitch." I'm truly pleased my sister has found her happily ever after, but today isn't the day to shove it in my face. "I'm destined for spinsterhood. I'm sorry, but you got the last good one. They're all fuckwits and liars. Besides, guys don't want a woman who can kick their ass." I suppose that's not strictly true. Married men apparently want me as their dirty little secret on the side.

"Some guys are into that shit."

"Not the kind I want to hitch my wagon to."

"I bet Linc could give you a run for your money."

"Stop! He's a roll-in-the-hay kind of guy, *not* the forever man."

"You're so judgmental, Dee. No wonder you haven't found the one yet. If you won't give someone a chance to impress you, how do you expect to find someone?"

I'm not in the mood for Dr. Phil tonight. Brooke knows nothing about my recent train wreck of a relationship. She's so damn happy, and I don't want to witness pity in her eyes for me.

"I've given more chances than you know. Trust me, I could use a break from all that. I'll see you in the morning at Central Park. Meet me at Strawberry Fields. Five o'clock." It's not an eloquent change of subject, but it'll do.

"See you then. Try not to be a grump tomorrow. Go play with that vibrator Mom thought was a good stocking stuffer for us last year. Matching vibrators. Only our mom, right?"

"She's mental, but I wouldn't trade her for some stuck-up, out-of-touch mom with a stick up her ass."

"Night, sis."

"Night, Brooke, and thanks for the pep talk."

"You're welcome."

As I hang up the phone, I know she's a better sister than I deserve right now. I'm like a bear with a sore head, blowing everything out of proportion. Hopefully, I'll feel better after a good night's sleep, and I won't get my ass handed to me on a platter tomorrow. Now isn't the time to hit a slump. There's too much riding on Vegas—entirely too much.

There's a part of me—I don't want to acknowledge—that knows Anthony will be watching the fight, probably with his wife, and I want him to see that I'm not a woman you fuck over. It shouldn't bother me, but it does. I pride myself on being a strong, independent woman, and he reduced me to a sordid affair. How dare he drag me down to his level.

By the time I finally fall asleep, it's fitful at best, and when I wake to my obnoxious alarm, the body aches of my session with Brenda yesterday are a stark reminder of the hits I'm taking this week—in and out of the ring. Gritty determination is all that propels me from my bed. If there's one thing I can say for myself, it's this—I didn't become a UFC champion by luck.

Diana Lexington isn't a quitter.

I am a machine.

I'm *not* a quitter.

CHAPTER THREE
LINC

THE UNIVERSE HAS a way of bringing you back down to earth with a bang when you soar too high. The first week after the win was phenomenal—partying, press, and a real sense of accomplishment. There's something about a team who wins championships together in any sport—a dynamic that's forged in fire. When you pull off the feat a second time, that bond becomes life-long. All these guys have become my brothers, and we had an amazing week celebrating.

This week, however, was a whole different ball game. I was asked if I'd make an appearance at my old high school. It's been a long time since I've been back, so I figured how bad could it be?

The answer was a sharp slap in the face. It was bad. Not the school event—it was fun. Most of these kids come from the same background as me and suffer from the same limitations that my mom tried to impose on me. Poverty and desperation are a recipe for mediocrity for most of the population of this town, but for me, it was the catalyst to get me to the major leagues.

I convinced Anders to tag along, which was great when I strolled in as the World Series high school alum, being cheered and heralded as the biggest star ever to walk the halls. Now that we're standing outside my mom's place, I wish I'd come alone.

"Is this where you grew up?"

"Yeah. When I signed with the Yankees, I offered to buy my mom a house and take care of all her expenses, but apparently, she hates me enough not to want my money."

"Then not to be insensitive, but why are we here?"

"Because she's my mom." My mom always hated that I wanted to play baseball professionally. The kid in me still wants her approval, and even though she wasn't forthcoming with praise after last year's win, I'm hoping this year is different. I hit the winning shot. Maybe now she'll understand and find it in her heart to be proud of me.

I gingerly rap my knuckles on the flimsy door, waiting at the bottom of the makeshift front stoop. I didn't think to check if she'd be home or not, assuming she still works the same shifts as always. The second I hear her shuffling around inside, my heart drops into my stomach, and as the door swings open, I'm no longer the World Series-winning baseball star, Lincoln Nash.

"What are you doing here, and who the hell is he?" she says, pointing at Anders.

Her voice is ice water trickling down my spine, paralyzing me as I take in the sight of her never-changing appearance.

"I suppose you want to come in?"

As I cross the threshold, it's as if I'm being dragged kicking and screaming against my will through a portal in time, and suddenly, Anders is no longer behind me, and when I catch sight of myself in the crusty old mirror on the counter, I'm seventeen again.

"WHY ARE you wasting your time with that bat and ball? Baseball won't pay the bills, Lincoln." She always seems so mad when I come home after a win.

"Coach thinks I could get a full ride through college if I hit well

this year. You should've seen me tonight... I was on fire." She never comes to my games.

"He needs to stop filling your head with nonsense. Your grades are disappointing at best, and my wages at the diner couldn't put you through community college. I don't know why these teachers want to get your hopes up. We're not a college family. The sooner you accept that and decide what trade you're going to pursue, the better off you'll be."

I bust my tail morning, noon, and night on the field, and when I'm done with that, I work shifts at the local coffeehouse. There's no time for good grades, which you'd think my mom would understand, considering she's the reason I need to work. Her job doesn't cover the rent on this shitty trailer, and even if I didn't need a job, I wouldn't want to spend time at home.

My mom is a single parent, and my father is a blank spot on my birth certificate. All I know is that he wanted nothing to do with my mom when he found out she was pregnant. I never felt the need to know his name or whether they were in love, but on nights like tonight, when my teammates' fathers are in the crowd cheering, I wish I knew the man whose absence ruined my mother. He must have been quite a guy.

All I know is I'm never going to let someone have that kind of power over me—not today, not tomorrow, not ever.

IT'S a hell of a lot hotter in Vegas than it is in New York right now. The sun is shining, and I'm ready to roll the die and continue my winning streak after the World Series win. We flew in ahead of the big fight tomorrow night, and after my trip down memory lane this week, I'm looking forward to letting loose and shaking it off. The woman of the hour, Brooke's sister, is supposed to be joining us for dinner, but I'll believe it when I see it.

Diana and I met once before at Brooke and Anders' wedding, but she wouldn't give me the time of day. She had a lame date at the reception, but when has that ever stopped a woman from diving into my pants. So, if I were a betting man—and I am, as evidenced by my current stack of chips—I think she'll be a no-show. A less confident man might assume she actively avoids social occasions with her sister if she knows I'm going to be present, but how little self-control can the woman have? Is she so worried she'd jump my bones that she can't be in the same room with me?

Brooke and Anders disappeared up to their suite over an hour ago to 'freshen up' before dinner, so I'm sure they're at it like rabbits. I am, however, killing it at the craps table, and the blonde to my left is easy on the eye. All in all, it's a decent start to the weekend.

"Showing off already, Linc? I'd expect nothing less." Her voice cuts through the adoration like a knife through butter, and I don't even have to look up to know it's her.

"Says the woman who's here to show off to a crowd of what, sixteen thousand?" I hold the die up to the cute blonde's lips to blow on for luck as I meet Diana's gaze across the table. She rolls her eyes at me, but there's a hint of something else—dangerously close to the green-eyed monster.

She can bring it outside the ring, looking gorgeous in a tight-fitting dress that hugs in all the right places with her long black hair cascading down her back like Niagara Falls. She's stunning, and she knows it.

I gather my winnings without taking my eyes off her, the blonde all but forgotten as I make my way round to greet Diana.

"I'm not going to lie, I didn't think you were going to show up for dinner." I can't help drinking her in from head to toe.

"Trust me, it's not for your benefit. I want to see Brooke for an hour, eat my dinner, and head back to my room to prepare for tomorrow."

"Do you need me to tuck you in? I'd be happy to help, all in the name of sport, of course." I give her a sly wink, making her blush, but she quickly brushes it off, her eyes cast to the ground.

"Dream on, Linc."

I lean in close, enjoying her sharp intake of breath at my proximity. "Say it like you mean it, Diana."

"Ugh. Is this how you get women? Smarm, charm, and that chiseled face?"

"So, you concede that I'm charming and dashingly handsome." I run my hand over my jawline, doing the smoldering eyes that photographers always ask for at a shoot, but she's not impressed.

"Of course, you cherry-pick the parts you want to hear and leave out what you don't. You're smarmy, Linc. I don't like it, and we're *never* going to happen."

"You realize you don't need to like me to have sex with me, right? What happens in Vegas stays in Vegas." She eyes me warily.

"I don't have sex the night before a fight." I hear her words, but her eyes say different as she rakes the length of me like a ravenous lioness, and I am her prey. She's considering it. If I'm honest, I am kind of surprised and so turned on my balls ache.

"What about after fights, when you're celebrating a win?" I take a step toward her, leaning in, my lips close to her ear. "One night of wild, crazy fucking between two insanely hot people isn't the worst way to revel in a win."

Her breath quickens, giving her away for just a fraction of a second before Brooke and Anders arrive, killing the moment.

"Is everything okay over here?" Brooke pulls her sister close while giving me the stink eye.

"Yeah, your sister was just watching me clean up at the craps table. I guess I'm getting lucky this weekend. Maybe if she blows me, she'll get lucky too." Anders shoves me in the back. "Sorry, did I get that wrong? Silly me. I meant if I blow on her, like the die in craps, it'll bring her good luck. If your minds went anywhere else, that's on you. It was a simple slip of the... tongue."

"Bullshit, bro. I know your mind. It's a dark and twisted place. My sister-in-law is out of bounds unless she tells me otherwise." So, I need his permission to sleep with a consenting adult woman who knows her own mind?

"Thanks for the chivalry, Anders, but I can say no to your friend here just fine by myself." Diana is feisty—it's hot as hell. "Now, can we go and eat? Gray has me on an early curfew tonight. Tomorrow is going to be a long day."

"Coaches can be such a buzzkill the night before game day. You should have a drink and some great sex just to be defiant." I wiggle my eyebrows, and she cracks the smallest of smiles.

"You may have a point. I should just go in search of a man who could sate my needs."

"I'm right here, baby."

"Never. Gonna. Happen." I'd believe her if she weren't devouring me with her eyes as she says it.

I hold her gaze as I speak. "Then let's eat because I'm *ravenous.*"

"Anders, I think we might need to eat at another table. These two are making me gag." That's rich coming from Brooke.

"I'm always the third wheel to your ooey-gooey slop fest of suck face."

"Amen to that." Something Diana and I finally agree on. "He's not wrong, sis. I love you, and I'm happy for you guys, but being the third wheel at dinner or even walking down the street with you two is... painful. You're so in love it makes my teeth hurt."

"Preach, Diana. It's great for you guys, but it's so sickly sweet for the rest of us. Like I worry I might become a diabetic because I'm friends with you."

Some strange, hybrid snort-laugh escapes Diana, and I decide it's best to ignore it. If I draw attention to it, she might legitimately kick my ass. Besides, it's kind of cute. She's quick to throw up her guard and compose herself. I guess she never really steps out of her gilded cage.

"Let's just eat. I need to be out of here and in my room an hour from now."

I offer my arm now that we have a common ground of sorts.

"Then let's get you fed. You have a fight to win, and the longer you spend around these two, the more likely it is you won't be able to keep your dinner down." This time she giggles, aware not to let herself slip. Heaven forbid anyone sees a glimpse of Diana, the woman, rather than Dee Lex, the MMA goddess.

"Maybe we should just leave them to suck face and whisper sweet nothings and get a table for two."

"I'd be down for that, but I know it would be a hardship for you. You know, considering how much you dislike me." With a sly wink, I lead her to the restaurant, where we're quickly taken to a secluded table in the back. It's odd because people aren't staring at Anders and me—star players for the Yankees. People are staring at Dee Lex, tomorrow night's big draw here in Vegas. I'm just the apparent arm candy for the evening, and it's a little disconcerting.

"Would you like drinks to get you started?" The waiter is trying to play it cool, but he immediately knows he's serving the biggest name in Vegas this weekend.

"Water for me, thanks. I'm here on business." The waiter blushes, and I want to slap it right out of him. What self-respecting man blushes?

"I'm rooting for you, Miss Lexington."

"Thank you."

The rest of us order drinks without any recognition. It's like the twilight zone compared to a night out in New York. Given menus to look at while the waiter goes off to get our drinks, there are hushed whispers as patrons begin to notice Diana. She's quick to use her menu as a wall to hide behind.

"This is why I usually eat in my room the night before a fight."

"I'd gladly have ordered room service with you." I can't help myself. The innuendos just keep falling out of my mouth when I'm around her.

"The next word out of your perfect, pouty lips better not be 'naked,' or I'll be giving you a fat lip." The lady doth protest too much.

"Admit it, you find me charming. I can see that hint of a smile dying to get out. Let it. I promise it won't kill you." Eventually, she relents.

"You're infuriating, Lincoln Nash."

"No one says my full name unless I'm being scolded, but it sounds so good coming out of your mouth. Like a dirty mistress or something. Say it again." She bites down on her bottom lip, and my cock twitches at the sight of it, but her expression quickly sours.

"I'm no one's dirty mistress. This is exactly why you and I will never get naked. You think women are expendable, for your amusement until you're done and ready to discard them like trash."

"What the fuck?" As soon as the words leave my lips, I realize the decibel level was way too loud. Brooke and Anders stop their conversation, their eyes snapping to me in unison.

"You heard me." She turns to her sister. "No need to stop me sleeping with him, Brooke. I wouldn't, even if you paid me."

"Care to explain?" I level the question at Anders because I can't stand to look at Diana *or* her sister right now. I didn't realize I was a problem to be managed this weekend, and they've clearly been instructed to run interference if I get too close for comfort.

"What?" He plays dumb.

"I've just been informed that your wife has been tasked with making sure Diana here doesn't give in to her animalistic desire to rip off my clothes and lick me from head to toe before begging me to make mad, passionate love to her for hours on end." I look to Diana. "Is that about right?" She has the decency to seem at least a little embarrassed that I've been designated minders for the weekend.

"I didn't mean it like that."

"Oh, my mistake. Is it that I'm so hideous, and you have a tendency to take pity on guys who resemble the hunchback of Notre Dame?"

"You're a jackass. A pain in the ass, hot as fuck, pouting playboy. I don't have any intention of losing tomorrow night, so yes, I asked Brooke to make sure I keep my mind on the task at hand. I won't apologize for it. I have a job to do, and just because I'm a woman, it doesn't make my goals and dreams irrelevant. Men like you disgust me. You're a self-absorbed, narcissistic, selfish womanizer." Whoa. Hold the fucking phone. Where did that come from?

"Message received, loud and clear." I don't have time for this shit. Diana may be beautiful and the best female MMA fighter of her generation, but bitchy isn't sexy. Whatever her damage is, it has nothing to do with me, and I'm not getting sucked into her man-hating brand of feminism.

"Linc..."

"Save it for someone who gives a shit. You don't need to worry about sleeping with me, Diana. Contrary to popular belief, I have standards, and women who get a kick out of being a bitch are a real turn-off. If you'll excuse me, I think I'll head back to the casino."

No wonder Diana is the UFC reigning champion. She goes straight for the jugular—unprovoked. At the first hint of a playful joke, she threw whatever shit she's dealing with in my face like a sucker punch. It definitely had maximum impact. I came to Vegas to get away from my own bullshit after visiting dear old Mom. Winning comes with its own demons where I'm concerned, and all I wanted to do was come here, have some fun, flirt, drink, and gamble. I'll settle for the last two. Back to the craps table, it is.

Anders knows better than to come after me, and I'd bet he's sinking his teeth into an eight-ounce fillet right about now. If he doesn't get me a to-go box, I'm going to nut-punch him.

Diana's venomous tongue is quickly forgotten as I lose myself in the crowd, ordering drinks for the high rollers and inviting a few for a private game of poker. Then, when Anders finally makes an appearance, it's time to play.

"Took you long enough. Did you enjoy your meal, Judas?"

"She's family."

"And I'm not. Good to know. Brooke leads you around by the cock now, and her sister is a colossal bitch. Thanks for having my back."

"Don't be pissy. It doesn't suit you."

"Poker?"

"Now, you're talking."

"Where's the ball and chain?"

"My wife has gone up to the room with Dee. Did you really have to leave?"

"Did she really have to be an ignorant, venomous shrew?"

"Valid point. My sister-in-law is somewhat..."

"Of a C-U-Next-Tuesday."

He rolls his eyes at me. "Abrasive. I was going for abrasive."

"You say potato... I say cunt. Let's play some poker. I've been watching these guys. They like to bet big with no real finesse."

"You know as well as I do that craps and poker have zero correlation."

"It's all in the body language, bro. Have I ever steered you wrong in Vegas?" He actually takes a moment to ponder it. What the fuck?

"No. You haven't. That bothers me, and there's a first time for everything."

"For fuck's sake, can we just play some goddamn poker?"

"Sure."

"Do I really come off as some womanizing dickhead?"

"No. She was out of line. She was projecting her shit onto you. You know I don't think like that, and neither does anyone else who actually knows you. She hasn't told Brooke any details, but I think there may have been a breakup recently and not an amicable one."

"I didn't know she was seeing someone."

"Just give her a break. She's nervous about tomorrow and has been a little off her game the past few weeks. She shouldn't have said that shit, but I don't think she meant it."

"Do you know what really grinds my gears about your sister-in-law?"

"I'm sure you're about to tell me."

"Even when she was tearing me a new one... there's just something about her. Fuck, she's hot, and it annoys me that I still want to rip her clothes off with my teeth."

"Are you on some thrill-of-the-chase mission now? Should I be worried? Because it's not your nuts that'll be in a vice if you fuck her over, Brooke will come looking for me."

"I didn't realize our cocks are linked. Is it like a superpower-type thing?"

"Shut up. You're both grown-ass people. If you want to have a night of love-hate sex and get it out of your system, just don't tell me or Brooke. Deal?"

"Deal."

He slings his arm over my shoulder and signals the bartender as we enter the private high rollers poker room. "Best whiskey you've got, on the rocks, keep them coming, open a tab for Verbeck. I'm in the Presidential Suite."

"Yes, sir."

"Tonight just got better. I get to drink my sorrows away on your dime."

"Only because Dee reduced your already tiny manhood to microscopic size."

"Don't diss the anaconda. You know better than anyone, there's nothing small about my manhood." He stares at me as if I just spat in his face. "That came out way different than it sounded in my head."

"Did it not sound like you want to be my life partner in your head? That's how it came out to everyone within earshot."

"You wish. I'm too hot for you."

"Dream on. I'd be in the major leagues of homosexual dating, and you'd be in the minors."

"What? You're insane. I'd totally be in the majors. What are you talking about?"

"You're a player."

"So were you until you met Brooke."

The waiter arrives with our drinks as the dealer shuffles the deck and our chips are set in front of us. I'm ready for a long night ahead.

"Here you are, gentlemen. The finest whiskey in Vegas, on the rocks, as requested. And if you don't mind me saying, Mr. Nash, you would definitely be considered the major leagues on the team I bat for." He gives a solemn, knowing smile, and I can't help but laugh. Anders was right, the entire room heard me.

"Well, you just doubled your tip tonight..."

"Derek."

"Excellent." I hold up a light blue poker chip. This small, insignificant-looking piece of clay is worth two grand. "Your tip will be whatever this chip makes tonight, my friend, as long as there's never an empty glass in my hand."

I'm true to my word. Derek walks away with ten thousand dollars at the end of the night, and I fall into bed with a lot of money and an impending hangover that could kill a lesser man. I'm almost asleep when my phone pings, and the second I lay eyes on the screen, I'm as sober as a judge.

Unknown: *One-time offer. Top floor, last door on the left.*

Me: *Who's this? And what's my one-time offer?*

Unknown: *Dee. One night. Wild sex. No feelings. And certainly no mention of this after tonight.*

Me: *You realize this is Linc? The guy you called a self-absorbed, narcissistic, selfish womanizer.*

Unknown: *You said we didn't need to like each other to have sex. I hate you. You hate me. Do you want to come up here and fuck me or not?*

Fuck me sideways and call me Judy. I know I should ignore her siren call and avoid what will inevitably be a toxic rebuttal in the morning, but fuck it, you only live once.

CHAPTER FOUR
DIANA

WAITING for the three little dots to appear is mortifying. He's not going to answer back. Shit. Shit. Shit. What was I thinking? I know better than to mess with a guy like Linc, and I've trained too hard to break the rules the night before a fight. Why did I think he was going to come running up here after the way I went off on him earlier?

The silence of my phone is deafening as I lie back in this huge bed, staring at the ceiling. Linc is probably in some other woman's hotel room right now, having just fucked her so hard she's forgotten her own name. In my head, he paused for a moment to answer my first text out of curiosity. Do men do that? Hopefully, not. Just the thought of him texting me while he's rocking some other woman's world is nauseating, and a guy like him won't have been short on offers. He looked impossibly handsome tonight, and from what I could see, he was on a winning streak when I called it a night.

I hate that I'm so attracted to him. He's an ass. A handsome, fit, glorious bad boy. The best kind of one-night stand. I'm horny, frustrated, and if I don't get some of this pent-up energy out, I'll never get any sleep, but I guess I'm on my own.

It's not like I can really blame him. He got two weeks of my frustration and anger that should've been directed at my ex. I'm sure it's for the best that he's blowing me off. I know that, although it doesn't mean I can't fantasize as I slide my hand beneath the sheets and between my legs.

His eyes are piercing blue, and the way his pants subtly highlighted his trouser snake tonight is enough to get me going. Imagining his lips on mine, trailing down my body...

Knock! Knock!

My frustration builds, but so does my anticipation as I leap from the bed and head for the door in nothing but a t-shirt.

"Who is it?"

"How many guys did you text for a booty call?" I can hear the self-satisfied undertone in his voice, but it's overshadowed by the deep rasping promise of sinful sex.

My pulse is racing as I twist the lock and open the door in my oversized t-shirt to find him leaning against the wall, his tie loose and the collar of his shirt unbuttoned. If he looked incredible earlier, he's mouthwatering now.

"Shouldn't you be sleeping?" He doesn't make a move, pinning me with his ice-blue gaze.

"I thought you'd be off fucking some fangirl you met downstairs."

"And yet you still hit me up. You must really want to fuck me, Diana." His tongue darts out to wet his lips, his eyes still firmly on mine.

"Were you with someone else?"

"Does it matter?" He's enjoying this.

My pulse is pounding so hard my ears are whooshing with every beat of my heart. Would I really sleep with him if he's just been in another woman's bed? "Were you?"

He runs the pad of his thumb over his bottom lip. "Why don't you taste for yourself? Go on, kiss me. You'll get your answer."

Fuck. I hate to admit that I'm so turned on my pussy aches. What happens if I taste another woman's arousal on his lips? Would I walk away? *Can* I stop myself? My breath is labored as I war with myself.

"Why did you even come? We didn't exactly hit it off tonight?"

"You want me here. I came running. I'm curious how you got my number, though."

"I may have swiped it from Brooke's phone. You still haven't told me if you were in another woman's bed ten minutes ago."

"Kiss me, Diana. You won't be disappointed."

With his eyes still locked on mine, I launch myself at him, my lips crashing down on his in a blaze of desire. The scent of his cologne invades my senses as our tongues twist and tangle in a frenzy of passion.

Without a word, he hoists me into his arms, kicking the door shut behind us as I wrap my legs around his waist.

He tastes like whiskey and mint, his lips soft but firm as he presses my back to the wall. His erection strains against his suit pants as he grinds against me, and I know he'll split me in two, and I'll love every minute of it.

"Diana." My name is a whisper on his lips—a song of praise as he slides one hand up into my hair, grabbing a fistful as he captures my mouth in a primal kiss. It's not the tender first kiss of young love or a hesitant caress between friends in hopes of something more. It's raw, powerful, and earth-shattering.

"Bed. Now." I claw at his jacket, fighting to divest him of some clothing.

"I'll take you to bed when I'm good and ready, Diana. You're not in the cage now. This is my arena." He grinds his hips against me, the friction of his massive erection causing a tornado of sensation to take hold and sweep me up in a haze of desire.

"God, you taste good."

"Just wait till you taste your arousal on my tongue." Kissing his way down my neck, he untangles my legs from his waist, setting me down just long enough to grab the hem of my shirt and pull it up over my head, leaving me naked.

"Is that an offer?"

"It's a guarantee." He drops to his knees, his large, firm hand splaying on my stomach. As he lifts his gaze to meet mine, the fire in his eyes is all-consuming. "Part your legs, Diana."

I do as he asks without hesitation, opening myself to him. Maybe I should be more bashful, but the moment for that passed when I texted him looking for a booty call. I slide one hand into his tousled hair, gripping it tight enough to pull his head exactly where I want him.

The second his lips press against my core, an explosion of sensation detonates, sending me spiraling into outer space. I groan his name, letting my hips grind in time with his tongue as he licks and flicks my clit. The warmth of his mouth is a delicious kind of wickedness.

"Linc. Yes! Right there."

The stubble on his chin pricks my skin in a stark juxtaposition of the softness of his tongue, but there's nothing gentle about the way he devours me. Every groan and rasp of his delight reverberates against my core, making every lick more intense, pushing me quickly toward orgasm.

His hands begin to roam, gripping my hips as he sets a punishing rhythm, forcing me to stay still, which isn't an easy task when all I want to do is ride his face until he can't take any more of me.

I hold on as long as I can, climbing higher and higher on a collision course with ecstasy.

"Not yet." His words are a command, holding me on the edge of where I want to be and where I *need* to be in this moment. "You come when I let you, Diana."

His words are my undoing.

"Oh fuck, yes! Yes." My mind is fractured, my senses overloading with the pleasure he rips from my body. Every kiss of his lips and flick of his tongue drive me wild.

"Yes. That's it. Let me hear you."

"Don't stop."

"Didn't plan to." He grips my calf and lifts my leg over his shoulder, spreading me wide as he continues his punishing rhythm. "Come for me, Diana."

"No... yes. *Oh God, yes!* No!" My orgasm comes crashing down, tearing right through me like a hundred-year storm, decimating my self-control.

Linc tries to pull away, but I grab a fistful of his hair and tug him back until I'm done riding the aftershocks of my explosive release. When I can't take any more, he looks up at me through hooded lashes, his lips glistening with the evidence of my arousal. Running the pad of his thumb over his bottom lip before sucking it into his mouth, I force my gaze upward, cursing the ceiling.

"*Fuck.*"

"Don't mind if I do. You taste so fucking good."

The second he gets to his feet and reaches for me, I dodge his grip. "No."

"What's wrong?"

"You."

He stares at me in shock. "You sounded pretty happy two seconds ago." I grab my t-shirt off the floor and shrug it over my head. I've lost my damn mind. Not only am I jeopardizing the fight, I'm about to make a huge mistake.

"I can't do this. You should leave." Flashes of past conversations, red flags, and barked orders of too many exes flood my thoughts as my traitorous body wants nothing more than to submit to his command.

"Are you shitting me right now? I literally have your orgasm on my face."

"No one *commands* my pleasure. Not you, not anyone."

"I beg to fucking differ. I'd go out on a limb and say that orgasm was one of the best you've ever had."

"Jesus, do you even hear yourself?"

"Funny you should ask. I couldn't hear shit when I was using your thighs as earmuffs."

"This was a mistake. You should go."

"What? You texted me. You wanted to fuck. I'm here for it."

"Yeah, and then you went all caveman, and 'you can come when I say so.' What bullshit."

He runs his fingers through his hair, and my body betrays me, desperate to slip my fingers back into his sex-mussed style. "I've literally never had a woman complain that I was being too masculine in the bedroom."

"I didn't say I dislike you being masculine but don't go spouting some archaic crap about making me come on command. I'm not a dog, and I don't do tricks."

His eyes go wide as saucers. "What the ever-loving-fuck? How the hell did you get to dog tricks from a little dirty talk? You want to be the one to bark commands, have at it." He throws his arms open, inviting me to continue. His lips glisten with the evidence of my arousal, and every primal urge is screaming at me to shut up, stop overthinking it, and fuck his brains out. Instead, I double down, forcing my desire into rage.

"We're not doing this. It was a bad idea in the first place. I should never have texted you." I start pacing, building myself up for verbal sparring, but it doesn't come. I expect him to protest, but without another word, he heads for the door.

"Good night, Diana." And just like that, he's gone as quickly as he came, and I'm left wondering why he brings out the worst in me.

I'm about to run after him when I think better of it. It's already so late, and I have the biggest fight of my career tomorrow—shit, it's one o'clock—today. Part of me wants to chase Linc down and explain myself, but the bigger part wants to forget that I just had the most intense orgasm of my life.

He's not the stroll-in-the-park, talking-for-hours type. Hell, he didn't even put up a fight. He just walked away, and that surprises me more than anything. I was expecting 'You can take me any way you want, sweetheart,' or a 'You know you want me. Give up some of that control you pride yourself on.' It's the same bullshit my ex would say to me, and I gave up control to him. It got me a scarlet letter on my forehead and a valuable lesson learned. I won't ever make that mistake again.

In my imaginary scenario with Linc, I was able to save face. I'd get him on the back foot, letting him know who calls the shots when it comes to my bedroom. Instead, he walked out without so much as a glance over his shoulder.

I've missed the witching hour. The window of opportunity has passed me by, and the acute ache between my thighs is less than satisfying. Now, I really do worry I'll be off my game tomorrow. Clearly, my judgment is skewed if I thought sleeping with Lincoln Nash was a good idea. And yet, the hint of his cologne still hanging in the air is delicious. The taste of his lips remains on my mouth. What the hell is wrong with me?

I head for the bathroom and switch on the shower, letting the cool tiles beneath my feet ground me as I grapple with the ghost of boyfriends past and an opportunity missed. The thought of going to bed with the smell of Linc on my skin is too enticing, and that's exactly why I need to wash away the evidence and erase what just happened. I'm not sure how denial will work when I see him at the fight tomorrow, but I'll be so focused in the cage, he'll be just another speck in the crowd—at least that's what I'm going to tell myself.

By the time I've washed all traces of Linc from my skin, I'm exhausted, mortified, and ready to crawl under the covers and forget tonight ever happened. Before I can settle my mind, I reach for my phone and type a quick message.

Me: *I'm sorry.*

Linc: *No means no. Never apologize to me or any other man for saying it.*

I wasn't prepared for a response, much less an understanding one.

Linc: *Go to sleep. You have a big day ahead.*

Me: *Good night, Lincoln.*

Laying on my back, I stare up at the ceiling, trying like hell to forget about tonight and focus on tomorrow. This is the biggest fight of my life. I need to be rested, and with every hour that ticks by, I wave goodbye to any meaningful sleep.

In the end, I get up and throw on some training gear before heading down to the gym at the arena. I may as well do a short workout and attempt to wear myself out.

The thing I love about Vegas is that no matter what time it is, the city is alive. It never sleeps or slows down. It's a constant, whirring, living, breathing entity, and I'm invigorated as I make my way to the gym, passing drunken gamblers having the time of their lives while they lose the shirt off their back.

My breath hitches at the sight of a familiar face across the casino floor. Linc is throwing back a drink while some pretty little redheaded bartender hangs on his every word. If she gets any closer, she'll be up on the bar with her tits in his face. A pang of jealousy courses through me—unwarranted and unwanted. Thankfully, he doesn't see me, so I drop my head and blend into the crowd before taking a sharp left toward the gym.

Swaddled in the bosom of an empty workout space, I can clear my mind. This is where I'm in control of everything. When I step inside the cage, I can't control what my opponent will do or how they've trained up until that moment. There are so many variables. But here, with a speed bag and thick red workout mats, I'm the queen of my domain.

I push myself, my muscles burning as I work them longer and harder than I should until I'm breathless, boneless, and laying starfish on the gym floor. As my eyes drift closed, my lids are heavy in the knowledge of what this fight means.

My brain carries me away to a place where life isn't measured in fights—in wins and losses. In that place, I'm not judged by my physique or left hook. No one cares that I'm a southpaw, and men aren't intimidated by my ability to hold my own in any situation life throws my way. Wherever I am, no man has deceived me or convinced me to make myself smaller to feed their own ego.

I don't know how long I'm out, but I dream of Prince Charming lifting me into his arms, cradling me like a delicate flower to be cherished. I can't see his face, but there's something familiar in his touch, and it soothes me in ways I find uncomfortable and unsettling. There's no prince for me, and even if there were, I wouldn't want him —wouldn't *need* him.

It's not until shards of light splinter through the drapes in my hotel suite that I realize I must have made my way back up here during the night. I could've sworn I slept soundly on that mat. I don't even remember getting up or navigating through the hotel, back to my room.

Every sinew and muscle fight a scorching ache as the alarm rings, and I grapple with my phone to shut it off. Last night was the worst scenario for fight preparation. Anvils hang where my fists should be, and the signature dance of my feet is hindered by concrete blocks instead of shoes. It takes everything I have to drag my ass out of bed and into the shower.

Standing under the water for what feels like hours, I let the heat and pressure massage my aches and pains until I feel somewhat human. Gray will be expecting me for our ritual pre-weigh-in pep talk in thirty minutes before we sit down for promo and interviews ahead of tonight. I guess there's no point worrying about aesthetics today. I could have a team of stylists this morning, but no amount of magic can turn this sow's ear into a silk purse. It's a sad day when I'm quoting my mom and her unconventional outlook on the world.

By the time I've tamed my hair into Dutch braids and made myself presentable, it's time to start this horse and pony show. The last thing I want to do on fight day is sit down with a bunch of journalists who are thirsty for blood. They want Dee Lex, the ruthless fighter, and I have the elevator ride down to the lobby to get into the right headspace.

Tonight could change the course of my life, and I won't squander that chance. Brands are lining up to endorse me if I pull this off. It's life-changing dollar amounts, and a chance to prove to my mom and dad that their support hasn't been misplaced all these years.

Winning a title is one thing, defending it cements my place in UFC history.

CHAPTER FIVE
DIANA

BANTAMWEIGHT REQUIRES me to be anywhere from 125-135 pounds, but I know I'm comfortably within range, so this weigh-in is just a formality to get out of the way. For most women, it's equivalent to the naked dream—a room full of people with cameras taking your photo as you stand on a set of scales. For me, it's par for the course.

As I step into a different kind of cage, my opponent is ready and waiting to get this over and done with. Kayla Dobrev and I go way back. We started out around the same time, but there's no room for friendship today. The crowd wants adversaries, and that's what they'll get.

Kayla is on the high side of our category, so she's probably going into today hungry. That's a small advantage for me, but at the same time, being the lighter of two fighters isn't historically the best if you're talking statistics. I know how to use my body and weight to my advantage, but she's an excellent fighter.

I'm up first, and as expected, I am right on target, pumping my fists in the air for the camera before stepping aside for my opponent. Brooke and Anders are standing at the back of the room, a small oasis of friendly faces in a sea of bloodthirsty strangers. There's no sign of

Linc, which I'm thankful for. I can't face him after last night. Making an ass of myself in front of him is made so much worse by the fact that he'll be a prick about it the next time I see him.

"No!"

A collective gasp ripples through the crowd as all eyes are on Kayla, her head in her hands, cursing like a sailor who just stepped on an anchor, pointy side up.

I turn to Gray, whose name is an accurate description of his face right now. All color has drained, and his eyes are bugging out of his head. Following his gaze, the penny drops, and heat spews out from my core, winding its way up and down my limbs before tightening its grasp, making it hard for me to move.

One hundred thirty-seven pounds.

My heart is thumping so hard it's as if it is about to leap from my chest and gallop off into the devastation of this moment.

"Miss Dobrev is two pounds over regulation for the bantamweight division, and therefore tonight's fight must be postponed until a later date to be determined." The official's words are cold, rehearsed, and yet the furrow of his brow indicates the chaos he knows is about to erupt.

Microphones come at me from all sides.

"How do you feel, Miss Lexington, knowing that all these preparations are for nothing?"

"Do you have anything to say to Miss Dobrev?"

"Will you agree to another challenge to your title from your opponent?"

"When will this fight take place now?"

I'm dumbstruck. It takes everything I have to hold my tongue, but Gray has given me shit for it in the past, and I'm in no fit state to keep a level head. Thankfully, he steps in front of me and signals for my bodyguards to escort me out, but I'm not moving. I want her to face me, to know that if and when we finally get in the cage, I'll be coming for her.

"No questions at this time, please. We'll be making a formal statement later today, but in short, we're extremely disappointed, as you can imagine. Dee prides herself on the dedication and hard work she puts into preparation for a title fight. We're grateful to the MGM Grand for putting together a fantastic event, and I hope they'll consider rehosting when and if Miss Dobrev can take this as seriously as my fighter. Rules are in place for a reason, and we've adhered to the letter. Thank you for coming, and we'll let you know of any further press conferences with your reigning champion, Dee Lex, later in the day."

Another wave of questions come hurtling our way, but this time I'm flanked by Gray and the bodyguards as they usher me out the room and quickly toward the elevators. As soon as the doors close behind me and we're heading for my suite, I finally let it out.

"What the ever-loving-fuck? She didn't make weight! This wasn't just some nobody fight, and even then, you make the damn weight. It's humiliating."

"You have nothing to feel embarrassed about, Dee, you did everything right. This is all on her. Fucking unprofessional is what it is."

I'm pacing the confined space like an animal climbing the walls. "This can't be happening. I've been working my ass off for this. The endorsements, the press, not to mention the physical side of it. All that shit is gone now because of two fucking pounds! Let me fight her anyway."

"You know that's not how it works. We have to reschedule, and that's only if you want to. You have grounds to refuse her if she comes knocking."

My fists ball at my sides, an electrical current running through them, buzzing with unfettered rage. I swing for the mirrored back wall of the elevator, watching it shatter the moment my knuckles connect. Shards splinter in a cacophony of sound, suspended for a fraction of a second before slamming to the floor of this speeding box.

"Jesus Christ, Dee." Gray covers his ears, his eyes wide as saucers taking in the carnage at our feet. Transported from a hotel elevator, I'm lost in a glass forest, locked in by my own frustration. I can't take a breath, an invisible force pressing on my chest—overwhelming disappointment.

As the elevator comes to a halt and the doors open, I'm met by familiar faces. Brooke, Anders, and Linc are waiting at the entrance to my room. "How did you get up here so fast? And why the hell is *he* here?" I gesture in Linc's direction.

"Good morning to you too, Diana. Lovely to see you again."

Brooke reaches for my hands, turning them over in her palms. "You're bleeding." Her face contorts as she takes in the damage behind me. "What were you thinking?"

I snatch my hands back and grab the keycard from my back pocket. "I don't know, sis. Maybe that I've been working toward this for months, and I just watched a life-changing amount of money flushed down the toilet over two-fucking-pounds."

She follows me inside, along with everyone else. "It'll still happen, just not today. I know it's disappointing, but..."

"Do you? You're already set with your sponsorships, ad campaigns, marriage to a two-time World Series-winning multi-millionaire. I'm alone, Brooke. If I don't get paid, I've nothing to fall back on."

"If it's about the money, we can help you out until they reschedule the fight."

"It's not about the goddamn money! I can pay my bills just fine, thanks. I'm still the reigning champion. I just... this was supposed to be... *fuck!*"

"Can you at least sit down so I can clean up your hands? You're dripping blood on the floor."

Gray is already fielding calls in the background while Anders and Asshat disappear into the bedroom. Guess their bromance is more serious than I previously thought.

"I just need everyone to get out, Brooke. Can you do that? Get rid of them. I don't want to hear Gray yelling at Kayla's manager or trying to calm down sponsors. Bodyguards really aren't necessary now, and I'm sorry, but Tweedle Dee and Tweedle Dum have to go. I don't want Linc in here being smug."

"Why would he do that?"

"It's a long story. Trust me. I just want to be alone."

"You're not getting rid of me. I'll tell everyone else to bounce, even my husband. But, if you call him Tweedle anything again, you and I are going to have a problem."

"Sorry. I can't believe this is happening. I'm going to go soak my hands in the bathroom. When I come back, it better just be you in here."

"I'll be here with a bottle of tequila."

I throw my phone on the couch before heading for the bedroom and the massive tub waiting in the bathroom to drown my sorrows.

"When you boys are done trying on my underwear and making out with each other, can you leave? I have a tub that's calling my name."

"That's weird. I thought I heard it saying my name a few seconds ago. Do you need company?" I don't know if he's trying to lighten the mood, but I have no patience for him today.

"Go away, Linc."

"Are you sure?" He gives me a sly wink that fills me with contempt. I spin on my heels and shove his chest, walking him backward to the open door, forcing him out of the bedroom.

"Get out. Get out. Get out!"

Anders stares me down as he follows behind. "I get that you're upset, Dee, but it's not his fault that your fight isn't happening. He's a good guy, and I know there's no love lost between you two, but damn, girl, give him a break."

"Then why don't you fuck him, and maybe that'll stop him trying to get into my panties."

Linc scrubs his hand over the scruff of his jaw with a chuckle. "Don't worry, Diana, I no longer have any interest in your panties or lack thereof. I figured all the hype about you being a cold bitch was just that. Hype. It's rare that the press pegs someone's personality, but with you, I think they nailed it."

"Fuck you, Linc."

"You wish, sweetheart. Guess you'll be zero for two today."

As he disappears out of sight, Anders hesitates just long enough to chastise me some more. "Get yourself together, Dee."

I slam the door to the bathroom, turning the faucet on full power to drown out the muffled voices in the living room area of my suite. I don't bother with bubbles, shrugging out of my clothes as soon as the tub has filled and immersing myself until I'm staring up through the rippling surface of the water.

My vision is slowly clouded red by the cuts on my knuckles, spreading through the water like a disease. I've never had a fight canceled like this before, and I have no idea what to do with the store of adrenaline my body is desperate to unleash. I'm literally spoiling for a fight.

I hold my breath as long as I can, attempting to calm myself in the cocoon of the bathtub, but eventually, I have to come up for air, and the reality of the situation crashes over me like a tsunami. It's not just me who'll be affected by this. There are going to be bars that have organized extra stock for fight night—small business owners who could suffer much worse than I will due to something like this being canceled. The MGM Grand can afford it, and they're able to sit back and wait on whenever this can be rescheduled, but there's a domino effect.

"Brooke! Brooke, can you come here a minute?" Within seconds, she's on the other side of the door.

"Are you okay? Can you let me in?"

"I'm fine. I just need to talk to you about something. Is everyone else gone?"

"Yeah. You drove them off with your warm and fuzzy personality. What the fuck did you say to Linc? He and Anders left before I even got a chance to throw them out."

"I'm sure Anders will fill you in later."

"Are you going to let me in or not?"

"I'm naked in the tub with no bubbles, and it's like a scene from a horror movie."

"What?"

"The cuts on my hands. Calm down. I'm fine. I'll be out in a few minutes. I have an idea, and I need your help. Start searching for small bars around here that were doing a fight night event."

"What did your last slave die of?"

"I didn't bring my phone in here with me. I don't need it pinging all damn day with commiserations and notifications. Let Gray deal with all that bullshit."

"Fine. Just so you know, he was *not* happy at being kicked out. I think he's aged ten years in the space of an hour."

"Yeah, it's a crapshoot all around."

"Hey, sis, I'm sorry about today. I know how hard you've been working toward this."

"Thanks."

"Do you want me to change our flights home? We can fly back to New York in a couple of hours."

"No point in wasting a weekend in Vegas, so let's have some fun. You know what they say about Sin City, little sis? When in Rome and all that."

"Why do I think we're going to regret this in the morning?"

"Because we most definitely will."

BROOKE and I found a few bars outside the strip that were planning to show my fight tonight and covered all their expenses for lost income. I may not be set for life yet, but I'm more than comfortable, and it's nice to turn this weekend around.

I wanted to visit a few incognito, but Gray insisted on the bodyguards coming with me. The owners were all so grateful, and it was awesome to give back a little of the support places like that have shown me in the past. Brooke tagged along, leaving the boys to fend for themselves for the day, but when we hit up the last bar, it had such a cool vibe, we decided to rent it out for the night. I told the owner to allow a crowd of no more than fifty at a time, with a VIP section for my team and me.

A thrill courses through me as Brooke and I step into the lobby. Anders and Linc are waiting at the bar with the same redheaded bartender I saw him hitting on last night. Anders can't take his eyes off his wife and rightly so. She's a knockout tonight. On the way back from the bar, she convinced me to go all out. We stepped it up a gear with killer heels and outfits that could make grown men beg. By the goofy grin on Anders' face, he's ready to drop to his knees for her.

As we strut across the casino floor to where they're sitting, I love the sight of Linc picking his jaw up off the floor at the sight of me. After last night, he has the upper hand—he's seen me naked—and I plan to take it back tonight.

"Wow." He runs his hand through his hair, and a jolt of desire goes straight to my core, remembering what it felt like to fist my hands in his mussed-up locks and ride his face. "You look…"

"Pick your jaw up off the floor, Linc." I take great delight in grabbing his drink and downing it while he devours me with his greedy stare. "Are we blowing this popsicle stand or what? I've been sober for far too long. I plan to get really drunk and maybe even a little slutty tonight."

"Don't look at me, southpaw. My cock is off limits to mean girls."

"Bullshit." I link my arm with Brooke's and prise her away from Anders. "Come on, sis, time to get drunk."

I can feel his eyes on me as I walk away, burning me up like a fever. I'm going to enjoy shamelessly flirting with anyone but Linc tonight. I don't need his cock to get off. There are plenty of hot men in Vegas who'll be more than happy for a bit of rough and tumble with a jilted UFC champion.

By the time we reach the bar, there's a cue wrapping around the block to get in. Word must have spread that there's a party going on.

I'm used to crowds cheering from afar in the arena, but it's a little intimidating to have people chanting my name and reaching for me when I'm within grasp.

"*Dee Lex! Dee Lex! Dee Lex!*"

Phones are pointed at me from every angle, but one guy manages to catch hold of my arm and pull me toward him for a selfie. Before I get a chance to snap his grubby little paw, Linc grabs his wrist and twists his arm off me and up his back.

"Take your fucking hands off her."

"I just want a picture, man. I didn't mean anything by it."

"And I won't mean anything by it when I knock your teeth out."

My bodyguards are quick to step in and herd me inside, the others hot on my heels. When Linc appears, I go toe to toe with him. "I didn't need your help. I'm more than capable of taking care of myself."

"I don't doubt it."

"Then why didn't you just let me handle it? You're not my boyfriend."

"Thank fuck for that. What can I say, I'm a naturally chivalrous guy. When I see a dickhead laying a hand on a woman, I don't hesitate. Sorry if that offends your feminist belief system."

"Really? You say feminist like it's a dirty word."

"Not at all. I'm all about burning bras and women's rights. You'd know that if you took a minute to do anything other than assume the worst of me."

Brooke takes me by the hand. "Stop being so combative all the time. Just say thanks."

"I could've dealt with that guy myself."

"I know. We all know, Dee, but God, does everything have to be a fight with you? Can't you two call a truce for the night, and let's have some fun?"

"Fine."

"Shake on it."

"Are you kidding me?"

She stares me down with the same look Mom used to give me when we were kids, the one you don't mess with. "No."

I extend my hand out to Linc. "Thank you for defending my honor... even though I didn't need you to."

"You're welcome."

"Truce?"

"I'm not fighting you, southpaw." He takes my proffered hand, and the chemistry between us flares. I know he feels it too when he pulls away as if he's just taken a hit of 120V. "I need a drink."

"Now there's something we can agree on."

"Halle-fucking-lujah." Anders slings an arm over each of our shoulders. "Now that we're all friends, there's a bottle of whiskey at the bar with my name on it."

This place is packed. Fifty people didn't sound like a lot in theory, but it's wall-to-wall bodies as we weave our way through. I draw the line at the bodyguards hovering while we party. They're stationed at the entrance to the VIP section with strict instructions not to judge me tomorrow for whatever debauchery transpires tonight.

Brooke and I are quick to fall into our college days of tequila shots, lime, and salt. Nothing like a good salty lick before downing a shot. Three drinks in, and Anders is already trying to steal my drinking partner for a dance.

"I need my extremely hot wife for a while. She looks smoking in this dress, and I need her grinding against me in it."

"That's what the bathroom stalls are for."

As he takes her hand and pulls her to his side, he gives me a wry smile. "You don't really think I'd risk anyone else hearing her when she comes, do you? That shit is mine and mine alone."

They disappear into the crowd, and I'm left with Linc.

"Now I know where you get your chauvinist dirty talk from."

"I taught him everything he knows. How do you think he snagged your sister?"

"We need more tequila."

"Will you dance with me if I do a few shots with you?"

"I'm not that drunk." He doesn't even bother to reply but heads for the bar and re-appears a few minutes later with a bottle of Patrón.

He sets it down on the table and turns to leave. "Enjoy your drink."

"You're not going to drink with me?"

"No, I'm going to go and flirt with the cute blonde who was trying to give me her number while I was getting your tequila. I know it comes as a shock to you, but most women find me irresistible."

"One shot."

"Fine." He fills one of my empty shot glasses, grabs my hand, and shakes some salt on it. "You get one." Lifting my hand to his lips, he pins me with his ice-blue gaze as he licks the salt from my skin before downing the shot and biting a wedge of lime to chase it down. My traitorous body ignites at his touch and fills with desire.

CHAPTER SIX
LINC

IT TAKES every ounce of self-control I have to walk away. Diana is the most infuriating woman I've ever met, but she's undeniably sensual. She exudes sex with every move she makes, but when she opens her mouth, vitriol spills out like chemical waste.

There's one big problem with forcing myself to go flirt with the cute blonde at the bar—she's not the woman I want in my bed tonight. As much as Diana infuriates me, I can't shake the image of her naked, legs parted, her fists in my hair, and lost to the pleasure my tongue tore from her body last night. Every time I glance in her direction, I can taste her, and it has me rocking a permanent semi tonight.

"So, what do you do for a living? Do you work with Dee Lex? I heard this is her party." The blonde stares at me with a bright smile and nothing going on behind her eyes. She has no idea who I am. This is a rare treat. Maybe tonight isn't going to be so bad, after all.

"No, I don't work with her, just a friend of a friend. I work in... the entertainment business." It's not a lie. I entertain Yankees fans regularly.

"Like movies or TV?"

"Television."

"I don't suppose you could introduce me to Dee Lex?" I just want to get laid. Is that such a crime?

"I tell you what. Why don't we have a few drinks, and you can tell me about yourself? A dance or two, and if I haven't held your attention well enough, I'll introduce you."

She glances in Diana's direction as she slides her hand up my forearm. "I get the feeling you're more than skilled enough to hold a woman's attention." Giving me puppy dog eyes, she leans in a little closer. "Are you *sure* we can't say hello before we dance? I'm thinking we'll be heading back to your place before the end of the first song anyway." This girl knows what she wants and how to get it.

I steal a glance in Diana's direction, and some asshole with more hair gel than hair is inviting himself to sit with her. I'm more annoyed that she accepts and pours him a goddamn drink of the Patrón that I fucking bought for her.

"Sure, why not?" I order a couple of shots. "Cheers. Here's to an uncomplicated night."

"I'll toast to that." She slings her drink back like a pro before linking her hand in mine and pulling me through the crowd. This woman is hot, one hundred percent my type, and—nothing—not a twitch, a thrill, or the excitement that usually comes with a one-night stand.

Before we make it across to the VIP section, she starts swaying to the music, turning to face me. Sliding her arms around my waist, she slowly begins to grind on me, her eyes never leaving mine. "Maybe you're right. Dancing first." The sickly sweetness of her perfume overpowers the smell of alcohol that surrounds us as she darts her tongue out to wet her bottom lip.

She's not shy about getting up close and personal, and then it dawns on me I don't even know her first name. I lean down, trying to be heard over the pulsing beat and the hum of the crowd.

"What's your name?"

"Does it matter?" She turns and backs her ass up against my junk in the name of dancing.

"No." I'm usually all over this kind of hookup. In fact, I'd already be finding us a cab back to the hotel by now. But not tonight and not with this woman.

I can sense Diana's whereabouts as she slithers through the sea of people, with some fanboy following submissively behind. She's watching me, I know it, and her eyes do more to me than any amount of grinding from a cute blonde.

My fixed-to-one-spot dance moves suddenly flourish into twists and turns, anything to let me keep an eye on Diana. If she takes that prick back to the hotel, I have fuck-all recourse, but I'll be pissed. Every time our eyes meet, it's not the stolen glances of potential lovers. We glare at each other with disdain, and yet there's undeniable chemistry sizzling in the air between us.

The douchebag she's dancing with is getting way too friendly, his hands trailing down her back, making a play for her ass, and something in me just snaps.

"Where are you going?" The blonde shouts after me as I stride off in the opposite direction.

"Sorry... whatever your name is."

"Dick!"

I don't care if I'm being a dick. I know I should, but at this moment, I have someone else I need to go and be a complete prick to —priorities. I make my way toward Diana, and when she sees me coming, she's quick to intercept. "No. I don't need any more chivalry tonight. His hands are just fine. I'll tell him if they're not welcome."

My blood begins to boil as her oblivious dance partner moves closer again, grinding against her back, sliding his hands over her hips. She closes her eyes, and I lose it. If he touches her for another second, I'm going to knock him the fuck out.

"Diana, let's not make a scene. Why don't you just come with me, so I don't need to ensure this guy is drinking through a straw tomorrow."

"Why would I do that?"

"Because..." I realize that no words will convince her, so I do what I do best. I lean in, whispering in her ear, letting my lips caress her cheek. "It's not his hands you want running all over your body tonight."

In one fluid movement, I wrap one arm around her waist and extricate her from the douchebag's grasp.

"Hey, what the fuck, man?" I've got six inches on this guy, but good on him for attempting to stand up to me.

"Sorry... man... but you'll have to find someone else tonight. Might I suggest that pretty little blonde over there?" I point to my previous dance partner before waiting on a response.

Diana doesn't struggle against my arm, leaning into me as I weave my way through the crowd to the exit. "We're leaving? A tad presumptuous for a guy who told me a few hours ago that his cock is off limits to me."

A wall of heat slams into my chest as I step outside, still clutching Diana's waist. "Then go back inside and have some mediocre sex with Mr. Bland, or you can admit you want to ride my face again and get in a cab with me back to the hotel."

"God, you're so fucking full of yourself."

As a cab pulls up in front of us, I relinquish my hold on her and slide my hands up into her hair, waiting just long enough to know she isn't going to pull away. "Tell me you don't want to be *full* of me tonight, Diana. That you don't want this just as much as I do."

"I despise you, and I hate that you've seen me naked."

"Good, because you're not exactly likable either, southpaw. There's only one way to even the score."

Her breath is labored as she waits, unwilling to make a move, her lips a hair's breadth from mine. "And how's that?"

"You see me naked. It's only fair."

"What if I don't want to?"

"You do, otherwise you wouldn't still be standing here. You don't do anything you don't want to, Diana."

"Get in the cab, Linc." She lets her lips graze mine with the smallest of touches, almost imperceptible, but it's enough to make me groan.

Without another word, I open the door for her and watch as she slides in across the back seat, her dress hugging every curve to perfection. I don't want to risk saying something else to piss her off or have her cuss me out to the point it makes my cock flop. Not that I've ever had a problem in that department. She's so damn hot, I don't think anything could temper the raging hard-on I'm sporting right now.

As soon as I pull the door closed, Diana barks the hotel address at the driver, and the moment it leaves her lips, I capture them, silencing both of us with a kiss. Soft but firm, sensual, and full of promise for a wicked night ahead. She darts her tongue out, licking the seam of my lips, and my balls ache with an urgency and desire I've never felt this acutely before. Every nerve ending in my body is on fire, desperate to sink inside her and fuck her so hard she can't walk tomorrow.

She fists her hands in my hair, tugging me toward her. It's a power play, and I'm not ashamed to say it's working. Short of murder, I'd do anything to fuck her right here, right now. I may even consider killing the cab driver if it came down to it. Either my balls explode, or someone dies—I'm saving my balls.

"Tequila looks good on you, southpaw," I moan between kisses.

"Don't talk. You'll ruin it." Fuck, even when she's being a bitch, it turns me on. Our tongues twist and tangle in frenzied anticipation. My hands begin to roam, crying out for her flesh. She doesn't shy away when my fingers blaze a trail up the inside of her thigh, hitching her dress just enough to ghost my thumb over the lace of her panties.

"*Fuck!*" She's already wet for me, and as she circles her hips against the pad of my thumb, I crave her more than my next breath. "You're wet."

"And you're hard. Now stop talking and kiss me." She runs her hand up my leg and over my erection straining beneath my pants. I revel in her sharp intake of breath as she caresses my cock.

"Think you can handle me? *All* of me."

"I never walk away from a challenge." She wraps her hand around me, teasing me with the friction of her hand against my pants. Fuck, I could come like a fourteen-year-old seeing a *Playboy* center-fold for the first time.

Baseball. Baseball. Baseball.

The cab comes to a halt outside the hotel, and I pay the driver a healthy tip for his discretion before trying to get Diana inside without being swarmed by photographers. We slipped the bodyguards at the bar, so we're on our own to navigate the casino floor and upstairs.

I know the minute someone clocks us, camera shutters go off like crazy. I shrug out of my jacket and drape it over Diana to shield her face from making front-page news, especially with me in the shot. She definitely wouldn't take kindly to being associated with me.

"I can't see anything."

I tuck her close at my side. "Just hold on, southpaw. Trust me. I'll get you where you need to be."

"Does everything that comes out your mouth have to be a double entendre?"

"You realize your booming voice isn't helping with the whole incognito thing? Just hush for a minute until we get to the elevator."

"Did you just shush me?" Her fingers dig into my side as we hustle through the casino with reporters hot on our heels.

"Technically, I *hushed* you."

"I'm about to punch you, Linc. We couldn't just get back here in silence."

"Don't worry, I've got a mouthful for you as soon as we're behind closed doors." It's not lost on me that she squeezes her thighs together the second we hit the elevator. "You like that? Trying to alleviate the ache between your legs, Diana. Can't you wait just a little longer?"

The moment the doors close and the familiar lilt of upward motion kicks in, she throws off the jacket and glares up at me. "Why can't you just be quiet? When you say shit like that, I want to go to my own room and flick the bean rather than let you fuck me."

In one fluid motion, I back her against the wall, bracing my hands on either side of her, careful not to touch her. "You can hate every damn word that comes out of my mouth, but you're going to love the way my mouth feels when it's kissing every... fucking... inch of your body. Send me away again. But if you do, know that this isn't baseball. Two strikes, and you're out. I won't be coming back a third time."

As the elevator doors open on her floor, she ducks under my arm and out. I stand firm, awaiting an answer to see if she'll send me away again. She stares me down with her hands on her hips, but as the doors begin to close, she reaches out to stop them. "Are you coming or not?"

That's all I needed to hear. I want to play it cool, but the second I get the green light, it's like a red rag to a bull. Diana holds her keycard to the door, and the familiar click as it unlocks is the gunfire, heralding go time.

She goes straight for my zipper before the soft-close hinge of the door is fully shut. My lips crash down on hers as I reach for the hem of her dress. If it weren't so fucking gorgeous on her, I'd rip the damn thing off. We stumble through the living area to the bedroom, kisses broken momentarily along the way, clothing discarded on the floor in a trail of desire.

Diana isn't holding back tonight, shredding my shirt in a haze of urgency and passion. Buttons scatter in all directions, and I'm quick to shrug out of it while she reaches for my already unzipped pants. Shoving them over my hips, she grabs the waistband of my boxer shorts and slides her hand inside, her fist wrapping around the shaft of my achingly hard cock. *Fucking hell!*

Any conscious thought disappears with every stroke, sparking a fire so intense I can barely keep it together. I back her toward the bed, capturing her mouth in a fever pitch—a frenzied fuck that sends shockwaves rippling through every fiber of my being.

Our chemistry is a palpable entity, enveloping us with an undeniable need to fuck and fuck hard. It's primal, raw, and unrelenting—a driving force to claim, kiss, and explore every inch of her body.

"Condoms. Tell me you have condoms, Linc."

"I'm not a rookie, Diana." Sliding my hands into her hair, I pull her close, trying to play it smooth as I consider where the hell my wallet is. *Crap.* It's by the door in my suit jacket.

"What are you waiting for?"

"Wait here. Do *not* move. I know where they are." I run out of the bedroom toward the door with my junk stiff as a board and grope around in the dark for the elusive foil packets. I've never been so relieved to set hands on a rubber in my life.

I quickly head back to the bedroom, but I'm not prepared for the sight before me. She's fucking transcendent—her legs spread wide, teasing herself with one hand, her other cupping her breast. "Took you long enough. I started without you."

"I can see that, and I'm more than happy to watch."

She continues to circle her fingers over her clit while devouring me with her eyes, coming to a grinding halt when she sees how hard I am.

"You weren't kidding about the size of you cock. No watching. Get over here and fuck me, Linc."

"Haven't you heard of foreplay, southpaw? All good things come to those who wait. Well, all good *cum* is worth the wait."

"Foreplay is overrated."

"Oh, baby, then he's not been doing it right."

"And you can?"

"Is that a challenge?"

"Maybe."

"Game on." I quickly close the space between us, capturing her mouth in a voracious kiss, my hands roaming her body until she's panting and ready for me. Then, and only then, do I slip one hand between her legs and thrust two fingers inside her. She's so fucking wet, I could come right now. "Are you turned on, Diana?"

"Less talking, more sex." I pull out, leaving her bereft and desperate as she watches me lick her arousal from my fingers.

"You want it, come take it." Without another word, she's up off the bed, launching herself at me like a spider monkey. Gripping my arms with more strength than any woman I've ever known, she pushes me down onto the bed before crawling on top of me, straddling my thighs.

"Give me the condom packet." I do as she says, taken aback by how forthright she is. It's hot as hell. She tears it open and fists my cock before rolling it down my length. Wearing a condom has never been so fucking erotic.

I drop my head back against the pillows, savoring every moment of her touch. She's so goddamn hot, and I'm not prepared when she positions my cock at her entrance and sinks down onto me, taking every hard inch inside.

"Fucking hell. You're so tight." She circles her hips, sending me into a tailspin of sensation. "Slow down. I'll shoot my load in two minutes if you don't calm it down."

She doesn't relent, enjoying the fact that I'm at her mercy, worshiping at the altar of her slick, tight little pussy. *Jesus Christ.* I grab her hips to temper her rhythm, entranced by the way her breasts move with every thrust. God, she's so beautiful, like a Botticelli painting come to life.

Bracing her hands on my chest, her hair cascades in waves, teasing her nipples as she rides me hard. I need to get her under me so I can set the pace and enjoy exploring every inch of her lean, toned body, but she won't relinquish her control.

"Oh God... you're so big, Linc... yes!"

I arch up on the bed, pulling myself into a sitting position before taking her with a fierce kiss, setting the same punishing rhythm of her hips. Sliding my hand between us, I circle her clit with the pad of my thumb with just enough pressure to make her moan.

"You like that?"

"Don't stop." She bucks wildly against my hand, milking my cock with every stroke, pushing me closer to the edge.

"Kiss me, Diana." She doesn't hesitate, her lips crashing down on mine. There's a moment she lets her guard down, her muscles relax, and her breasts press tight to my chest as she wraps her arms around me, digging her nails into my back.

Our bodies are slick with a sheen of sweat as I continue my ministrations, her hips keeping time as she climbs higher and higher.

"Oh God... I'm so close... oh fuck... Linc. Oh God... yes!" One final flick of my thumb and she crashes over the edge, her pace quickening as her muscles tighten around me.

"That's it, baby. Let me hear you." She silences me with a kiss, her pulse racing as she rides the aftershocks of her orgasm, pulling me with her until I can't hold on any longer.

I come so hard I'm seeing white, her pussy contracting around me with every wave of pleasure, the ebb and flow sending ripples of ecstasy throughout every nerve ending in my body. It's intense, amazing, and almost painful but in the best fucking way.

We collapse in a heap of tangled limbs, but Diana is quick to extricate herself from my embrace, pulling a sheet around herself as if we haven't just shared the most intimate of acts.

"Wow." I wait for her to say something else, but apparently, that's all she's got. For a woman who doesn't know when to stop berating me, I'm a little stunned.

"Yeah. That was... intense."

"I'm going for a shower."

"Is that an invitation? I'm down for round two being wet and wild, just give me a second to catch my breath."

She turns to me with an almost mystified expression. She's not an easy woman to read.

"Are you okay, southpaw? Did I hurt you or something?"

"No. It was... good."

"Good? Well, shit. I definitely need to up my game this time around." I don't believe that was just 'okay' for her. She came so hard her legs were shaking uncontrollably, but if she wants to goad me into riding her harder and longer, I'm down for that. I stalk her into the bathroom, and the second the water is running, I lift her into my arms, forcing her to drop the sheet and hold on tight. "Good isn't what I'm going for. Get ready for amazing."

I lose myself in seconds and thirds, fucking in the shower, going down on her on the bathroom countertop before finding our way back to the bed for the finale. Holy shit. By the time we're done, I don't think I have any cum left in my balls. She's a spitfire, to say the least, and I'm exhausted. Closing my eyes, I turn to face her, but the blissed-out smile of only moments ago has been replaced by the firm set of her brow and a stern glare.

"Time to go. You're not sleeping here."

"What?"

"I don't sleep with a stranger in my bed."

"We're not exactly strangers now, are we?"

"Fine. Acquaintances who shared a handful of orgasms."

"Have it your way." As I root around the bedroom on a treasure hunt for my clothes, I glance back at the bed, Diana tangled up in the sheets looking ethereal in her beauty.

"Remember, Linc, what happens in Vegas stays in Vegas."

"It doesn't have to be just Vegas. Haven't you heard? What happens in Manhattan..."

"I'm going to stop you there, lover boy. This was a one-time thing. We're not going to call each other with giddy excitement and go for picnics in Central Park together. You're..."

"Dashing? Sexy? More than any one woman could handle?"

"One hell of a one-night stand, but once is enough." A wry grin creeps at the corner of my lips, hidden in the shadows of the room. She'll be in touch. A woman doesn't orgasm like she just did and pass on the offer of a rematch.

"I'll see you around, Diana."

"No, you won't." She calls after me as I start the walk of shame back to my room. The only problem with that is I have no shame. There's no way this is a one-time thing because I haven't gotten near enough my fill of Diana Lexington.

CHAPTER SEVEN
DIANA

HE HAUNTS MY DREAMS. Linc and his giant cock have ruined sleep for me, not to mention my self-inflicted pleasure. *Ugh.* Ever since I got back from Vegas, I've been jonesing for his disco stick, and it's driving me nuts. He has to be the most arrogant, alpha-douche, and skilled lover of any man I've ever slept with. It's infuriating that all his bluster when it comes to sex is completely founded.

It's been three weeks since the fight of my career was postponed, and all I can think of is that night with Linc. He's like a leech I can't shake off, sucking my pleasure and hoarding it for himself. I've typed a handful of messages for a second round of rough and tumble, but the thought of his smug face is enough to stop me in my tracks. I can't give him the upper hand.

I'm meeting with Gray to discuss a new date for the fight. I've been putting it off, not because I'm concerned about winning but simply to inconvenience Kayla. She screwed up big time, and I want her to feel the weight of pressure that's squarely on her shoulders. I went into the last event as the reigning champion—that's already a huge boon for me—but next time, the crowd will be out for her blood.

When I arrive at the gym, Gray's face lights up as if I just walked in holding the winning lottery ticket. "You're here. Great timing. I'm just off the phone with the MGM Grand, and we have a few prospective dates to choose from. Kayla's management got in touch yesterday about setting a new date."

"Why are we letting them dictate any part of the reschedule? She's the one who fell short last time. I want her to sweat it out a while before agreeing to anything."

I can see the idea percolating. "Good point. We should be using this to our advantage."

"I don't need an advantage to kick her ass, but I certainly don't feel the need to be helpful in any way."

"Semantics. Replace the word *advantage* with *being a royal pain in the ass*. It comes easily enough to you, Dee."

"Unless you want to be my sparring partner today, I suggest you keep your jibes to yourself."

"Get out of bed on the wrong side this morning? Or is it that you got out of it alone?"

"Says the only man I know whose virginity has grown back. When was the last time you caught some action, old man?"

"Old man? I'm only ten years older than you."

"That's the part you're focusing on." A chuckle bubbles to the surface. "Damn, Gray, how long has it been?"

"Let's just get down to business."

"Is that your pickup line? It could use some work."

"God, I don't know what's worse. You in a bad mood, or you being playful. Both are equally terrifying."

"Don't poke the bear."

"Your pickup line needs work, Dee. It's supposed to be, 'please poke my...'"

"Finish that sentence, and I'll break your arm." Gray and I have always had a fun working relationship, but I draw the line at this discussion, mostly because it makes me want to call Linc. I shouldn't be counting the days since he rocked my world, but damn him, it was that freaking good.

Twenty-one. It's been twenty-one days.

"Get in the ring, work off your frustration, and stop questioning mine."

He's right. All I need to do is focus my energy on training. If I tire myself out, there won't be time or the inclination to replay my night with Linc over and over on a loop. It makes me dislike him even more.

I throw myself into my workout, hitting longer, harder, and faster than usual. I want to be so exhausted I don't dream tonight. It's the only way to get Linc out of my traitorous brain. Then it dawns on me —maybe I need to find someone else to scratch the itch.

When I'm done for the day, I pull up Brooke's number.

Me: *Drinks tonight? I need a wingman.*

Me: *Wingwoman.*

Brooke: *Can I bring Anders?*

Me: *NO! What don't you understand about being my wingperson?*

Brooke: *No need for shouty capitals.*

Me: *Viper at eight?*

Brooke: *Fine, but I get to veto your prospective man friends.*

Me: *Man friends? Really?*

Brooke: *What? Your twig and berries for the evening? The manger-ines you want to mount? The stallion you plan you ride reverse-cowgirl?*

Me: *Stop!*

Brooke: *The stick you want to dip...*

Brooke: *That doesn't work. You're the dipped, not the dippee.*

Me: *I've changed my mind. Forget it.*

Brooke: *Grumpy much? You really do need to get laid. I'll be there at eight, trying not to look as hot as you.*

Me: *You get one veto. No more.*

Brooke: *Deal.*

When did my sister become a dork? Marriage has scrambled her brains. I can't think of anything worse than a night out playing third wheel to her and Anders. I'd rather take off all my clothes and walk down Fifth Avenue.

"SO, do you have a new date for the fight? I need another weekend in Vegas."

"We don't need an excuse. Call it a sister-bonding weekend, but we could go anytime. You and me."

Brooke takes a long draw of her margarita. "I know, I'm totally lame now, but I don't really want to go without Anders."

"I'm glad I don't need to point out your lameness. Seriously, you're going to be that girl who never hangs out with friends or your own *sister* without your husband?"

"I know! It's disgusting, right? I'm the loved-up idiot we used to mock."

"Yep, and if you mention his name again tonight, you're doing shots. Every time you gush over your husband, you're doing a tequila shot."

"Not fair. When do you have to do shots?"

"I don't need a reason. I'm going to drink a little, flirt a lot, and find a cute guy to make out with."

"Okay. Let operation wingwoman commence." She picks up her drink and casually scans the bar. "What about that guy over there? He's cute." She nods to her left.

"Brooke, there are like ten guys where you're nodding your head. I'm going to need some descriptive words."

"Tallest guy, dark hair, cute butt."

"No, clearly loves himself. I'm not in the mood for a guy who's more attracted to himself than me."

"What about the blond one? He has a nice smile.'"

"He's short. I have four-inch heels on."

"Then he'll be at the perfect height to motorboat you."

I spray a mouthful of my drink. Brooke caught me off guard with that one. "Oh my God!"

"He's out. He just saw you spitting your margarita all over me."

"Tell me I have other options. The rest of this crowd is scraping the bottom of the barrel. Maybe we need to look elsewhere."

"Just give me a minute." Brooke grabs a napkin off the bar and wipes at her top where I showered her with my margarita. "There are plenty of guys in here. What are you looking for?"

"Hot, fit, and taller than Danny DeVito. Is it too much to ask for a single guy who knows his way around a woman's body?" She surveys the rest of the bar. When did it become impossible to find a hot guy for the night?

"Anders."

"Stop gloating. You're doing a shot for that, maybe two."

"Linc?"

"Definitely not. He might know his way around a woman's body, and he's unbelievably sexy..."

"I knew I was sexy, but *unbelievably*? You're too kind, southpaw." A shiver runs down my spine at the sound of his voice, sending a jolt of desire straight to my core. The deep rasping tone with a hint of wickedness that's so sensual when he's groaning my name as he comes.

Shit.

I turn to face him before realizing his proximity. The scent of his cologne is delicious, and the way his crisp white shirt highlights the planes of his chiseled physique should be illegal. "What the hell are you doing here?"

Brooke is too busy sucking face with Anders to explain why she invited them to join us.

"I should be asking you the same question. Are you stalking me, Diana? Anders and I just came out for a few drinks, and here you are, dressed to kill, waxing lyrical about how sexy I am."

"God, you're awful."

I signal the bartender for another drink. "Make it the fishbowl, frozen margarita this time. And a whiskey for the jackass. Just double up the order. My backstabbing sister and her man will want a drink when they come up for air."

"Buying me a drink. Are you planning to get me drunk and have your way with me?" My insides turn to Jell-O with one sinful wink of his ice-blue eyes.

"I'd rather smother myself in honey and punch a beehive than take you home to my bed."

His wicked grin sends my pulse racing. "Then come home to mine."

"Did you not hear the part about the bees?"

"I heard something about you smothered in honey. Everything else after that is a blur. Just so we're clear... you're naked in this scenario, and I'm the beehive."

"So I can punch you?"

"Whatever turns you on, southpaw." He leans in, his lips ghosting a caress on my cheek. "Whatever you want."

I hover for a moment, letting him make a move before grabbing my drink from the bar behind him and heading for the dance floor. The beat of the music is all I hear as I repeat the same sentiment over and over.

Do not take him home. Do not take him home. Do not take him home.

As much as I try to ignore Linc, my eyes are drawn to where he stands, leaning against the bar with effortless finesse, his steely gaze fixed on me. I'm mesmerized as he lifts his glass, his tongue darting out to meet the amber liquid before it reaches those perfect lips.

My heart is hammering in my chest, so far past a gallop, I'm worried I'll drop dead of a heart attack at any moment. I can just see the headlines now.

MMA fighter killed by horny overload.

UFC fighter loses battle with her own libido.

Dee Lex - Death by shameless desire to mount Lincoln Nash like a bucking bronco.

MMA fighter spontaneously combusts. Point of origin – between her thighs.

Dee Lex slips and breaks her neck on her own arousal. Lincoln Nash to blame.

I DRAIN MY FISHBOWL, taking way too much at once, giving myself the worst brain freeze. Stumbling toward the nearest surface to prop myself up, I close my eyes and will it to pass. I've taken hits in the cage that hurt less than this.

"What's wrong?" Linc wraps his arm around my waist, holding me up.

"Brain freeze," I manage to choke out.

"Put your tongue on the roof of your mouth."

"What?" I grip my head, trying to ignore the warmth of his hand on my back.

Without another word, he captures my mouth with his, the warmth of his tongue twisting and tangling with mine. I can't breathe, my whole body sparking to life as the brain freeze subsides. I let myself enjoy him for a moment before coherent thought returns, and I pull away.

"What are you doing?"

"Getting rid of your brain freeze. You seem to have an inability or an unwillingness to accept my advice, so I got rid of it for you."

"A likely story."

"I hate to tell you, southpaw, but you were kissing me back. I know that doesn't play into your narrative of me being a colossal dick and you maintaining optimum bitch status. Sorry you're attracted to me."

"So..." Really? That's all my brain can come up with? "You're attracted to me too."

"Yes, I am, which is why you should come home with me tonight."

"What happened in Vegas..."

"Was hot." He closes the space between us, fisting his hands in my hair but stops just shy of my lips. "But it's just the tip of the iceberg, Diana. We could have earth-shattering, dirty as you can handle, mind-altering sex together, and still hate each other in the morning."

He searches my gaze, begging entrance before his lips find mine with a desire I can't ignore. I want him, and I don't want to want him, but holy mother of all that's good and pure, his kiss is soul-destroying.

"Privacy." I only manage one word before devouring him, giving myself over to the desire burning like an inferno, destroying all my resolve to ashes.

We weave our way through the bar toward a roped-off area in the back, barely breaking our kiss long enough to see where we're going.

"This isn't the exit."

"I know." Slipping behind the rope, Linc leads me down a dark hallway to a heavy steel door. "I need you now." The moment we're inside the plush office, he twists the lock. "We won't be disturbed in here."

His cock is already straining against his pants—hard, thick, and ready for me. Reaching for his belt, I walk him over to the deep red sofa against the far wall, unbuttoning his fly and freeing his erection before forcing him to sit.

"For a woman who says she doesn't want to fuck me, you're quick to whip it out."

"Don't talk yourself out of a blow job, Linc." His eyes flare at the mere mention of it, drifting to my mouth as I bite down on my bottom lip. I drop to my knees as gracefully as I can manage in this dress, enjoying the surge of power I have over him right now.

"I'm shutting the fuck up now." The rapid rise and fall of his chest betray his calm exterior as he watches with bated breath. I wrap my hand around the thick base of his cock, leaning in close enough for him to feel my breath on the shaft.

"How much do you want it, Linc?"

"Wrap that pretty little mouth of yours around it and find out."

I flick my tongue over the crest of his cock before pressing an open-mouthed kiss to the tip, teasing him as I pull away. "Tell... me."

"If I die with my cock in your mouth, I'll die a happy man."

"That's a weird thing to say." I crank my neck back to catch his gaze, puzzled by his lack of smooth-talk.

He fists his hands in my hair, holding me steady. "I want to fuck your mouth so bad my whole fucking body aches right now. Is that what you want to hear? Or that my pulse is racing so hard it's pounding in my ears. I *want* you, Diana. I have to know what it feels like to thrust my cock into that smart mouth of yours."

My lips part around the tip of his cock before taking as much of his length as I can into my mouth. He's so big that even as he hits the back of my throat, it's still not all of him. He doesn't let go of my hair, but I'm still in complete control, setting the pace, letting my tongue explore his cock—steel encased in velvety-soft skin.

"Oh fuck... Diana." He can't take his eyes off me as I move up and down, relishing every thrust in and out of my mouth, his groans of pleasure spurring me on to take more, faster, harder. "Holy shit."

Running my hands up the inside of his legs, I brace them on his thighs, giving myself over to sensation, moaning with delight, letting it vibrate along the length of him. I'm consumed by lust, desperate to watch him fall apart beneath me.

When I know he's close, I still myself, waiting for him to set his own rhythm, a thrill coursing through me. There's a difference between giving a guy a blow job and letting him fuck your mouth.

"Don't stop. You look so fucking good when you're on your knees."

I press soft kisses from the base of his cock, up the length of him, stopping shy of the tip. "If you want it... take it."

With his hands still fisted in my hair, he tightens his grip. "Open those pouty lips of yours." I do as he asks, gasping as he takes me with a hard, sharp thrust of his hips. "Fuck me, that's it."

He circles his hips, easing almost out of my mouth before sliding back in, slowly picking up the pace, his head dropping back as he relishes every thrust, ripping his pleasure from my lips. Heat pools between my thighs, wet and ready for his big, beautiful cock.

"Jesus, your mouth is so damn perfect. If you don't want a mouthful of cum, I suggest you pull away because, holy shit, I can't. It's too fucking good." He continues to thrust, and I take it, pumping him harder, swirling my tongue over the crest on every upward stroke.

I don't know why, but I need this—to watch him splinter into a million pieces because of me. He sets a punishing rhythm, climbing higher and higher until he can't hold back any longer. His orgasm pulses through him, a warm shot of cum hitting the back of my throat, but I still can't relinquish his cock, my eyes fixed on him as he crashes over the edge, shouting my name as he comes hard.

"Diana... oh fuck... yes... Diana." My name is a plea on his lips as he rides the aftershocks, his whole body undulating beneath me. I sit back on my heels, the sight of him undone in the afterglow causing a physical ache between my legs.

The moment his eyes find mine, they're dark, sexy, and clouded by desire. Holding his hand out to steady me, he wets his lips, raking the length of me as I get to my feet. Without a word, he hitches my dress up to my waist, discarding my lace panties in one fluid motion, tapping my left leg to step out of them.

I expect him to slip on a condom or thrust his fingers inside me, but instead, he takes my hands and places them either side of him on the back of the sofa. "Hold tight, southpaw." He grabs me by the thighs and hoists me up his body, taking my weight as if it were nothing more than a feather. I cling to the sofa, curling my fingers over the top to steady myself.

When he has me where he wants, he slides down between my legs, parted wide as they'll go as he positions himself so I can ride his face. "Fuck, you taste good, Diana. You're already soaking wet and ready to ride me."

I begin to move, letting the scruff of his jaw tantalize me while the wet warmth of his tongue sends me spiraling. Whatever shred of control I thought I had is gone in a haze of animalistic need. He devours me, groaning as he licks, nips, and sucks my pussy, reveling in the pleasure he knows I crave from him at this moment.

Within seconds, I can feel the familiar beginnings of my release unfurling deep in my core. I'm so turned on, I was on the brink before he even touched me. Using the back of the sofa for leverage, I ride his face with wild abandon, any thoughts of tomorrow discarded on the floor next to my panties.

"Oh God... Linc... fuck... oh God, yeah." It feels too damn good, and when I find myself on the edge, there's no holding back. Linc sends me roaring into the abyss, freefalling as my release takes over, radiating through every fiber of my being. My legs are shaking uncontrollably, my voice hoarse, and I scream his name. "Linc... yes... oh fuck yes... Linc."

I collapse against the sofa as Linc continues to rain featherlight kisses between my quivering thighs. Struggling to catch my breath, I can't take anymore, shifting away from his touch.

"Fucking hell, you taste like honeydew melon when you come."

My limbs are so weak, I can't even right my dress, exposed to Linc's hungry gaze. "Holy shit, that was... intense."

"Still don't want to take me home tonight? I don't know about you, but for me, this was just an appetizer."

"I'm not taking you home." I try to say it with conviction, but even my voice is shaking.

"Say it like you mean it. I'm going to fuck you tonight, Diana, and that's not up for debate. We both know it, so the only real question is where. I can fuck you right here, quick and dirty. You can take me back to your place, and I'll use both of the condoms in my wallet. Or... I can take you back to my place and fuck you in every room, on every surface, and the orgasm you just had will seem like nothing more than a good French kiss by comparison."

I know I'm going to regret this in the morning.

"Your place it is."

CHAPTER EIGHT

LINC

RUNNING IS the best way to clear your head. When I disappear into Central Park, I become just another jogger out there trying to stay fit. With my ballcap on and earbuds in, the rest of the world falls away, one stride at a time.

Temperatures are barely above freezing today, and every breath forms a perfect puff of visible air, disappearing before my eyes as quickly as it forms. I've been lax on my exercise lately, but then, I've been getting plenty of private workout sessions with Diana. Ever since the night at Viper, we've been drunk dialing each other regularly, and I hate to admit it, but she's growing on me. She's made it pretty clear that she has nothing but contempt for my personality. However, my giant cock seems to be winning her over to my other standout traits.

The park is busy this morning, more so than usual, which I like. It's even easier to disappear in here when there are twenty other guys in a ballcap pounding the running trail. With Diana on my mind, I push myself harder, picking up the pace, my jog turning to a run as I force the air in and out of my lungs, my chest aching with the cold.

I haven't hooked up with anyone else in the time that Diana and I have been casually becoming steady booty-call buddies. We don't acknowledge it or discuss any other potential partners we have, and as much as I want to be nonchalant about the whole thing, I'm not. With every passing night we spend in my bed—never hers—the less I'm interested in anyone else. Even Candy has noticed. We've never been anything more than a mutually convenient speed dial, but I haven't called her since before I went to Vegas. Since before Diana.

My mind is racing, torturing myself with the 'what-ifs' of Diana's personal life. What if she's seeing other people? What if she doesn't feel the same inexplicable draw I do? What if some other guy has had his hands on her? I have no right to an opinion, but the rage that courses through my veins at the mere thought of it has me flat-out sprinting by the time I reach the end of my run.

"Fuck."

Maybe I should just call Candy or go to Viper tonight *without* calling Diana at the end of the night. It's not like I don't have other offers. Not to blow my own trumpet, but I have women falling over themselves for one night with me. And yet, I can't get the only woman I want to even let me set foot in her apartment.

As I head back to my place, I pull out my phone and make the call I should have before now. I'm letting this mess with my head, but I'm done.

"My apartment. Eight o'clock."

MY LITTLE DOG, Tink, is excited when she hears a knock at the door, finally getting out from under my feet in the kitchen. I'm going all out tonight with my signature carb-loading fettuccini pomodoro.

She's a sight for sore eyes when I open the door, and as always, she launches herself at me with very little preamble. "I'm supposed to be at Brooke's by nine, so this'll need to be a quickie." She reaches for my shirt as her lips find mine, but as much as I'd like to lose myself in her, I have to draw a line and hope she wants to cross it with me.

"Hey, I made dinner."

"You can reheat it after I'm gone. I'm on the clock, Linc. Take off your pants."

I hold her at arm's length. "I made dinner for *us*. I thought maybe we could eat before we fuck."

"Why?" She tries to stare me down, but I know her well enough to see a fleeting moment of vulnerability in the firm knit of her brow. "We don't do that."

"Just because we haven't doesn't mean we can't. Look at me, I'm wasting away from all the sex and none of the dinners, lunches, or midnight snacking that usually comes along with it."

"I can better assess your need for calories when you're naked. From memory, I think you're fine. Better than fine." Diana has this way of looking at me like I'm the meal and she's ravenous.

"I made the pasta from scratch. Have one mouthful."

"You really called me to come have dinner with you?"

"Yes. Is that so weird? I know every inch of your body intimately, so I figured it might be time to hang out."

"I have to be at Brooke's in an hour."

"Then I guess you better eat fast if you want to get your rocks off."

"If I don't eat, I don't get sex? Really?"

"No, because you look fucking hot, and I have no self-control, but I'm asking you to sit down and eat a meal with me. You might even find some small redeeming quality of my personality."

"Why do I feel like the bad guy right now? You're the one changing the rules."

I hold a chair out for her to take a seat. "I thought the beauty of us is that we don't *have* any rules."

"It does smell pretty good. I guess it can't hurt."

"There's the enthusiasm I was looking for." She cracks a smile as I grab a few glasses and pour us some champagne. While I plate up the dinner, I jump right in on the small talk. Something we're not accustomed to. "So, how's training going? Have you got a new date for the fight?"

"Training is fine. I'm not going full tilt right now which is nice. That's one of the annoying things about having the fight postponed. I was ready and in peak physical condition. Now I have to pull back and then get myself back in that space again. I swear to God, if it gets put off again, I won't need a venue or a crowd to watch, I'll just go and kick her ass myself."

"If you need some cardio workouts for fight preparation, you know I'm here for you... as a fellow athlete."

"Do you think about anything other than sex?"

I set her plate down and take a seat across from her, laughing at the absurdity of her question. "I'm trying to feed you dinner. You're the one who doesn't want to have a real conversation with me. Hell, we've been sleeping together for a while, and I don't even know what the inside of your apartment looks like."

"Sorry, I just wasn't expecting... this." I watch as she winds the pasta around her fork and lifts it to that beautiful mouth of hers.

"Yeah, I can do other things besides rock your world and be a baseball god."

"And there's the Linc I know. I swear your head's as big as your cock."

I choke on my half-chewed mouthful, trying not to laugh. "You're not helping the problem when you're reinforcing the fact that I have a huge cock. I know you love it, but some polite dinner conversation wouldn't go amiss."

"Sorry, these limp noodles got me thinking about your junk. My bad." A sly grin spreads across her face, and her cheeks flush with a carefree ease I've never seen before. It looks good on her.

"I guess you won't need dessert, then?"

"Let's not be hasty."

"Then, talk to me. Tell me something about yourself."

"What do you want to know?"

"Anything."

"My mom made me dance ballet for six months when I was a kid until I refused point-blank to put on the tutu one day. That's the closest I've ever been to a conventional girl."

"You're more conventional than you think."

"Oh really? Why is that? Pray tell, oh wise one." She sits back, crossing her arms over her chest—defensive rather than combative. This is something she's sensitive about.

"For a start, look at you. You're a knockout."

"Ha-fucking-ha."

It takes me a moment to understand her ire. "There was no pun intended. Shit. I was trying to say that you're gorgeous. You have the figure of a goddess. Your breasts are..." I scrape my hand over my jaw, considering my next words carefully. "Perfection."

"Wow, that was the most superficial observation of my femininity. You really do know me."

"You didn't let me finish. As usual, you want to berate me before hearing me out. Looks aside, I think I know you better than you think."

"Enlighten me."

"You act like it pisses you off that people assume you're masculine because of your chosen profession, but I think you hide behind that physical strength. You keep guys like me at arm's length, so I'd venture to say the last guy you dated broke your heart."

"Everyone's had their heart broken."

"Okay. You want specifics." I rest my cutlery on the empty plate, mirroring her body language as I lean back in my chair. "We've slept together countless times, but you still get shy when I go down on you. You bite your bottom lip when you're uncomfortable, just like you are right now. You always wear your hair down when you're on a night out, and my guess would be that you want to be as feminine as possible. It's also why you never wear pants when you turn up at my place after you've been to a bar."

"I know I'm a woman, Linc."

"Do you? You know you're female, but when I call you a woman,

I mean that you have curves in all the right places. I mean, you have a softer side you don't like to show people. You play with your hair when you're turned on, and you lick your lips when you want me to lick you out. You like it when I hold doors for you but always think better of it and berate me for being a gentleman."

"I wouldn't use the word 'gentleman' to describe you."

"Only because you won't let me. That's why you're itching to leave right now. I'm sitting here trying to tell you that I see you, and not just as a fuck buddy."

"We're not even buddies."

"We could be. We *are* if you choose to acknowledge it. Yes, we spend ninety-nine percent of our time together fucking, but I've started looking forward to the one percent."

"You're tired of me?"

"This is what I'm talking about. How do you get that from what I just said? You add two and two and come up with five. I enjoy your company. I like the quiet moments when we're boneless and breathless, and you make me laugh. When you let yourself be vulnerable, you're fucking resplendent."

There's a visible change in her demeanor the moment she puts her walls up. I've pushed her too far, too quickly. Standing from the table, she grabs the finished plates and takes them into the kitchen.

"You can leave that. I've got it."

"You cooked, so it's the right thing to do. Clean up. I have time before I need to go."

I follow behind her, standing at her back as she rinses the dishes off in the sink. "What are you afraid of, Diana? That maybe I see you, and I like what I see?"

She turns to face me, sliding her hand over my crotch. "You see what I want you to see, Linc. *This* is what I'm here for, pretty boy, so do you want to fuck me or not?"

Tucking a loose tendril of hair behind her ear, I caress her cheek, willing her to give me a chance. "You know I do, but what if I want more? A date. Dinner and a movie, maybe some drinks after. *Then,* all the sex you can handle." I lean in, pressing my lips to her in a chaste kiss. "One date." I continue to kiss her between each word. "You... might... like... it."

"No." She drops her hand from massaging my cock to a raging boner, my balls aching as she shoves me away and walks over to the living room. "This is me... take it or leave it." She grasps the hem of her dress, pulling it up over her head before tossing it on my couch.

"Diana."

"Stop with the Diana. You're the only person who calls me that. It's Dee." She unhooks her bra, letting it slide off her shoulder and down to the floor.

"It's never bothered you before, especially when I'm shouting your name as I come inside you. Tell me you don't love the way it sounds on my lips."

She snakes her fingers under the sides of her panties and pushes them down her hips, standing naked in nothing but a pair of sexy as hell heels. "Take me... or leave me."

It's taking every ounce of strength I have to try to resist the urge to fuck now and talk later. "I want you. I want more of you."

"And if this is all I can give?" She parts her legs, letting her hand slip between them, blazing a trail of fire to the apex of her thighs. "You don't want it?"

I may be attempting to cultivate something more with this woman, but I'm not a fucking saint. Unzipping my fly, I close the gap between us, my cock aching to be inside her. Any coherent thoughts of attempting to be a gentleman are gone—forgotten.

My lips crash down on hers as I pull her into my arms, her naked flesh like manna from heaven. She unbuttons my shirt with expert fingers before shoving it off my shoulders and moving to my pants. I can't get enough of her, wanting to taste every inch of her at once.

"Fuck, Diana, I need you."

Her hand fists my cock as she shoves my pants and boxers just low enough for me to spring free. There's no softness in her touch, only raw, desperate hunger for more. "Fuck me, Linc. *Hard*."

I see red, all sound judgment out the window as I hoist her into my arms. "Wrap your legs around my waist."

She does as I ask without question, her slick pussy grinding against my erection. *Jesus Christ.* It's too fucking good, we're not going to make it to the bedroom tonight. Finding the nearest wall, I press her back against it for purchase, circling my hips as her arousal coats the length of my cock.

"You feel so fucking good. I could fuck you right now, no holds barred."

"Then do it." She slides one hand between us, positioning my cock at her entrance, rendering me helpless to resist. "I have an IUD. Fuck me."

I take her in one sharp thrust of my hips, the warmth of her pussy tightening around me as I sink balls deep, making her take every hard inch of me. I've never taken a woman bareback before, and the fact that it's Diana only serves to heighten the sensation to a fever pitch. A guttural roar escapes me in a voice that's unrecognizable.

"Fucking hell."

"Oh God, Linc. Yes... fuck... yes!" Every move, every twitch of her muscles is a lightning rod of ecstasy, igniting me as every nerve ending in my body sparks to life. There's no room for gentle, slow, or steady. This is a primal, unbridled, uncontrollable fuck.

"You're so fucking tight. Jesus... Diana." Her name rings out in a litany of worship as she grinds against me, pushing me higher and higher, her moans of pleasure almost too much for me to handle.

"Linc... I'm so close. I can't. I need. Oh fuck, please." I hammer into her, driving harder with each thrust until she loses control, screaming my name as she orgasms, milking my cock, ripping my release from the very core of my being.

Wave after wave, I slam her, begging for more, giving her every-thing I've got. I've never come so hard or so long in my life. As the aftershocks pulse through me, her muscles spasm around my cock, the pleasure so intense it's on the verge of painful, but I don't fucking care.

When I can't hold us up any longer, I withdraw, bereft, before lowering us to the hardwood floor. Her breath is labored, her cheeks flushed with the blissful afterglow of a screaming orgasm.

"Holy shit, I was *not* expecting that tonight." I roll onto my side, drinking in the sight of her naked and sated. "That was..."

"The last time."

"Yeah, should probably go back to the condoms from here on out, but Jesus, you feel so fucking good." I reach over, tracing circles on her stomach. "You're breathtaking, Diana."

I'm not prepared when she recoils from my touch, scrambling for her discarded clothes. "I need to go."

"I'm sure your sister won't mind if you're a little late." As she wrestles her dress on, the inside of her thigh becomes slick with my cum as it spills out of her. It might be the single hottest thing I've ever seen. "Stay, we can take it to the bed for round two. You know you want to."

She can't even look me in the eye as she slips her panties on and stuffs her bra in her purse. "I don't want to. When I said the last time, I meant us. Whatever this is between us just stopped being fun."

"I beg to fucking differ." I don't bother with modesty, jumping to my feet as she heads for the door. "When you say it with a voice so hoarse you'll still be feeling it tomorrow, I don't think you have a leg to stand on."

"You're a great lay, but this..." she gestures to the dinner table, "... I don't want this. You couldn't just keep it light."

"I just fucked you bareback. I hate to tell you, southpaw, but we're way past light."

"Consider it a goodbye."

"Is that how you say goodbye to all the guys?"

"Fuck you, Linc."

I follow her out into the hallway as she slams the button for the elevator. "How did we go from my cum dripping down your leg to you never wanting to see me again?"

"I told you this was just sex, but as usual, you don't listen. Guys like you never do."

"Hold the fucking phone with the *'guys like me'* bullshit. I made you a goddamn dinner, and now I'm literally standing here with my dick in hand. I didn't exactly propose. What did I do that was so wrong?" I may not have my cock in my hand, but it's hanging in the breeze right now as the elevator doors open, and she disappears inside.

"I didn't want dinner. I don't want some fake shit about how you'll be a reformed man and won't still fuck everything with a pulse. Let's be realistic, you're a player, and I enjoyed the game, but I'm done."

"I promised you nothing, but I'm standing here offering you something, and you're making excuses not to give me a chance. I've never been a cheater, and I fucking resent the implication. Can you say the same thing, Diana?"

"Go fuck yourself, Linc." Tears well in her eyes as the doors close, and I have no fucking idea what just happened.

"Too late, you already did that for me." As the familiar whirring of the elevator springs into action, the faint sound of her voice—cursing me out—echoes as I stand shellshocked and buck naked outside my front door. I wore my heart on my sleeve tonight, taking a chance on something more for the first time, and it bit me in the bare naked ass.

I won't be doing it again any time soon.

CHAPTER NINE

DIANA

"CAN you grab the steaks out the fridge, Dee?"

Brooke has been trying her hand at cooking since she shacked up with lover boy. Most of the time it's a disaster, but how bad can it be frying a steak? Ever since I turned up at her door a few weeks ago looking disheveled and thoroughly fucked, she knows something's up.

"Earth to Dee. The steaks."

I grab the raw meat from the refrigerator, and the smell is overpowering. "I think they might be off." I hold the plate as far away from my nostrils as possible, urging her to take them. "Seriously, take a whiff."

She lifts them right up to her face, making me gag at the sight. "They don't smell like anything. I got them fresh from the butcher earlier today."

I pour us both a glass of wine while she starts prepping the stinky steaks, but when I bring it to my lips, another wave of nausea washes over me. Setting it down, I pull up a barstool at the end of the kitchen island, propping myself up on my elbows.

"Where's your limpet tonight?" I ask with a sickly-sweet smile.

"If you're referring to my super-hot, super-sexy husband, then he's at the batting cages with Linc."

"Those two need to just give in already and get it on. Their bromance isn't fooling anyone."

"Very funny, but..." she says, staring off into the distance, "... how fucking hot would that be?"

"Nothing involving Linc is sexy." Just the mention of his name has my stomach in knots, and I'm not too thrilled when Brooke starts cackling.

"I smell... bullshit! I don't care if you're not a fan of the guy's personality, but you'd have to be freaking blind to say he's not sexy."

"Does Anders know you have the hots for his boyfriend?" The bite in my voice is bitchy as hell, but I can't seem to rein it in when it comes to Linc.

"What's the deal with you two? Why can't you just get along already?"

"I don't know what you're talking about."

"Again, with the bullshit. Did you have a fight or something? I thought you called a truce in Vegas. He bristles at the very mention of your name, and you're a catty bitch when it comes to him." He doesn't even want to hear my name now. I can't blame him, but I also can't give him what he wants, not after I made such a mess of things with Anthony.

"Does it matter? We don't move in the same circles."

"What the hell am I, chopped liver? You *are* going to see each other, and I need you to be civil at least. I'd rather you were friends, but that seems impossible. Maybe you're just oil and water."

"More like oil and a lit match."

"This is exactly what I'm talking about. What the hell happened in Vegas?"

"Nothing. I just don't like the guy. Do I need a reason?"

"Yeah, actually. He's my husband's best friend, and he's a really good guy once you get to know him. He has a heart of gold beneath all the bravado."

I know this only too well, and that's why I have to distance myself from him. I'm not going to fall for another player. Maybe his game is a little different to my ex, but the end result is the same —heartache, disappointment, and me left alone picking up the pieces.

"Is this why you asked me over, to lecture me about Linc?"

"No. You're my sister, and you seem... off lately. I know the stuff with the fight threw you, and you haven't set a new date yet, but you're back training. What's going on with you? You can talk to me, Dee."

No, I can't.

"I'm fine."

Just as she's about to launch into some lengthy speech about being my sister and the fact that I'm emotionally stunted in some way, the key turns in the lock. I've never been happier to be the third wheel for the night.

"That screwball was too good for you, admit it." *Shit.* I know who Anders is talking to before the door opens wide, and my worst nightmare walks in.

"It was a fucked-up pitch, bro, don't try playing it off like you meant it." The deep rasp of his voice is like a fan to a flame, igniting the desire I've been trying to stamp out for weeks.

"Brooke." I glare at her with daggers in my eyes. "What the fuck?"

Shaking her head, she welcomes them both. "Hey baby, I didn't know you were going to be back so early."

I turn to see Linc staring at me as Brooke wraps her arms around me. "Sorry, Lexington, I have a date, so I called time on our session at the cages. He was throwing out those whack screwballs he loves so much."

"You mean the one only I can hit? Does it hurt you deep down in your soul to know I'm the superior hitter in his life?"

The breathy sound of Linc's laugh causes a physical ache in my chest.

"Cruel. All I've ever done is love you. I let you share my best friend, and this is the thanks I get?"

"You know I love you."

"I love you, too, Lexington." His eyes drift in my direction, but I divert my gaze as my stomach lurches up into my throat.

"Excuse me." I run to the restroom, losing what little lunch I had earlier today. You know a relationship in any form is toxic when it literally makes you sick. It takes a few minutes for the retching to stop, but when it subsides, I splash some cold water on my face and rinse my mouth out with mouthwash before heading back to the kitchen.

"Are you okay?" Linc studies my face, worry etched in his brow.

"I'm going to go home. I think I might have food poisoning."

"You haven't even eaten yet. My cooking's not that bad," Brooke jests.

"I think it was my lunch. I'll leave you guys to the rest of your night. I'll call you tomorrow." I grab my purse and make my way to the front door.

"Do you want me to drop you home, Dee? You look a bit off-color." Anders is a good man, but he suffers from the same macho overprotectiveness as Linc.

"I'll be fine. I can manage by myself."

"I'm heading out just now anyway, so I can drop her home," Linc interjects.

"You're talking about me as if I'm not standing right here."

He makes a big show of turning to face me. "I can take *you* home, Diana. It's on my way, and you look like ass. It won't kill you to be in the same car as me for five fucking minutes."

Brooke steps in before I can respond.

"*Enough!* I hate this. Both of you. I don't know why you dislike each other so much. I actually think you'd be great friends if you just got over yourselves for two seconds. I'm tired of the back-biting every time you're in the same room. When you're in my house, you play nice. Got it?"

"I can get myself home. I'm a perfectly capable woman." My argument loses all credibility when my stomach roils, and I drop my purse and run back to the restroom.

By the time I make it back to the front door, Linc is ready and waiting with my purse on his arm. "I'm not debating this with you, I *am* driving you home."

"Fine."

Brooke pulls me into her arms, worry marring her sweet face. "Do you want me to come with you?"

"No. You have a steak to massacre and force-feed to Anders. I'll be okay in the morning."

"Call me when you're tucked up in bed."

"I'll try to remember."

"Linc, make sure she gets into her apartment."

"Will do."

The ride down to the parking garage of their building is excruciating. Silence spans out like the sands of time, endless and as uncomfortable as bringing home half the beach in your butt crack. It's only made worse by the car journey to my apartment and the fact that Linc insists on walking me up to my front door.

"Are you sure you're okay, Diana?" There's genuine affection in his voice. "I can stay for a while if you need me to."

"You've done enough. Thanks for bringing me home. I don't want to keep you from your date." Saying those words out loud makes me want to puke again.

"Of course, you don't."

"That's not what I meant."

"I got the message, Diana, you don't have to freak out. I'm a decent guy, and you're obviously sick. I'm just making sure you're okay, nothing more. And you're right, I have a date with a woman who actually wants to spend time with me, so I better get going."

Watching him walk away, knowing he'll be warming another woman's bed tonight is gut-wrenching, but I don't have time to think on it too long as another round of toilet hugging takes hold. There's nothing left in my stomach now, and the dry heaving is painful, to say the least. When it finally lets up, I strip, slip on my favorite pajamas, and crawl into bed, pulling the comforter up over my head. This clusterfuck of a night needs to end. Exhaustion finds me in the darkness, coaxing me into a dreamless sleep. Hopefully, tomorrow is a better day.

EVERYTHING I'VE EATEN this past week, I've thrown up. Training is on hold, and Gray has been badgering me to go see the doctor. I finally relented when I figured I'm way past a bout of food poisoning. This is some stomach flu on steroids, and at this point, I need relief. I'm miserable, and seeing Linc again makes it worse. He didn't have to bring me home or walk me to my door. Not after the way I treated him.

Since the night I walked out on Linc, I've busied myself with anything and everything to stop from calling him. He wanted more than I could give. This week, I miss him. Lying around in my pajamas and camping out on my bathroom floor, I've had way too much time to think, running over that night a million times in my head.

That was the first time I've been with a man without a condom and knowing it was a first for him only made it harder to leave. It was selfish of me because I knew it had to be the last time I slept with him, and I couldn't walk away before experiencing him without barriers— skin to skin—pleasure at its most raw.

Today, I'm out of the house, if only to go to the doctor's office, but I take the opportunity to focus on the task at hand rather than torturing myself about Linc

"The doctor is ready for you, Miss Lexington." The receptionist leads me down the hall to an exam room, where everything is so clinical and sterile. "He'll be right with you."

"Thank you."

God, whoever the cleaners are for this place, they went overboard on the chemicals last night. The scent is so strong that my stomach starts churning. There's a stack of those sick bowls that look like hats sitting on the counter in the corner, so I grab one, just in case I lose the single slice of dry toast I managed to eat before coming here.

When the door opens, my shoulders sag, my relief palpable as my doctor appears. Being an athlete, I'm a frequent flyer in here, and I have a good rapport with him.

"How's my favorite patient?"

"Hey, doc. I think I've got the stomach flu."

"How long have you been feeling sick?"

"About a week."

"Any fever or chills?"

"No."

"Sickness *and* diarrhea?"

"No, thankfully, I'm not exploding from both ends. Just the vomit comet for me." He starts tapping away on the keyboard, his brow furrowed as he notes down what I assume is my symptoms."

"Okay, so the sickness... is it constant?"

"Yes, and my sense of smell is super intense. Everything makes me want to blow chunks, and then whenever I eat something, I can't keep it down. It's godawful. Please tell me you can give me something for it."

"Well, before we do that, let's run some tests. I'd like to get some bloodwork and a urine sample."

"We share such a special relationship, you and I." That gets a smile out of him.

"I want to get you feeling better as quickly as possible. I'd like to have the nurse come in and give you some IV fluids after we get the samples. If you haven't been able to keep anything down for a week, you'll be dehydrated. Have you got time?"

"The only plans I have right now are centered around my apartment, and more specifically, my bathroom."

"Okay, I'll be back. The nurse will be in shortly, and we'll get you fixed up."

"Thanks, doc." He leaves me to be poked and prodded, drained, and refilled. By the time the nurses are done with me, I actually feel a little better. The fluids have worked wonders, and I'm hoping this will get me over the hump with this flu.

I've read every poster and pamphlet in the room by the time my doctor comes back, his face oddly blank—schooled. *Shit.* What's wrong with me?

"How are you feeling?"

"A lot better after that IV. Thank you. So, your face has got me a little worried right now. What's up?"

"I've sent your bloodwork to the lab. We'll get those results in a day or two. Your urine analysis did flag something which I think could explain all your symptoms."

"O-kay. Let me have it."

"You're pregnant."

My chest constricts as the wind is knocked right out of me. It's wrong. *It must be wrong.* I have an IUD for crying out loud. My pulse begins to race, pounding so hard I can hear it whooshing in my ears, the doctor's voice becoming white noise.

This can't be happening. I've always been so careful. I have two years left before my IUD needs to be changed. It's impossible. A wave of nausea sweeps through me, washing over me. I cling to my sick bowl as my stomach muscles tighten, forcing that single slice of toast up and out of me in a gross projectile.

Only when I stop retching does the doctor speak again, this time with a soothing, consolatory tone. "I'm assuming this wasn't planned?"

"Not even close." Another wave hits me.

"I'd like to admit you for twenty-four hours, just to get you feeling a little better."

"No. If I don't have the flu, and it's not a bug, then I'm stuck with the sickness until I hit the three-month mark, right?"

"Most likely. Your bloodwork will give us a better picture of how far along you are, and we can coordinate with your OBGYN for further treatment. The good news is that I can give you something to help with the nausea."

"Thank God for that."

"Do you want to discuss your options?"

"No, I already know them and what I'm going to do. It's a no-brainer for me."

"Okay. Can I at least have one of the nurses accompany you home? I don't like the idea of letting you leave in this condition. You'd really benefit from more fluids."

"Now that I know what I'm dealing with, I promise to hydrate, even if I don't feel like it."

"I'm going to arrange someone to take you home."

"It's okay, I'll call my sister. She lives a few blocks from here."

"If she can't come, you're not leaving without an escort."

"Fine." I grab my phone and tap out a quick message.

Me: *Can you come pick me up at Dr. Schneider's office?*

Brooke: *What's up?*

Me: *Just the stomach flu. I'll be fine, but he doesn't want me taking a cab home alone. I need you for twenty minutes tops. Can you come?*

Brooke: *On my way.*

Me: *Thanks, sis.*

By the time Brooke arrives, I'm glad she's here. My limbs are weak, and my stomach is still in knots, only now I don't know if it's nausea or knowledge. One thing's for sure, I'm not telling Brooke.

She gets me home but won't leave when I tell her I'm fine, clucking around me like a mother hen. "You've been sick all week, and you didn't think to call me?"

"I just need to rest. There's nothing you can do for me, so why bother you?"

"Because I'm your sister, and I love you. Or maybe because if you're sick enough to go to the doctor, then you shouldn't be alone."

"Single people get ill all the time. It's not like you were going to rock up here and find my rotting corpse or anything."

"Wow, you just took a dark turn. I was thinking that you need someone to bring you soup or give you a trashcan to puke in. Maybe even give you towels to kneel on when you're hugging the toilet. *Now* I'm worried about finding you croaked. I'm staying until you feel better."

"No, you're not. You have a life and a husband to go home to. I'm just going to be sleeping. The doc sent a prescription to the pharmacy for some anti-sickness drugs. They'll be delivered in an hour, and I'll be on the road to recovery. Thank you for helping me home, but honestly, you can go."

"I don't like this, Dee. Maybe I should call Mom to come hang with you."

"Fuck, no. Are you kidding me? She hovers more than you. How am I supposed to rest with you guys staring at me?"

"Fine, but promise you'll answer the phone when I check in on you. I'm going to be calling every few hours to make sure you're okay."

"Seriously?"

"It's the only way I'm going home right now. You answer your phone, and if you don't, I'll be back over here with Mom, Anders, and I'll have him bring Linc, too, just to piss you off." At the mention of his name, I grab the trashcan at my side and heave a whole lot of nothing. He's the last person I want to see. He can't know about this.

"Not funny." I echo into the steel can.

"Not kidding."

Brooke hovers while I change into sweats and my favorite hoodie—apparently, privacy isn't a thing. After I'm curled up in bed, she fusses for another thirty minutes, making sure I have the television remote, phone and charger, tissues, crackers, and a dozen bottles of water. What does she think I am, a camel? No one needs this much water in one sitting.

"Okay, do you need anything else before I go?"

"You've thought of everything. I'm just going to get some sleep now."

"I'll leave you to rest, but I'll wait in the living room for your prescription to arrive."

"You don't have to do that."

"It saves you getting up. If you're asleep by then, I'll leave the pills on your nightstand."

"Thanks, sis. I know I'm a crotchety bitch, but I really do appreciate you."

"You get a pass right now on the bitchy. I'm a bitch when I feel like crap too. Rest, and I'll talk to you tonight."

I must find some small respite from the nausea because I wake to find my prescription bottle sitting on my nightstand, and it's dark outside. How long did I sleep? Grabbing my phone to check the time, my heart stutters to a halt when I see the name on my screen.

Linc: *Brooke says you're still really sick. Are you okay?*

Tears well in my eyes. After the way I've treated him, how can I face him now? It's better for both of us if things stay as they are—nonexistent.

Me: *Please, don't message me again.*

I can't deal with this, crying until my eyes are almost swollen shut. I've come out of fights looking and feeling better than I do right now. I need time to think and figure out my next step. I'd be a terrible mother and doing it alone would be a million times harder. This isn't supposed to happen to me. Brooke is the one who has her life together. She's got the guy, the marriage, and the capacity to bring a baby into the world and raise it properly. What do I have to offer? I'm a fighter. It's all I've ever known. I'm not ready to be a mother.

I know what has to happen, even though it'll be the hardest thing I ever do. With the decision made, I cry myself to sleep after gagging on my own snot and tears with my head in the trashcan for an hour. It's fitful at best, plagued with visions of Linc holding our baby. I try to get close, but with every step I take, they get further and further away until I'm running to catch them, but they're always out of reach. *Forever out of reach.*

CHAPTER TEN
LINC

"ARE you still not over her? You didn't even hook up. If you were never under her, why can't you get over her? Seriously, bro, she's not worth it." I know Anders is trying to be a good friend, but he's just pissing me off.

"I'd really appreciate it if you didn't weigh in on this particular topic."

"Have you hooked up with anyone recently? What about Candy?"

"I'm bored of Candy."

'She's your go-to girl."

"*Was.* I'm fed up with the same old, same old. What if I want more than one-night stands?"

"Shut the front door. As I live and breathe, Lincoln Nash has gone and grown a heart. I wasn't prepared for this today."

"A man can change. You did."

"Yeah, but that was because of Brooke. It didn't come out of nowhere. I had a reason, a catalyst for change. Dee isn't encouraging you to be a better man. She's not dangling a carrot and saying, 'come get me,' is she?"

"Who says this has anything to do with her? Maybe I'm just ready for a relationship. I'm a grown-ass man. I'm sick of one-and-done. I want something more substantial. Candy isn't the kind of woman you find forever with. She's great for no strings attached but not for a lifetime."

"Holy shit. You're serious."

"Is it so hard to believe? Am I that shallow? Is your opinion of me that low?" Anders knows me better than anyone. If he doesn't see me as capable of a meaningful relationship, then maybe there really is no hope for me—with Diana or anyone.

"Jesus, you're becoming a real boy, Pinocchio."

"Fuck off." I knew it was a bad idea to come to the gym with Anders today. I woke up with Diana on my mind, and I'm quickly learning that I'm not fit to be around others on days like this. I fucking hate it.

"Why don't you bite the bullet and ask her out?" If only he knew.

"You and your wife are the ones who've been telling me I'll be turned into the first eunuch the Yankees have ever had if I go near her." This is exactly why I haven't told them Diana and I hooked up for months. It would be different if she'd taken me up on the offer of more, wanted to date me, and made an honest man of me, but apparently, she only wanted me for my anaconda.

"I didn't realize you wanted a girlfriend. I just thought you were looking for a roll in the hay."

"It doesn't really matter what I want. She has nothing but disdain for me."

"Because she doesn't know you. Given the chance to see the real Linc, you guys would get along like a house on fire."

"I doubt it." I can't tell him that she had ample opportunity and decided I wasn't someone she wanted in her life.

"What makes you say that?"

"Can we drop it? I want to work out and *not* talk."

"Fair enough. But, if you change your mind, I'm always here if you want to talk."

"You mean you're around if I want the shit ripped out of me."

"*No!* I get it. It wasn't easy for me to admit I wanted more with Brooke. I had to step way out of my comfort zone, and I was scared out of my mind. It's not for the faint of heart, and I admire you for wanting to give it a go."

"Fuck, I think I'd rather go with option A. Having you admire me is disconcerting."

"Make up your mind, bro."

"I did. Silence." I put my AirPods in and set the treadmill to an uphill gradient.

"I'm shutting up now."

"Five miles and then lunch."

"Sounds like a plan."

I turn up the volume on my favorite playlist and allow the music to carry me away, letting my mind clear as I pound the treadmill at a steady pace. I need to start going on dates. Real ones, with women who are looking for a relationship. Not the Candy girls of Manhattan.

When we've run our five miles and worked up a sweat, I've earned a long, hot shower and worked up an appetite. We head for our favorite pizza place just off Central Park and grab a few slices.

"I know we're going to have a night out with the team for my birthday next week, but Brooke's parents are insisting on a dinner at their place in the Hamptons this weekend. Do you want to come? It would be less of a snooze fest."

"Are you kidding?" He can't be serious. Why the hell would I want to spend a weekend with his in-laws?

"No. You like Diana. What better way to spend some time with her and let her get to see a different side of you? Her mom loves you."

"She's not exactly one for being swayed by her mom's opinion, or her sister's. She'll just be pissed that I'm there."

"Then fuck her."

"I want to."

"You know what I mean. If it annoys her, then that's her problem.

We'll have some laughs, go out on the water, drink some ridiculously priced whiskey, and have some laughs. I think Carter might be up there this weekend too."

"Of course, he has a house in the Hamptons."

"The man is making money hand over fist from idiots like us who run up tabs for thousands of dollars, paying for copious amounts of alcohol whenever we drink in his clubs."

"To be fair, we're generous motherfuckers. We pay for everyone's drinks, and his clubs are the bomb."

"So, are you going to come? We can go hang out with him one night and drink his top-shelf liquor."

"If Diana gets catty, you're the one who's taking the talons to the face."

"Whatever. She likes me."

"Well, isn't that fucking lovely for you? The only Lexington that loves me is an octogenarian married mother of two."

Anders' pizza becomes a projectile that I manage to avoid by less than an inch as he descends into a fit of laughter. "She's in her late fifties. If she finds out you thought she was in her eighties, you'll be on her shit list too."

"I was exaggerating for effect. Besides, your wife loves me."

"She does, but if you tried to snake her from me, I'd kill you."

"You'd try, but you wouldn't succeed."

"You underestimate my rage."

"Dream on, Beck."

"Shut up. Are you coming or not?" I pretend I'm thinking about it, more to convince myself than Anders. Who am I kidding? The opportunity to see Diana even though I know it's going to hurt, means I'm going.

"Fine, I'll come. But when Diana tries to kick my ass, you better have my back."

"Did you just ask me to help you if a girl tries to fight you?"

"No, I just asked for backup when a fucking UFC fighter, who hates my guts, wants to kick my ass."

"Good point. She could kick both our butts without breaking a sweat. We may have to enlist Brooke. She knows the right things to say when it comes to her sister."

"Yeah, I'm sure she's up for helping me get laid."

"Sure, she wouldn't be happy about that, but she'd be on board if she knew you were looking for the real deal. Plus, if nothing else, if you two become friends, it will at least make it easier for us all to hang out."

"I forgot, the world revolves around you and Brooke. The rest of us merely exist in your orbit."

"Now you're getting it. My orbit's a happy place, come join the party."

"You're a dick."

"I'm a fucking happy dick." I can't argue with him. He and Brooke are sickeningly blissed out.

"Seriously, we'll have a good time. I'll make sure of it."

"You better, or your birthday present will be a swirly in the locker room at practice next week."

"You're a thirty-two-year-old man. Swirlies aren't a thing at our age."

"Bullshit. If I'm physically still capable of it, then it's fair game."

"And you wonder why you haven't found a woman to settle down with yet. Could it be your maturity level?"

"You love me. I'm sure there are plenty of women out there who have the same kindergarten maturity level that you do. Don't be so down on yourself, Anders." I snigger as I take a long swig of my drink. Maybe it's a bad idea to go to Diana's parents' house this weekend, but I miss her. I admit it—I'm a sad schmuck of a man, and I crave her with every fiber of my being. If there's even the slightest chance I can get a second chance with her, I want it.

THE DRIVE UP here has been an episode of insanity—a lonely kind of crazy. Anders and Brooke drove up earlier today with Diana, but I figured that wasn't a good way to start the weekend, and I had a few things to do before heading up there.

I've gone through every possible scenario. Her being less than happy to see me. That one grew arms and legs, playing out in ten different ways, all of which came to the same conclusion, and it wasn't good for my balls.

Then, there was the possibility we make peace and become friends, or at least amicable acquaintances. That may be enough for her, but even as a hypothetical, it leaves a sour taste in my mouth. I know I'd always want more from her.

Finally, there's the fairy-tale Disney outcome. I'm not going to lie, this is my favorite. It gets me all the sex and happiness I can handle. I appear in the Hamptons with the charm and good looks God saw fit to bestow on me, Diana can't resist, and finally admits she wants me just as much as I want her—*and they lived happily ever after*.

Pulling up at the address Anders texted me this morning, I realize Brooke and Diana didn't exactly have to pull themselves up by their bootstraps to get where they are today. It doesn't lessen their achievements at all, but observing the difference in our childhood experiences is a little intimidating. The Hamptons is a far cry from the trailer Anders had the pleasure of visiting with me the week after our World Series win.

I've never been the woe-is-me guy, which is why I don't really tell people about my journey to the major league. Everyone's path is different, but we all ended up on the same team and worked our asses off to get there. I'm not better or worse than anyone else because I ate shit microwave dinners for one most of the time, and my mom's idea of a nanny was handing me the television remote.

I have multi-million-dollar contracts and endorsements, and I live in a very nice penthouse in Manhattan, but I'm still a little intimidated as I sit in the driveway staring out at the mansion before me.

The Lexington family is obviously, *extremely* wealthy. I take a few minutes to gather my thoughts before grabbing my overnight bag from the trunk and the bottle of single malt I brought for Mr. Lexington.

There's a vintage-looking knocker on the door which is heavy as I take it in my hand, rapping it three times before standing back, half expecting some Lurch butler to welcome me in. I'm surprised when Brooke's mom opens the door.

"Lincoln! I'm so glad you could join us."

"Hello, Mrs. Lexington. Thanks for having me. It's a pleasure to be here."

She ushers me inside, the smell of home cooking wafting through the foyer. "None of this Mrs. Lexington nonsense. Call me Martha. You're practically Anders' brother so that makes you family."

"I'm good with that."

"You've got perfect timing. Dinner will be ready in ten minutes. Can I get you something to drink?"

"Is there somewhere I can put my bag out of the way?"

"Of course. Of course. Upstairs. First door on the left. There are fresh towels in the bathroom. If you need anything, don't be afraid to ask."

"Thank you."

She pats my shoulder in what I believe would be a very motherly way, and I find it comforting. "Sweet boy."

"Can I do anything to help when I come back down?"

"You're here to relax. Everyone is in the living room when you're ready. Just follow the sound of Brooke and Diana bickering about God knows what."

"Will do." Knowing that she's a few feet away has my pulse racing. Fuck, I've turned into a teenage chick. Before I come back down, I better check I'm not growing tits, and my cock hasn't been replaced by a pretty pink pussy.

As I thought, the room is bigger than the trailer I grew up in, and the bathroom is on a par with the one I have in my apartment. Martha has impeccable taste, but that doesn't surprise me. Both her daughters are beautiful and know how to dress to impress. There's a difference between wearing something expensive for the sake of it and knowing how to wear something simple and elevate it in an elegant way. Diana doesn't see herself as elegant, but I do.

I grab the bottle of single malt from my bag, take a deep breath, and head downstairs. I'm hoping Mr. Lexington wants a drink tonight because I think I'm going to need one. The last time I saw Diana, it didn't go so well. I can only imagine her reaction when she found out I was crashing the family party.

"Hello! Fear not, the life and soul of the party has arrived." Anders and Brooke spring to their feet to greet me, followed by Mr. Lexington.

"Welcome to our humble abode, young man. Glad to have you."

"Thank you, sir. I brought you a small gift for letting me come along to celebrate Anders this weekend." His eyes light up at the sight of the label.

"A man who knows his whiskey. I like you already. Would you like a glass?"

"I wouldn't say no."

He looks to Anders. "I know you won't refuse a good whiskey."

I chance a glance in Diana's direction. She looks different, but I can't quite put my finger on it. When she meets my gaze, that same electric chemistry sparks to life between us, and she stands to greet me. "Hi, Linc. How are you?" Her voice is quiet. Reserved. Unlike her. She holds out her hand to shake, which feels awkward as fuck, but I guess she's trying, so I reciprocate. Even this smallest of touches is enough to make both of us jump. Vibrations course through my body, and I can't take my eyes off her.

"I'm good. It's nice to see you, Diana."

Her dad chuckles as he hands me my drink. "God, I haven't heard anyone call her that since she was in kindergarten."

"Well, sir, it's a beautiful name befitting of a lady."

Diana drops her gaze, fidgeting with her foot, raking it back and forth in the plush pile of the carpet. "No one's referred to me as a lady in a long time either."

"You are, so don't let anyone make you feel otherwise. Being fierce doesn't mean you're not feminine. They're not mutually exclusive. If anyone really studied your movement in the ring, they'd see how elegant you are. I'd say that's the essence of being a lady." I take a gulp of whiskey, realizing I'm not playing it cool at all. Everyone is staring at us, jaws on the floor. I've gone past small talk and maybe some harmless flirting to pouring my heart out for everyone to hear.

Thankfully, Anders reads the room and steps in to save my ass as I drown in the ocean of my own making. "There's a pool table in the study. Fancy a game?"

"Sure." He knows as well as I do that we don't have time for a game, but we can rack it and get the hell out of this room for a hot minute. The second we hit the hallway, he pulls me through the door to the study, the smell of old books cloaking me in a comforting blanket of wisdom.

"What the hell was that?"

"I don't fucking know. It's not like I planned it. I saw her, and my brain stopped communicating with my mouth."

"Then you need to rewire that shit. Dee isn't the kind of woman who responds to the lovey-dovey crap."

"What if you're wrong? Maybe that's exactly what she needs. Everyone treats her like a dude because she's a fighter, but does anyone stop to think that she has a softer side?"

"You've met her. What you see is what you get with Dee."

"You're wrong. So fucking wrong it's laughable."

"What's laughable is that you think you know some big dark secret about my sister-in-law. Brooke knows her better than anyone. You're reading way too much into it. Sometimes people *should* be taken at face value. Dee is a hardcore fighter. If you want a woman who needs a man to come in and sweep her off her feet, you're barking up the wrong tree."

"Dinner's ready."

"I didn't hear anyone shouting at us."

I can't stomach another minute of his short-sighted view of Diana. "I guess you can add hard of hearing to your list of shortfalls."

"What the fuck? I told you I'd help you this weekend. I'm just offering you some friendly advice."

"Yeah, well, this is something I know you're wrong about." I'm showing my hand—giving too much away, too early. I stride out the room, my thinly-veiled attempts to pass off my faux pas as righteous indignation.

Storming down the hallway, I run into Brooke on her way to tell us dinner's ready. "Hey, food's ready. Where's Anders?"

"Still in the study."

She eyes me warily. "Is everything okay?"

"Peachy."

"Then why do you seem so ticked off?"

I try to blow off the tension coiling in my muscles. "I just think everyone needs to remember that your sister is more than her persona in the ring. He disagrees."

"I thought what you said was sort of sweet. If I were her, I'd jump your bones."

"You would?" I wiggle my eyebrows with a wicked grin.

"Not when you do the creepy brow thing, but when you let yourself be genuine, you're a catch, Linc. She'd be lucky to snag you. I tell her all the time that she should give you a chance."

"You do?"

"Why do you seem so surprised? I'm mildly offended."

"I don't know. I just figured you see me the way everyone else does. A player who's not good enough for your sister. That's what Anders thinks."

"Don't listen to him. He's lucky he snagged me."

"Never a truer word spoken." We share a conspiratorial laugh. "Thanks, Brooke."

"For what."

"For not thinking I'm a douche nozzle."

"I didn't say that." She gives me that cute smile of hers, and I can't even pretend to be mad. "Now go and show my sister what a catch you are. I'll grab Anders and be there in a minute."

"You really are a keeper."

"I know." She wraps her arms around me, hugging me as tight as she can. It's like getting a bear hug from Tinkerbell, but I appreciate the sentiment.

Leaving her to deal with her husband, I follow the sound of voices to the dining room. The view of the water is incredible, surpassed only by the sight of Diana laughing, carefree with her mom.

"You seem to be having a good time in here."

Martha has a radiant smile as she guides me to the seat next to Diana. "I was just trying to press this one for details on her latest conquests, but she's not giving me the juicy details, so I'm resorting to making her laugh."

I think my eyebrows just became part of my hairline. "Okay. Is this something you generally talk about with your daughters?"

"Brooky never gives me the good stuff, but Dee and I can have a few laughs over a glass of wine. That's the problem tonight. She's on the soft stuff for some unknown reason, and she's no fun when she's sober, isn't that right, Dee?"

"Thanks, Mom. It's good to know my personality is so lacking without alcohol." Diana rolls her eyes, which I find adorable, but I'm trying not to stare, so I take my seat at her side, heat coming off me in waves.

"I think you're just fine without wine, but why the abstinence tonight? Worried you'd be unable to resist my charms?"

Martha slaps my arm with a familiar snort. The same one her daughter gets when she's nervous. "Oh, I love this boy already. You have to snap him up, Dee. He'd make a perfect son-in-law, and your babies would be gorgeous."

All color drains from Diana's face, and she can't meet my gaze. "Mom! Could you be more inappropriate? Can we go back to talking about the matching vibrators you got Brooke and me for Christmas? They'd be much better dinner conversation. The third setting is particularly pleasant."

"Another whiskey?" her father interjects.

"Can you make it a double?"

"Great idea." He disappears out of the room shortly before Martha departs for the kitchen, leaving Diana and me sitting side by side at the table.

"Did you mean what you said earlier about me being a lady?"

I turn to face her, my whole body desperate to close the distance between us. "Every word. I've missed you, Diana. Why do you think I'm here?"

"For Anders."

"I can see that jackass any day of the week. I came to see you. I know you don't want more, but I can't stop thinking about you."

"I'm glad you came. We need to talk."

"We do?" Shit. That came out like a giddy schoolboy. Way to play it cool. I have zero moves when it comes to Diana. I'm about as smooth as sandpaper that's been coated in thumbtacks and blasted with porcupine needles.

"Okay."

"After dinner. When they're all three sheets to the wind, they won't notice if we disappear for a while."

"How are you doing after your bout of sickness? Is that why you're not drinking?" I've been worried about her ever since that night I dropped her at her apartment. I had to assume she was okay when Anders didn't mention her being unwell weeks later.

"I'm okay. Thanks for asking. Not that I deserve your concern. I was a total bitch to you that night... and every time before that. I have no idea why you would still want to talk to me."

"Maybe I'm a sucker for a pretty face, or I have a high tolerance for bitchy." I give her a playful wink and nudge her shoulder. Thankfully, she takes it in the manner it's intended, that shy smile of hers creeping at the corner of her lips. It's rare, but when you see it, it's so fucking beautiful.

I'd slay dragons for one more glimpse of that smile.

CHAPTER ELEVEN

DIANA

AS PREDICTED, my lushy family is good and drunk by the end of dinner. I'm not judging them because usually, I'd be on that train. Heck, I'd be the conductor. I am not ready to tell everyone I'm pregnant, but I won't be able to hide it much longer. The baggy clothes are barely covering it now.

The tension between Linc and me is palpable every time our legs brush against each other under the table, whether by accident or on purpose. The same chemistry that landed us in this situation is about to change his entire life. Conversation flows, and we talk about anything light and inconsequential. I'm the only one who knows the world is about to be turned on its axis when Linc and I find a few moments alone. I've talked myself out of telling him at least five times throughout dinner.

During the starter, I convinced myself it would ruin Anders' birthday weekend, which is a ridiculous reason not to tell Linc about the baby. The main course was a running loop of *walk before you run*. We should become friends before I upend his world with this bombshell. Holding off on telling him isn't going to be a concrete foundation for a lasting friendship. During dessert, I had the most ludicrous of ideas. Basically, I had myself in a Jason Bourne scenario, where I go on the run with a new name, new passport, and no one ever finds out. The fundamental fly in the ointment is that I don't want to do this alone, and I'd never see my family again. Like I said—ridiculous.

"Could we go somewhere and talk?" I make the mistake of leaning in, whispering in Linc's ear, breathing in the intoxicating scent of his cologne. Every pregnant bone in my body wants to climb him and rut until I sate the beast that's been desperate to get out. This heightened libido during pregnancy is no joke. My vibrators have been getting a workout. Stock in Duracell is probably on the rise because of me.

"I warn you it might not be a good idea for you to lean in this close."

"Why is that?" I know the answer, but I want to hear him say it. Apparently, I like to torture myself.

"Because I may not have the wherewithal to stop myself from kissing you." Butterflies take flight in my stomach, their wings fluttering until they keep time with my racing pulse.

"Maybe I wouldn't stop you."

He offers his hand, his eyes never leaving mine. As our fingers intertwine, a jolt of electricity courses through me, making me feel more alive than I have in months. He waits for me to take the lead, knowing the house better than he does. It only takes a split second for me to lead him upstairs to my room. It's a bad idea, but right now, I want him in my space.

"I thought you wanted to talk. It's a little presumptive to bring me straight to your room, southpaw." He takes in our surroundings, cataloging every detail. I've never been happier that this isn't some childhood time capsule. My parents bought this place five years ago, so there aren't any embarrassing relics of high school lurking on the walls.

"It's quiet." My head is spinning. Morning sickness has been brutal and shows no signs of stopping anytime soon.

"It is. A good place to... talk." Running his hands through his dark messy hair, he glances at me with those ice-blue eyes, and I'm mesmerized by him as he darts his tongue out to wet his lips. The things those lips can do. There's a growing ache between my legs, and I convince myself our conversation can wait a few hours.

I don't jump him because, honestly, I'm so exhausted all the time that an all-out attack would sap the energy right out of me, so instead, I stand in front of him and stare up into his eyes. My breath is labored, and my hands are shaking, but I force myself to remain still, to let him take the lead, even though it goes against the grain for me.

"You look beautiful tonight, Diana." My gaze drifts to the floor. "Why can't you look at me when I say that?"

"Because I'm wearing a hoodie and jeans. Not exactly beautiful." He slips his hand under my chin, gently lifting my gaze to meet his.

"You could be wearing a trash bag and look beautiful to me. When are you going to understand that? Now, tell me what you want to talk to me about." He searches my eyes for answers that are stuck in the depths of my stomach, churning like a washing machine on spin cycle.

"Before I do, can you do something for me?"

"Anything."

"Kiss me." He doesn't hesitate or sweep me off my feet, but I'm definitely swept in every figurative sense of the word. He slides his hands into my hair, taking his time, letting his fingers tangle in my loose curls. I'm nervous, and yet there's a serenity in his touch I've never felt before.

As he dips down to kiss me, he stops just shy of my lips, so close I can feel his breath as he speaks. "With pleasure." His lips descend on mine in the softest of kisses with an intensity so great I feel it in the depths of my being. This goes beyond a passionate kiss. It's a connection of some sort. Maybe I'm feeling it this way because I know we're having a child together, and I wish I could stop time right now, at this moment, suspended in the perfect kiss.

Linc groans as he darts his tongue out to lick the seam of my lips, begging entrance which I willingly give. He could ask anything of me right now, and I'd give it to him.

Taking his time, he lavishes me with his kiss, his tongue gently caressing mine, sending waves of desire rippling through my body all the way to my toes. I breathe him in, letting my body relax for the first time since the doctor told me I'm pregnant.

I reach for his pants, desperate for the same slow fuck he's giving my mouth. God, I've missed him. I didn't even realize how much until now. He doesn't stop me but doesn't move to undress me. "I want you, Linc."

"I don't have a condom on me."

"It really doesn't matter." I can't stress that fact enough.

"Right. IUD. I'm not sure I can watch you walk away again after feeling you skin to skin."

"I'm here asking you to fuck me." He swallows my words, reaching for the zipper on my jeans before shoving them to the floor along with my panties. He's about to reach for my top when I distract him, leading him to the bed. I'm scared to have his imposing frame bearing down on me in case he squishes the baby somehow, so I bend over the end of the bed, spreading my legs for him.

"Is this the porno version of that movie with Julia Roberts, where she says she's standing in front of a boy, that English twat, asking him to love her?"

"Do you want to talk chick flicks or have sex?"

"Does a bear shit in the woods?"

I'm bent over, half-dressed, with my ass in the air, and he's talking shit, literally talking about shit. "Linc, how can you go from being insanely sweet and romantic to having verbal diarrhea?"

"You make me nervous."

"You? Lincoln Nash." Looking over my shoulder, I catch his gaze, watching as it darkens and the nerves fall away, leaving only the fierce lover I know him to be. As he moves toward me, taking his cock in hand, a jarring realization dawns on me.

"What's wrong?"

"I didn't say anything."

"Your face is saying something."

"How many women have you slept with since the last time we were together?" I don't want to shame him, and I *really* don't want to know, but I can't sleep with him unprotected if he hasn't been tested recently or, God forbid, slept with another woman bareback. I don't think I could handle knowing that.

"You're slut-shaming me right now? I asked about condoms, and you said it's fine. Fucking hell, Diana, you're the most infuriating woman on the planet."

"I know, and I'm sorry."

"How many guys have you been with? I don't even want to know the answer because it would shred me. *I fucking care!*"

"No one. There's been no one since you, Linc."

He breathes an audible sigh of relief, dragging his hands through his hair as he begins to pace the floor. I turn and perch on the end of the bed, reaching down to the floor for my jeans and panties. I ruin everything I touch.

"It's been months."

"I know. I can count."

"Is that normal for you?"

"You still haven't answered the question. How many women?" I put one foot into my panties, but he stares me down.

"Not so fast."

"What?"

"There's been no one else, Diana. Since that night when I felt you skin to skin, you ruined me. I haven't slept with anyone." I'm struggling to understand, to take it all in. Linc isn't the kind of man who goes months without sex, and rarely goes a day without offers.

"Why?"

"I haven't even thought of sleeping with another woman since I got a taste of you that first night in Vegas."

"Really?"

"You're exquisite, Diana." He stops pacing and walks over to the bed, offering his hand when I stand to face him. "Give me a chance to get to know you." He reaches for the hem of my hoodie, but I'm quick to stop him.

"Can I keep it on?"

"What's wrong?"

"I'm just feeling self-conscious."

"You shouldn't. Your body is perfect." It's different than the last time he saw it and felt it beneath his fingers.

"Please, just for tonight."

"Whatever you want. Tell me what you want." I slip out of his grasp and turn and place my hands on the bed, offering myself to him. My head is spinning. "I can't see your face."

"You can see it next time. I just want to feel you deep inside me, Linc. All of you. I need that tonight. Please."

He doesn't take me by force or with the disconnect that normally comes with this position. Instead, he slowly steps behind me, running his hands up my quivering legs, pressing an open-mouthed kiss to my entrance before standing and letting his erection spring free of his pants and boxer shorts.

"I've missed you, Diana," he says as he slides his cock inside me. It's one long fluid motion, gentle but commanding, firm, and all-consuming. When he's seated to the hilt, he rests his hands on my hips. "Fuck... you feel even better than I remember."

God, he's right. I've been dreaming of the way he filled me, but it's a pale imitation of this. My memory is black and white compared to the glorious Technicolor of this moment. I'm seeing stars as he begins to move, slowly thrusting inside me, circling his hips with expert precision until my arms begin to shake. "Oh God, Linc."

"You need to keep the volume down. We're not alone in this house." His voice is distant as if he's at the end of a tunnel. Heat begins to rise in my cheeks so fast it's like an inferno, enveloping me, pulling me into darkness before I know what's happening.

Then, everything goes black.

Silent.

"DIANA, can you hear me? Shit, please say something. I should go get Brooke or your mom." Every muscle in my body screams in exhaustion, protesting any form of movement. I attempt to open my eyes, but overwhelming nausea stops me in my tracks.

"No."

"Thank God, you're awake." It takes me a few moments to get my bearings. I'm in my bed under the covers with Linc hovering over me.

"What happened?"

"You passed out. We need to go to the emergency room."

"No, I'm fine." I'm mortified.

"You're not fine. I need to get Brooke in here." Worry is etched in his brow, marring his masculine features.

"Don't. Please. How would we explain why we were in here together?"

"I don't care. You're ill, Diana. Getting you to a doctor is all that matters. They can stake me through the heart if they want, as long as you get the proper care."

"They're drunk. If we slip out, they won't even know we're gone. We'll be back before they wake up in the morning. It'll be like it never happened. Please, Linc. They're really overbearing, and I don't like being at the center of their attention."

"I'm worried about you."

"Can you drive? How much have you had to drink?"

"I'm okay. I didn't drink the second glass your dad brought me. A certain someone left me sort of dumbstruck." At times like this, Linc has an almost goofy charm that's so damn cute I can hardly stand it. It could make a girl fall. Hard.

"Okay, so we go to the emergency room, and they won't know we're gone."

"If I feel like we need to call them after the doctor checks you out, then I'm doing it. Take it or leave it."

"Fine." I shift over to the side of the bed, but I'm light-headed the

124

moment I try to pull myself up into a sitting position. Taking a few deep breaths, a wave of nausea washes over me, and I stumble into the bathroom in nothing but my hoodie, only making it to the toilet bowl with a second to spare, losing what little dinner and dignity I had left.

Linc runs in after me. "Jesus, Diana. Have you been sick this whole time?"

"Can you grab my pants?" I wretch again. "Actually, there are sweats in the top drawer in the closet. The gray ones."

He retrieves them for me and returns to find me propped against the tub with my head leaning back. If only the room would stop spinning for a few minutes, we could blow this popsicle stand.

Dropping down to his knees at my feet, he slips one foot and then the next into my sweats and slides them up my legs before lifting me just enough to pull them the rest of the way.

"You're not sneaking anywhere, southpaw. You'll need to make peace with me carrying you out of here."

"Yeah, I'm okay with it, but can you hand me the mouthwash first?"

"Good deal."

"And yet again, I'm providing the ultimate sexual experience." I quickly rinse my mouth and spit into the toilet bowl. I'm long past trying to be sexy at this point. The man just watched me puke sans pants, and then had to put the damn things on me like a toddler or some ancient relic.

He slides his hands underneath me. "Wrap your arms around my neck." I do as he asks, but I have no strength to hold on tight. As he lifts me into his arms, my shoulders sag, exhausted from weeks of constant worry. "I've got you, southpaw."

I nestle my head into his chest, breathing him in as he navigates to his room. "Can you grab my keys?" He nods his head toward the tall dresser by the door, and it takes all my strength to pick them up. I hold them close to my chest and close my eyes, letting him take care of me for once.

I'm not sure how he gets us out of the house without alerting the Lexington clan, but he does, and for that, I'm eternally grateful. He buckles me in, and I curl up in a ball, resting my head against the window as he drives us to the nearest emergency room. I drift in and out of sleep, so physically and emotionally drained. I've been trying to hold everything together since I found out about the baby, knowing my career isn't conducive to motherhood. There isn't a maternal bone in my body.

When we arrive, I'm still too weak to walk, and I'm growing more and more anxious by the second. He needs to know. I have to tell him. He cradles me in his arms, striding into the emergency room like I'm the most important person in the world.

"I need whoever's in charge here. She needs to be seen. Now."

"Sir, you need to fill out insurance forms, and then she'll be triaged and seen according to priority level."

Tension radiates off him, his body coiling like a spring, ready to pounce at any moment. "Listen..." he peers at her name tag, "... Karen. An apt name for her. She looks like a Karen. I'm going to need you to have someone see her now. She passed out, and I'm not carrying her for shits and giggles. She can't fucking walk."

"Sir."

"Look, I don't want to be that guy. The asshole. But I will. For her, I will. We were being... intimate, and she went limp in my arms. I'm good, Karen, but I've never been capable of literally fucking a woman until she passes out."

He did not just say that. If the ground could open up and swallow me whole, now would be the time.

"I... I..." Karen is officially speechless.

"If you knew her, I guarantee she's a ballbuster of epic proportions, and under normal circumstances, she'd rather be carrying me in here in a fireman's lift, and I'd let her, Karen." All eyes are on us, and whispers begin to fill the waiting room.

"Linc..." I whisper, "... people are starting to pull out their phones."

He lowers his voice. "Also, I should've led with the fact that we're both sporting celebrities, and if we hang around the waiting room, our pictures will be all over *TMZ* and Instagram within the hour."

She rolls her eyes in resignation, ushering us to a back room and away from prying eyes, but I'm afraid it's too late for that.

"You're the man, Mr. Nash!"

"I can't wait to watch your fight, Dee Lex."

Suddenly, my head is a bowling ball attached to my neck, too heavy to hold it up.

"I fucked up." Linc's voice is suitably filled with contrition.

"Makes sneaking out of the house pointless. I'm sure Brooke and my parents will love reading about you 'fucking me until I passed out.' Good breakfast conversation for sure."

"Okay, new plan. We don't go back to the house. I drive us to the airport, and we leave the country."

"Now that sounds like something I'd come up with."

"See, we're made for each other."

When the triage nurse comes in to see us, she asks Linc to leave the room. He's not happy about leaving me, but it's part of their protocol. It gives me a chance to let them know I'm pregnant before they take me back, and hopefully, I can pluck up the courage to tell him before we speak with the doctor. I need to be the one to tell him.

I go through the motions, answering their questions and letting them take my blood pressure, which they aren't too happy with. I'm quickly taken back to a room and hooked up to an IV for fluids.

After that, everything becomes a little hazy. Flashes of nurses. A doctor who's insanely hot and yet doesn't come close to Linc. I'm so tired I let my eyes rest a while, waiting for them to bring Linc back to sit with me. The scent of his cologne lingers in the air at some point, but I can't quite put the smell with an image of his face in the room with me. I hear his voice, but I don't know what he's saying.

There's a blanket that surrounds me, but it's not a physical thing. It's him. I feel safe when he's around. Wanted and cherished, even though I've done nothing to deserve it. Eventually, I give up trying to grasp the strings of broken conversation, letting myself rest in the knowledge that he's here, protecting me.

It's okay to let my guard down, if only for a few moments.

JARRED by the unfamiliar smells and sounds of the emergency room, I awake with a gasp, my body trembling.

"It's okay, Diana. I'm here."

"Linc?"

"The one and only." His voice is flat, the warmth of only moments ago nowhere to be found.

"Have they said when the doctor might be in?"

"You don't remember talking to him?"

"He was in earlier before you were here. I don't remember them bringing you back."

"I've been here for a few hours."

"Hours?"

"You've been asleep for a while. And yes, the doctor came by about an hour ago."

"Oh."

He scrapes his palm over the stubble on his jawline, considering his next words carefully.

"Were you ever going to tell me?"

CHAPTER TWELVE
LINC

"LINC, I CAN EXPLAIN." Hollow words coming far too late.

"That might have been a good thing to do a few months back when you realized you were pregnant."

"I was in shock. It was one time. I have an IUD, and I told you it was okay not to use a condom for that very reason."

"Are you keeping it, or are you planning to have an abortion?" It takes every iota of self-restraint in my body to keep my cool right now. I know what I want, but I'm not going to force her. She didn't even see fit to tell me, so that's a pretty clear indicator of where she's at with this curveball. Anger radiates through every muscle in my body, adrenaline curling my hands into fists. I can't even look at her right now.

"Is that what you want? For me to have an abortion?" Her voice is smaller than it's ever been—fragile.

"You don't get to put this on me. You've had months to talk to me about this. How long have you known?"

"Since about a week after I got sick at Brooke's place. The night you drove me home." *Holy-fucking-shit.* I shoot to my feet, unable to sit and listen to this, and start pacing the room like a caged animal.

129

My chest is tight with the weight of a thousand hopes and dreams, dashed and trodden beneath her feet.

"You never once thought to call me and say, 'Hey, Linc, you're going to be a daddy. Want to talk about it?' That's kind of a big deal, Diana."

"I know. I picked up the phone a million times, but I couldn't find the words."

"*I'm pregnant.* Those are the words. Pretty simple. I'm not a fucking monster. The night we obviously conceived, I was begging you to give me a chance. I wanted more. I was right there. You didn't think that two weeks later you could've called me, and I'd come running?"

"I treated you badly."

"No shit, Sherlock! You're a pain in the ass. It's not exactly breaking news. You have berated me since the day we met, and I still wanted you. Didn't that tell you something? But this... you left me in the dark all this time, fully expecting me to move on. Hell, you asked the question tonight. *How many women?*"

"And you said no one." She reaches for my hand as I pace past the bed, but I keep moving.

"It's not the fucking point, Diana. You set us up to fail. What if I had gone off and slept with five women in that time?"

"I don't know."

"And what if I liked one of those women enough to start a relationship? Did you stop for one second to consider that scenario, or is it just a given that no woman in her right mind would want to date me?"

"No. Please sit down."

"I can't."

"Linc..." The anguish in her voice is a dagger to my heart, but her betrayal is a deathly blow to my fucking soul.

"If I were dating someone, and you eventually told me we were having a kid together, what then? I get to see them on weekends? That's bullshit. I'm the dad. I want to be there. I have the right to be involved. You don't get to take that away from me, Diana. You don't want it, fine, then I'll raise it alone, but I suppose I have to wait for you to tell me if you're keeping it first."

"I'm keeping it."

Relief washes over me—or rather slams into me like a tsunami. I can finally meet her gaze, but what I see breaks my heart. Her eyes are glassy as she struggles to hold back tears, and I crack like a pair of cheap stripper's heels.

Perching on the edge of the bed, I pull her into my arms and hold her for the longest time before whispering in her ear. "Thank you."

Her entire body shudders as the tears I suspect she's been holding in for a while trickle down her cheeks. I don't move, giving her the dignity of crying without my eyes on her. I know she'd hate that, and as conflicted as I feel right now, I don't want to hurt her. I'd never want that.

We sit in silence, locked in this embrace until the doctor reappears.

"You're awake. How are you feeling?"

"Still pretty rough, if I'm honest."

"As I explained to your boyfriend..." Her body stiffens as she realizes how I came to know I'm going to be a father. *I'm going to be a father.* "You have something called hyperemesis gravidarum. It's a severe form of morning sickness. I called your OBGYN, and she will follow up with you."

I've been googling this shit while Diana was asleep, and it can get nasty. I'm worried about her, and I'm mad that she has been dealing with this alone. I'm just angry and terrified.

"Luckily for you and baby, you were in peak physical condition before pregnancy, so with some added dietary supplements on top of the regular prenatal vitamins, your OB can monitor your electrolytes and hydration. At this point, I can let you go home on bed rest, but I want you to be aware that you may end up with a hospital stay if it gets any worse. As I said before, your previous healthy lifestyle has gone a long way to keep you going up until this point, but once your own stores are depleted, the baby will take everything first, and you'll be running on empty. We need to get you doing better."

"Bed rest? Really?" She can't even protest with any gusto, she's that weary.

"Where do you think you're running to, southpaw? I had to carry you in here, and the toilet bowl was holding you up prior to that. If bed rest is what's needed, then that's what we'll do."

"We?" The doctor chuckles as Diana's eyes bug out of her head.

"I'm going to be watching you like a hawk. Get used to it. If I cook, and you puke, then..."

"We're in a bad Dr. Seuss book?" There's a little spark of the Diana I know and, she saved my ass there. I didn't have anything to rhyme with that.

"So, I can take her home, doc? Are there certain foods she can eat that may be easier for her to hold down?"

"I'll have one of the nurses bring down the medication and some information on things you guys can try. Make sure you follow up with your OBGYN. It's vital they monitor you closely from here on out."

"I'll call them myself," I interject. I'm aware Diana is probably rolling her eyes at me right now, but I don't care. I'll be making sure she and the baby are healthy whether she likes it or not.

Once we have the prescriptions and my reading for the night—or early morning now—I drive us back to Diana's parents and slip inside as if nothing ever happened. The lights are out, and the house is quiet.

She managed to walk with my arm around her waist, supporting her weight, so that's a big improvement on where we were earlier tonight. It seems like a lifetime ago we were here, in her room, having sex, and then she was ill. Now she's pregnant, and I'm going to be a dad.

I wait until she's under the covers before taking my leave, but her voice is a whisper in the darkness. "Could you stay in here... with me?"

"I don't want my ass handed to me on a plate in..." I check my watch, "... five hours."

"My family are notoriously lazy. I'm sure Brooke will be having puke-worthy morning sex with Anders while I just puke on command at six o'clock."

"Well, that sounds lovely. How could I refuse such an enticing offer?" Humor is all I've got right now because my entire world is upside-down. Lying down next to her, knowing she's pregnant with my child might be the most torturous, soul-destroying, *amazing* thing that I could imagine at this moment. Anders can keep his epic sex. For now, I'll be content with Pukey Patty and our Peanut.

"I know I made a mess of this, and there are a million reasons why you should walk across the hall right now, but please, for a few hours, can we put a pin in all of this, knowing that we *will* talk it all through when we get back to Manhattan?"

There's no point in putting up a fight because when it comes down to it, I don't want to leave this room. I want to watch over her every second of every day. When she collapsed in my arms tonight, I was petrified. I'm not sure there's ever been a time in my adult life that I've been more scared.

Without a word, I slide under the covers and settle at her back, pulling her against my chest. I don't know what any of this means for us, but tonight, I need to feel the warmth of her skin on mine and rest in the knowledge that she's safe in my arms, no matter how precarious that illusion may be.

"Linc, what are we going to do when pictures from the emergency room surface tomorrow?"

"I took care of it. There won't be any pictures. Everyone that saw us can now buy themselves a new car tomorrow, on me."

"You did that, for me?"

"Of course. I'd do anything for you, Diana." She doesn't respond. "Diana?"

Her soft breaths become shallow, and she seems so fragile in my arms. She's sound asleep.

My mind is racing, unable to slow down—a freight train of fractured moments. Every minute Diana and I have spent together. The night we conceived this baby. The months that have gone by between her finding out and where we find ourselves today. Where we go from here. The fact that I'm going to be a father.

My entire world has been spun on its axis tonight, and I have no idea which way is up. Since the moment I first laid eyes on her, I've been drawn to Diana. It wasn't a moth to a flame because that doesn't do justice to the visceral effect she has on me. There's a magnetism when I'm in the same room as her, and no matter how bad I know I'm going to feel when she inevitably leaves, I can't pull away. I want her in ways I've never even contemplated with any other woman, but every time I get close, she walks away.

She feels that magnetic chemistry between us, but it's different for her—it's only skin deep. She wants my body, I know that much. I can tell if a woman is faking it, and there's nothing fake about the way she moans for me. *Shit!* What if that's something else I'm wrong about? There are many things I can recover from in this life—shitty parenting, growing up in the armpit of existence, heartbreak, defeat—but if a woman faked an orgasm, that would tear a hole in the space-time continuum or something. I'm Lincoln-fucking-Nash, for God's sake.

Sleep doesn't find me, so I savor the soft scent of Diana's hair on the pillow next to me. It's coconut or something similar. When the digital clock on her nightstand reads five o'clock, I reluctantly leave her room, stopping in the doorway for just a second to take in the sight of her. Diana is Sleeping Beauty—if Sleeping Beauty could kick your ass. At this moment, she's serene, curled up in the covers, growing my baby inside her.

Nothing will ever be the same again.

THE LEXINGTONS MUST THINK I'm the worst house guest on the face of the planet. I turned up just in time for dinner last night, disappeared, and resurfaced at lunchtime today. Way to make an impression on the future grandparents of my child.

Anders doesn't let anything slide. "You're a lazy fucker, Nash. And don't think I didn't notice you and Diana both went to bed early last night." He's gracious enough to mumble under his breath as we all sit down to lunch.

"I didn't get my rocks off last night." My statement is one hundred percent true. I can't say we didn't have sex. We had the most unsatisfactory sex of all time. Unless your fetish is a woman passing out while you're inside her, it's not a good way to keep a stiffy.

I couldn't say I didn't 'sleep' with her because although I need The Clockwork Orange to keep me awake today, Diana was sound asleep in my arms in her bed. So, I opted for a true statement of fact. My balls are purple, and I couldn't jack one out in the shower because now this is the grandparents' house, and it would be inappropriate.

It was wrong to hammer their daughter yesterday while they were downstairs getting drunk.

It's clear to me that my lines of morality are hazy at best and need some work before I'm responsible for another human being. What's also clear is that Diana and I have to start making nice around Brooke and Anders because we're about to blow their minds.

Diana is sitting across from me, trying not to stare, but it's obvious she's overcorrecting herself. "Morning, southpaw."

"Don't you mean afternoon?" I consider her for a moment. There's a softness, a trepidation no one else notices. "What are you staring at?" She attempts derision, but I'd give her a three for effort.

"I thought I saw a Cheeto in your hair."

"I'm saving it for later. I might want a snack."

Brooke sniggers next to her. "You two would be such amazing friends..." she gestures between us, all flailing arms and smiles, "... if you used your humorous powers for good."

I hear Martha trying to contain a snort-laugh at the other end of the table, covering her mouth as she stares down at her glass of water.

"What do you say, Diana. Will you give me a chance to use my impeccable wit and earn your friendship?" My wry grin sobers as I meet her gaze. What started as a playful jibe is becoming one of the most important questions I may ever ask.

The rise and fall of her chest quicken, her sultry smile falters, and a fleeting hint of the Diana I'm intrigued by is in the driver's seat. "I'm game if you are, ball boy."

"Fuck me, I never thought I'd see the day." My best friend seems to have forgotten the table we're currently inhabiting.

"Anders!" Brooke slaps his arm, making Diana laugh, which is music to my ears today.

"Your mom buys you sex toys, so I think she can handle a cuss word or two." He flashes his pearly whites at his mother-in-law and winks, making her giggle like a schoolgirl. "Isn't that right, Martha?"

"You boys need to frequent our dining table more often, don't they, darling?" Mr. Lexington seems less amused by our conversation, but I get the sense that he subscribes to the mantra, *happy wife, happy life*.

"Welcome to the jungle, Linc." Diana proceeds to move food around her plate in an attempt to convince everyone else at the table that she's fine. How none of them can see the differences in her is beyond me. Since the last time I watched her walk out of my life, she's lost weight, and yet there's plumpness to her cheeks that makes her all the more stunning. Although she's tired and run down, there's a soft glow to her skin, a vibrancy that lights up her face.

We spend the rest of our meal in easy conversation, talking baseball for the most part, but when Diana's dad starts asking when a new date will be set for her fight, a chill runs through me. It didn't occur to me that my sperm has changed the trajectory of her career. I thought maybe she had an injury or her sickness bug—what I thought was a bug—had left her needing more time to train. This changes everything. She won't be able to fight for a year or so. I've fucked her—literally and figuratively. Holy Mother of God—I might have the most powerful swimmers in the universe, and apparently, they're intent on being a one-man wrecking ball for Diana Lexington.

Thankfully, Diana is skilled in the art of diversion with her family. They tend to see what she wants them to see. She flies under the radar for the most part, and today she's done it with practiced ease.

Her parents have plans with friends for the afternoon, and I can see that Diana is struggling to keep up the façade of anything close to normal. She's supposed to be on bed rest.

"Why don't you girls go put your feet up? We can take care of clearing away the dishes."

"Good idea," Anders seconds my suggestion. "Go have some sister time."

The second they're out of earshot, he's on me about last night.

"What the fuck happened last night?"

I gather the plates, piling them one on top of another. "Nothing."

"Bullshit. You're... you."

"Nothing happened. You saw us today. We're turning over a new leaf, and we'll try to be friends from here on out."

"Are you shitting me?" He follows me into the spacious kitchen. Any closer and he'd be crawling up my ass.

"No. I love you guys. It's been nice being up here with the family this weekend. You've met my mom and seen where I grew up. Is it such a stretch to think that Diana and I could be friends, and I could have a little slice of the happy that everyone else seems to have going on?"

"Bro, you hit me right in the feels. Now I feel like a tool."

"Good. I'm a sad trailer park boy with no family, and you're over here crying your diamond tears."

His face goes blank, and I know I went too far. "You're a multi-millionaire baseball legend. I'd say you've got your own diamond tears going on."

"Whatever, just help me load the dishwasher."

By the time we're done and go in search of the girls, Diana is fast asleep on the couch with Brooke flipping through a magazine at her side.

"Something's going on with her. She's never like this."

Anders' phone beeps at the same time as mine, and I'm quick to fish it out of my pocket so it doesn't disturb Diana.

Carter: *Sorry, boys. Change of plans. See you in Manhattan.*

"I guess we don't have plans for the rest of the day anymore."

Anders reads the same message before allaying Brooke's fears. "She trains hard. Sometimes too hard. Let her sleep. Why don't we go down to the marina and have a few drinks?

"Okay. I'll leave her a note to join us when she wakes up." Grabbing a pen off the coffee table, she starts looking for a pad of paper.

"Why don't you guys go? I'll hang here for a bit and walk down with her when she wakes up."

"Who are you, and what have you done with Lincoln Nash?"

"What?" They say it like I'm incapable of chivalry. "I'm a good guy."

Brooke jumps up from the couch and runs into my arms. "You're wonderful. It's just weird that you guys finally listened to me and decided to try being friends, and now this. I really appreciate you making an effort with her, Linc. It means a lot to me. I know she can be difficult."

I'm not sure she'll be so grateful when she finds out I'm going to make her an auntie.

"You don't need to thank me. She's funny. I like her sense of humor. It would be infinitely more hilarious if her dry wit was aimed at someone other than me, but I know how to roll with the punches. Honestly, go have a few drinks, do your happily married thing, and I'll keep my third wheel up here until number four wakes up."

"Are you sure?"

"Yes."

"Okay. Come down as soon as she's up."

"Will do."

Anders practically drags her out of the room, and the moment I hear the front door close, Diana sits upright on the couch. "What the hell?"

"I wasn't asleep. We need to talk, and Brooke would *not* stop talking. I love her, but I have other things on my mind right now. Can we sit and have a conversation?"

"Yeah." My pulse quickens as I take a seat across from her. There's a war raging inside me right now with Diana at the center, tangled up in a million different emotions. "So... talk."

"There are so many things I want to say, but I'm not good at this stuff, so I don't know where to start."

"How about the fact that you have an IUD, you're about three and a half months pregnant right now, and I didn't know until last night. Pick a point and go from there." Frustration builds, coursing through my veins as I replay the moment the doctor mistook me for Diana's boyfriend last night and spoke to me candidly about our baby.

"I'm so sorry. That's not how I wanted you to find out. I took you upstairs yesterday to tell you. I know that sounds lame and convenient."

"Yes, it does. You were going to tell me, but then you accidentally fell on my cock and forgot?"

"I don't know how to explain it. You and me... we have chemistry... this phenomenal physical connection, and whenever I'm around you, it takes over. It's like all rational thought goes out the window." That's the first thing she's said to me that actually makes sense.

"Okay, so you're attracted to my body but not my personality. I get it."

"Yes. No. That's not what I meant."

"How about skipping to the part where you found out you were pregnant and didn't call me?"

"I promise, I was always going to tell you, and no one else knows.

I was in shock, and I've been trying to wrap my head around it. This is a big deal. It's going to change our lives."

"I know. That's why it's good to have time to prepare."

"I thought if I had a plan, then it would be easier when I told you. And the night we conceived, I thought my IUD was still working."

"I don't care about that. We work with the situation we're in. Where do we go from here?" I'm trying to keep a level head. "What do you want to do?"

She wrings her hands in her lap, a shadow of her UFC persona. "Can we be friends?" My heart sinks. "I think that's probably the best way to do this. We don't know each other that well outside of..."

"Mind-blowing sex."

"That's one way of putting it. We had a lot of sex, we made a baby, and we're not a couple, so friends is a good option. What do you think?"

"Whatever you need, Diana." Every fiber of my being is fighting against me, urging me to claim her as mine—but that's the thing— she's not mine. She doesn't want to be claimed. I told her I wanted more, and she said no.

"I care about what you think. What do you need right now?"

"Do you care?"

"Yes. How do you feel?"

"I'm angry. I'm really fucking angry. You didn't tell me, and I'm so mad about it. I had real, genuine feelings for you, and you walked out. You left and didn't look back. Then last night, you scared the shit out of me, and you're having my baby. I'm a million different things right now, Diana, so I can't think about what I need because I don't fucking know. I'm mad at you. I can't trust you. I'm in awe of you for growing a person. I'm happy, I'm confused, and I'm terrified. None of that helps you in any way, and it sure as shit doesn't help me, so tell me... *what do you need from me, Diana?*" Overshare of the century, dickhead. At least one of us will still be getting a period while she's pregnant—me.

"I'd like to get to know you, Linc. I've heard you're a pretty awesome friend and a great guy to have around when the shit hits the fan. I think we can safely say the fan is on full blast, and a dump truck of manure was just unloaded directly in its path."

"The miracle of life. I've never heard it put so... colorfully." Taking a deep, steadying breath, I push my feelings aside and consider the life that's growing inside her. He or she is why I offer my hand to Diana with no regard for my heart's desire. "Hi, I'm Lincoln Nash. It's nice to meet you, Diana. I think we'll be great friends."

She takes my proffered hand, sending an ache of longing through every nerve ending in my body. "Nice to meet you, Linc. I'm preggers," she says with a playful smile.

"What can I say? He shoots, he scores." Her smile lights up the room, and yet as I withdraw my hand, a darkness settles in the pit of my stomach. If agreeing to be nothing more than Diana's friend is the price I have to pay to be a father, then I'll do it because I won't repeat the sins of my father, wherever the fuck he is.

CHAPTER THIRTEEN

DIANA

THE SCENT of his cologne invades my senses as he helps me back to bed. I've been so weak since getting back from the Hamptons, and now that Linc knows I'm pregnant, he's not taking no for an answer when it comes to sticking around. He wasn't joking around when he agreed to us being in this together and doing it as friends. I don't understand why he wants to be here with me right now, and I hate to admit that I'm scared to let him. He's hurt that I kept this from him for so long and pushed him away.

Now, I can't tell him how I felt that night before I collapsed and how his lips set every fiber of my being on fire. Because now, if I say I want that chance with him—the one he offered me months ago—he won't know if my reasons are genuine. Where does that leave us?

We can be friends who have a kid together.

Those words spoken from his lips were a balm to my fractured soul and a strike straight through my heart. One I wasn't prepared for.

"Oh God, I think I'm going to be sick again. I need to get to the bathroom." Linc rests his hand on my stomach with such tenderness before reaching over the bed and grabbing a trashcan.

"I'm prepared. You don't need to go anywhere. You can blow chunks in this, and I'll get rid of it."

"You don't need to be here. If my sparkling personality hasn't put you off already, then watching me vomit definitely will."

"Are you kidding? At least you have a good reason. Most of the women I've seen puke have been drunk as skunks and thought nothing of trying to kiss me after losing their dinner in the bushes."

"Gross." I can't hold it in any longer. "Don't look." My entire body retches as I lose the contents of my stomach.

Instead of doing as I ask, he gently sweeps my hair out of my face and slowly rubs circles on my back. "You're okay. I've got you. Besides, you forget I've seen you hug the toilet before. A trashcan isn't so bad."

"If this is what pregnancy is going to be like the entire time, this kid is going to be an only child."

"Didn't you know that the dewy glow everyone talks about is from morning sickness? Or in your case, the worst case of sickness in the history of pregnancy, in the chronicles of humankind."

"That's so nasty."

"You don't have to tell me. I can smell it. I'm a sympathetic vomiter. You have no idea how hard I'm fighting back my gag reflex right now."

My chuckle reverberates in the metal trashcan. "Don't make me laugh while I'm puking, I'll end up peppering you with chunks."

"Are you going to go all soft on me now that you're knocked up?"

"Fuck, no. How terrifying would that be?"

"True that. The only thing scarier than you hating me, would be you liking me. Christ, could you imagine if you actually enjoyed spending time with me?"

"God, no. Two assholes being assholes together."

He tucks a loose tendril of hair behind my ear, his fingers grazing my flushed cheek. "There's the girl I know and love. It took you a few hours to call me an asshole today. I was getting worried. For a second there, I thought you appreciated me for my personality rather than just man candy."

"I'm sorry. Linc, I..."

"Seriously, southpaw, I have to flush the contents of this trashcan before I fill it myself. You must have had something nasty for lunch. Fuck me." He grabs the can and disappears into the bathroom. There are some weird gagging noises before he returns a few moments later looking decidedly pale.

"Sorry." I'm mortified. "You sure you want to be my friend?"

"It takes more than a little vomit to deter me. So, do you want to watch some TV? What floats your boat for binge-watching?"

"I can't tell you. You'll judge me."

"Of course, I will. People judge each other all the time. Why is it a dirty word? Fans judge me on performance."

"That's fine and dandy when you're winning. Would you be so nonchalant about it if you'd missed that final hit?"

"Who are you kidding? They'd still adore me."

"Dream on, Nash." He pulls the remote out of my hand and starts flicking through streaming apps until he lands on *The Vampire Diaries*. "Seriously?"

"Judge away. Vamps are my guilty pleasure."

"I didn't have you pegged as a fan of teenage fantasy."

"I love the judgment dripping from every word, thirty seconds after you chastise me for judging you."

"Ugh. I'm a total bitch, aren't I?"

"Your words, not mine. I like to think of you as feisty. Come on, admit it. The vampire thing is hot. The intimacy of sinking your teeth into someone willingly offering themselves to you. Heightened senses that amp up arousal, making an orgasm ten times as intense."

I can't concentrate on anything other than his lips as he makes my mouth water. "Mmm."

"The Vampire Diaries it is." He settles in next to me, stretching his legs, his thigh brushing mine as his imposing frame takes up half the bed. There's a sly grin creeping at the corner of his lips. He knows

I'm watching in disbelief, desire unfurling deep in my core, turning into an ache that may never be sated.

"You're a nightmare. You know that, don't you?"

"More like your favorite wet dream, southpaw. Now, be quiet so I can hear the Salvatore brothers fighting over Elena."

He gives my shoulder a little nudge as we fall into an easy rhythm. "I'm sorry about... well, everything. I should've told you sooner, and you've been great about it."

"You're a walking, hormonal babymaker right now. I'm trying not to hold it against you."

"And about the other stuff..." I can feel my cheeks flush, but I need to say it if we're going to forge some kind of friendship.

"What stuff? Our fuck-buddy stage? The best orgasms of your life? One and the same, really. The pre-puke days? Good times."

"Your ego is so big..."

"And yet pales in comparison to the size of my anaconda."

My sides split as laughter erupts from my chest, causing a searing pain to spread throughout my body. "Oh God, you call your penis the *anaconda?*"

"Don't knock it because you've tried it. Big, hard, thick, and deadly. You would take a ride right now if I let you."

"I'll be going Hans Solo for a while. No one wants to bang a projectile-vomiting pregnant chick. Not even you."

He keeps his eyes firmly fixed on the screen without turning to face me. "Stop throwing yourself a pity party. It doesn't suit you. And FYI, I have the worst case of blue balls. Fucking agony. You got me all worked up in the Hamptons, and then you just left me hanging. Like you were actually hanging off my cock. If it weren't so disturbing, it would've been funny."

He can't look at me, his jaw tightening as he focuses his attention anywhere but on me.

"Was it disturbing? I don't remember anything, being the one who passed out."

Taking a moment to choose his words, he runs his hands through his hair. He does that when he's uncomfortable. "There are no words. You want the truth? There's no scenario in which that night would've been funny. I was a wreck. I didn't know what to do or if I'd hurt you. Scared out of my mind would be the understatement of the century." He physically shakes it off, a shudder running through his entire body. "Basically, I may never have sex again because you traumatized me."

"Well, if you're so mentally scarred by it, you won't miss us having sex. Our new friends-with-no-benefits situation will work out great." That didn't sound even slightly convincing.

"Yeah, yeah, southpaw. Easy for you to say. You don't know what it's like to fuck you. It's pretty addictive, and I'm not going to lie..." Now, he turns and holds my gaze as he darts his tongue out to lick his bottom lip. "You taste fucking divine." Without another word, he runs his hand over the scruff on his jaw before crossing his arms behind his head and focusing his attention back on the television.

"Thanks."

"You're wel... come." It's more of a question than anything. Oh my God, I'm an idiot. Who says 'thanks' after something like that? I'd never confirm to Linc, but he's not wrong when he said he gave me the best orgasms of my life. I'm not sure I could handle him knowing. His ego would be out of control.

I struggle to keep my eyes open as one episode runs into another. Eventually, I stop fighting it and let myself drift off with the comforting weight of Linc on the bed next to me. There's something about his presence that soothes me. I don't want to delve too deep into those feelings because, now more than ever, I need to shut them down before I get my heart broken.

"DO you know you snore like a trucker? And you drool in your sleep." His voice is deep and raspy in the morning.

"You told me you were sleeping on the couch. It's your own fault."

"I did the first night, then you started begging me for warmth. I know you have heating in this place, but you just love having my brawn in your bed."

"I didn't hear you protesting."

"You didn't? That explains why you didn't get naked when I asked last night."

"You, as a human being, are wrong on so many levels, Linc."

"You do want to get naked?" He squints his eyes open, flashing me a gorgeous morning smile."

"I don't need to. You're doing it all by yourself. The anaconda's loose." He quickly checks himself, the crest of his morning wood peeking out above the waistband of his gray sweats.

"Fuck. Not how you wanted to start your day. Sorry, southpaw." He adjusts and closes his eyes for a few moments.

"Didn't your mom ever tell you that when you close your eyes, people can still see you?"

"Ha-ha. I can't look at you. I need my brain swelling to go down, and you look hot in the morning."

"I bet." I'm about to lay into him for flirting with me, but like clockwork, my routine of hugging the toilet bowl first thing in the morning kicks in with a vengeance. I stumble from the bed, holding my stomach as I make a beeline for the bathroom.

Before every muscle in my body contracts, Linc is behind me, wrapping his arms gently around me, holding me together as I bring up nothing but stomach bile. "It's okay." I sag into him, letting him take my weight. Lowering us to the floor, he stays at my back, whispering soothing words. "I'm here. You got this, Momma."

Once I've stopped heaving, I slump against the broad lines of his chest. "The anaconda still has rigor mortis. You should really get that seen to or speak to a therapist or something. If hugging a pregnant woman while she vomits doesn't get rid of a chubby, there's definitely something going on."

"Shut up, southpaw. Just let me look after you without questioning me all day long. Can you do that? One day is all I'm asking."

"Brooke is coming over this morning, and you can't be here when she arrives. You're free." He sweeps my hair off my face with a tenderness I don't deserve.

"Awesome. Are you going to tell her?"

"Not yet. You and I are just figuring things out, and I want to have a plan of attack when I tell my family."

"Okay, but the sooner, the better. Anyway, I'm not going to push you right now, and I need to go check on my dog. My neighbor has been watching her, but she doesn't give her enough love."

"Why didn't you bring her here? She's cute and didn't seem to hate me when I used to turn up at your place during the... what did you call it last night... the pre-puke days."

"I didn't know if you were a dog person. Besides, it's presumptive to turn up on someone's doorstep with your dog in tow."

"I love dogs. And you turned up on my doorstep and started sleeping in my bed. You put a baby in my belly. I think we're past you being comfortable enough to bring your dog over."

"Noted. Has it really been that bad having me around?" He moves to help me up, but the cool tile feels good, so I tug him back down, resting my head against his chest.

"It's been great. You're not an asshole."

"I love the surprise in your voice when you say that."

"Give me a break. You're a known player, and you're just insanely hot. My experience with guys like you is that they live up their own ass and think the world revolves around them."

"*Guys like me*. If you haven't realized yet, I'm one of a kind."

"I'm starting to. But as much as I appreciate having you here, I can't let myself rely on you, Linc."

"Why not?"

"Because we live in the real world. We agreed to be friends and figure out this parenting stuff together, but you'll go back to training, start hooking up with non-pregnant women, and I'll still be here trying to sort out my life. I'm going to be a mom and a single one at that. The sooner I wrap my head around it, the easier it'll be in the long run." He stiffens at my back.

"You're not going to be a fucking single mom. I'm here. I plan on *being* here for everything. Whether you want me or not, you and the baby are my priority now."

"I don't expect anything from you, Linc. That's all I'm saying."

"Fine, and if I were a dickhead, then I'm sure you'd be the most amazing single mom on the planet. But I'm here, and I want to be part of this. We're friends now, get used to it."

"We know next to nothing about each other."

"Fine. If I tell you something personal, will that make our newfound friendship more legitimate in your eyes?"

"Depends."

"Okay, not my cock size or anything. That's way too personal and impressive to share with you. Oh wait, I've already done that." He gives me a sly wink and that panty-melting smile of his. He does make me laugh.

"Tell me something good."

"First, let's get you up and brush those teeth. Morning breath and puke is... just gawd awful."

"Your breath isn't exactly Tic Tac fresh right now either, buddy."

He leans in, pressing a kiss to my cheek. "Then, I guess we're not making out until post-mouthwash."

"Why do you say things like that?"

"Because I know you want to kiss me, Diana." He lifts me to my feet, the rise and fall of my chest betraying me. "I'm just waiting for you to catch up."

"Stop, Linc." I force myself to step out of his spell-binding orbit. "We're not a couple, and you saying stuff like this is confusing. I'm asking you... please stop."

His expression sobers as he runs his hands through his messy hair. "Sorry. It won't happen again. Friends without benefits. I'll leave you to get ready."

"Linc..." He closes the bathroom door behind him, leaving me staring at myself in the mirror, contemplating why I can't just let him be nice to me. I manage to keep it together long enough for the shower to heat up, but once inside, I brace my hands on the wall, letting the water rain down on me as silent tears spill from my eyes.

What am I going to do?

How did I end up here?

THE APARTMENT IS quiet when I emerge dressed, refreshed, and starving. Linc's shoes are gone from the living room, and his keys aren't on the kitchen island. I've managed to push him away, and now I'm left in the solitude of my secrets. I know I'll need to tell Brooke and my parents pretty soon, but I'm not ready for them to know yet.

As my eyes well with tears once more, the door to my apartment swings open, and in walks Linc with bags from the coffee shop across the street.

"I didn't know what you might be in the mood for, so I got one of every bagel. Caffeine is bad for the baby, so I got you some super-healthy herbal tea. The barista said it's amazing."

"I thought you'd left." I swipe the errant tear rolling down my cheek, but I'm not quick enough. Linc stares at me as if he's just witnessed someone delivering the knockout blow to a Labrador puppy.

"Because you don't want to sleep with me? I'm sorry. It takes more than that to get rid of me." He sets the bags on the countertop and strides over to where I stand, pulling me into his arms. "We're friends. End of. Get used to the fact that you're not alone in this, Diana."

"Why are you being so nice to me?"

He pulls back, wiping the tears from my eyes with the pad of his thumbs. "Truth time. Sit down, grab a bagel, and I'll tell you why I'm your new best friend."

"Okay, Lincoln Nash, spill." I do as he asks, expecting him to start joking around the second I probe him, but I'm shocked when he opens up.

"I have no idea who my dad is. My mom never told me, and I'm not sure if that's because he left her pregnant and alone at nineteen or because the role of daddy was a multiple-choice question."

"I had no idea."

"Why would you? I don't exactly share my private life with people. My mom wasn't thrilled about my arrival, and she let me know every day until I left for college."

"I'm so sorry."

"It is what it is. I wasn't part of her plan, and she saw me as the end of her chance to be somebody."

"So I'm your pity case? I remind you of your mom who didn't want you?" I say it with no malice in my voice, but it still comes out wrong.

"Not at all. I know you don't need me around. You're nothing like my mother, Diana. You're an accomplished athlete with drive and determination. You also have the capacity to be kind and sweet." I roll my eyes. "Okay, maybe not with me, but I've seen you with your sister."

"I guess."

"Not, *I guess*. It's time to realize that you have friends and family who are going to be alongside you and support you." He stops for a moment, visibly psyching himself up for whatever he's about to say. "I haven't thought to ask until now, but did you consider *not* having the baby?"

"I'd never get rid of it. Her. Him. I don't know, but there's a person growing inside me, and I want them. Surely, you understand that? If your mom had made a different decision, the world wouldn't have a Yankees legend, and there'd be sexually unsatisfied women all over New York." I try to make light of the moment because the reality is too heavy to bear.

"You're right about the unsatisfied women, but I'm not under any illusions about the choice my mom made. She was very clear when I was a kid, abortion was a dirty word back then, and given the chance, she'd have taken the out. Her life would've been very different and probably for the better. I wouldn't be here, but I wouldn't know, would I? The Yankees would have some other star batter. Sure, he clearly wouldn't possess my devilish charm and good looks, but the world keeps turning. You need to make the decision that's best for you, whatever that may be."

"Do you really think your mom would be happier without you?" I can't imagine anyone feeling that their life would be better without Linc in it.

"Yes. She'd have finished college, gotten a great job, and had the standard house in the 'burbs, two kids, a dog, and some guy she tolerated for the stability. An accountant or something equally as bland. I'd be that little blip she took care of and kept as a dirty little secret, never to be mentioned."

"That breaks my heart. I don't want my kid to think that when they get older."

"They won't. You'll be a great mom. You're *nothing* like the woman who raised me, Diana. Trust me, you will be amazing."

"I'm not so sure. What do I know about babies? I'm a fighter." I munch my way through four bagels while we chat back and forth. I seem to have become a nervous eater all of a sudden. This isn't going to be fun an hour from now when I have to see the rewind.

"They eat, poop, and sleep. How hard can it be? As long as we figure out how to change a diaper and make a bottle, they'll be fine."

"We?"

"Yep. I'm going to be here whether you like it or not. I'm the dad. It falls under the job description."

"You're going to regret this when we have a screaming infant, and I haven't showered in three days."

"Why are we giving up on personal hygiene? That's a deal-breaker. You forget that I've been here for days witnessing the puke, the morning breath, and the farts. I'm going to need you to shower at least every other day."

"I hate you."

"You love me." His words hang in the air between us.

"You're okay."

"Progress! Now, I've told you my deep dark secret, so do I get any details about the ex who broke your heart?" He stares at his coffee cup, unable to meet my gaze.

"Why do you assume there's an ex of significance?"

"Really?" He sips his coffee, letting the silence choke it out of me.

"The long and the short of it is, I thought we were dating exclusively. Turns out, he has a wife."

"Fuck."

"Yeah. I found out two weeks before the fight. I ended it immediately. I need you to know that I'd never knowingly sleep with a married man or be a part of cheating in any way."

"You don't need to explain yourself to me."

"I do. I feel so... dirty. And guilty."

"You have nothing to feel guilty for. That fucking scumbag is the one who should be held accountable. Did his wife find out?"

I hang my head in shame. I took the easy route and pretended it's not my place to tell her. "No. And I haven't contacted her. She deserves to know what her husband does when she's not around, but I'm selfish, and I don't want my name dragged through the papers as a homewrecking adulteress."

"Can I ask one thing?"

"What?"

"How long were you together?"

"A year. I had no idea. I thought I knew him, but in the end, I only saw what he let me. I've gone over every interaction I can remember, trying to figure out if there were glaring signs I chose to ignore."

"He's the douchebag from the wedding."

"You noticed my date that night?"

"I couldn't give two fucks about him. I noticed everything about *you*. If I'd had my way, you'd have been in my arms and my bed that night."

Oh, how I wish I could go back in time and change that one day. I'd have saved myself a year of regret and self-doubt. I felt Linc's eyes on me that night, but I'm not a cheater—or at least I wasn't until Anthony turned me into one. If I'd paid attention to the little ways he controlled me from the start, maybe I would've realized his deception sooner.

"In hindsight, I'd have let you."

CHAPTER FOURTEEN
DIANA

I'VE BEEN PACING my apartment since six o'clock this morning. Woken by an overwhelming need to empty the contents of my stomach, it's become the expected way I start my day. Today, the nausea is threefold—the baby doesn't seem to like my diet of nutritional food, I have my ultrasound today, and a wave of panic sets in every time I think about Linc taking me to my appointment.

Facing being a single mom is terrifying, but I'd made some kind of peace with it before Linc found out. Deep down, I knew I had to tell him, but I thought I had more time to figure it all out. Having him find out the way he did left a sour taste in my mouth, and I know he has reservations about all of this. How can he trust me when I kept this from him?

He's been encouraging me to tell Brooke since we returned from the Hamptons a few weeks ago, but there's something nice about having this secret with him. There's an intimacy to it that transcends the physical relationship that got us here in the first place.

When my phone pings with a message from Linc letting me know that he's idling on the curb outside my building, a wave of nausea takes over, and I have to run to the bathroom, forfeiting my breakfast before I'm ready to face him.

The second he spies me, he's out of the car and opening the passenger door. "Morning, southpaw."

"Hey, Linc. Thanks for coming with me this morning."

"I said I would."

"I know, but..." He stops me in my tracks as he closes the door behind me and jogs back around to the driver's side. As he slides in, I can't help noticing the way his lithe body moves—effortless—exuding sex appeal.

"But nothing. I'm the dad. I may not be your ideal choice for the role, but I promise you, I'll learn to be good at it. I'm going to be here every step of the way. Today is about two friends hanging out, and we just happen to be taking a look at your uterus to see my spawn growing inside you."

"God, don't say that. I'm nervous. What if the doctor missed something last time? Or something has gone wrong since then? What if it's squished, or they don't find a heartbeat, or it has two heads?" He reaches for my hand, resting the other on the wheel before pulling out into traffic.

"It's going to be fine."

"How do you know? Shouldn't I be showing more by now? Most women have a sizable baby bump at this point."

"I have a good feeling. And no, you're an athlete with a thick layer of abdominal muscles. Also, your hyperemesis means you've probably lost weight rather than gaining it over the past few weeks. It's completely fine that you've only got a small bump. You look pregnant."

"I do?"

He pulls away, planting both hands firmly on the steering wheel. "Not that people would notice when you keep wearing baggy clothes. But when we're at your place, and you wear tops that hug your curves, yes, you have a defined baby bump now."

"Is it unattractive?"

He keeps his eyes on the road. "As the guy who spent months being your booty call and memorizing your curves, I can say, hand on heart, that the sight of you with a baby bump is the furthest thing from unattractive. You look stunning."

It dawns on me that he must have done some research. Why else would he know about an athlete's body reacting differently? "You've been reading up?"

"In true southpaw style, breeze past the compliment and focus in on the mundane comment. Yes, I've been reading up. Haven't you?"

"I've been too scared."

"About what?"

"Telling you. Doing this on my own. The fact that my family is going to freak out. What are Brooke and Anders going to say?"

"We can tell them together if you want. Then maybe, you'll feel more excited after everyone knows."

"Thanks, but I think I need to tell Brooke myself."

"Sounds like a plan. Do you want me to tell Anders?"

"He's going to kill you."

"I can handle myself."

"I don't want to be the reason you and he fall out. Plus, this wasn't exactly planned, and I know we haven't figured everything out yet. I don't expect you to put your life on hold for me."

"Maybe I've just realized what life's all about."

"In all that research, you've learned that life is about a puke monster who craves rocky road over celery and yet can't keep the damn ice cream down for more than an hour?" I have to change the subject because, if I don't, the kernel of hope I've been ignoring may blossom into a rose bush. Beautiful while it lasts but with thorns that'll tear you to shreds in the end.

"To be fair, I know I'm supposed to want the celery, but eating healthy isn't always fun. You know how much I deprive myself of to look this good." He gives me a sly wink, and all seems right in the world.

"What I really don't understand is how you support your ego. Your neck muscles must be like Gaston from *Beauty and the Beast*."

"You could've gone with The Rock or Arnold Schwarzenegger, but no, you give me a Disney character. Really?"

"Don't you remember the song?"

"I'm not eight... or a girl."

"Keep your panties on. How dare you diss my favorite movie of all time."

"Shut up. No way. You're *not* that girl."

"I have a feminine side."

"Don't I fucking know it. I think it's you who underestimates your feminine wiles." When he says things like that, it's as if I'm laid bare, naked, and vulnerable, like he can see parts of my soul that no one else ever takes the time to notice.

"Back to the song. He breaks a leather belt with his giant manly neck muscles. It's all very charged with testosterone. You'd love it."

"I guess we know our next movie-night pick."

"You'd watch it with me?"

"I'd do anything for you, Diana." He thinks better of it the moment the words pass his lips. "Except put up with your middle-of-the-night leg twitches. You're a goddamn UFC champ, and those motherfuckers hurt. I was crying like a little bitch baby last time we spent the night together."

"I'd pay good money to see you crying like a bitch baby."

"I bet you would. I'm sure there are a few things you'd pay money to see me do. Sorry, southpaw, I'm not for sale."

"That's not what I've heard."

"You're feisty this morning."

"I guess you bring it out in me."

"The desire to knock me down a peg or two every thirty minutes or so?"

"Yeah."

He flashes that panty-melting smile just before the lights turn green. When we pull into the parking garage of the hospital, every nerve ending in my body kicks into high gear. "Time to meet our baby."

"COME ON IN, you guys. You can put your purse down on that chair and hop up onto this table for me." My heart is hammering in my chest, and I've never been so scared in all my life. Having Linc here makes this real in a way it hasn't been until now. I've had scans by myself, but this is different. His energy in the room sparks an excitement that hasn't been there before.

I gingerly set my stuff down, but Linc reads my face. "You got this, Momma. Now, get on the table and spread your legs," he says with a sly wink.

My OB is trying to stifle a laugh. "Not that kind of ultrasound, I'm afraid. We're far enough along that all I need is for Ms. Lexington to lift her shirt a little and just unzip the top of her pants."

"Now, we're talking." He sticks his tongue out at me, pulling funny faces.

I roll my eyes in mock distaste. "You have the maturity of a twelve-year-old. You know that, right?"

"Moving on up! The last woman who said something like that to me put me at around ten. Look at me, I'm growing."

"And when was that?"

"You, three days ago, when I couldn't stop laughing at you."

"You'll have to be more specific."

"You were laughing so hard while we were watching *Weird Science*, a fart slipped out, and your face was so stinking cute... pun intended."

"Oh my God." I clasp my hands over my face, but the OB just breezes past it as she squeezes some clear gel onto my stomach.

"Y'all are so sweet together, you'll make amazing parents."

We both stiffen at her assumption that we're a couple, but when I open my mouth to correct her, the strangest sound fills the room—a rhythmic whoosh, pounding, strong and steady. My gaze snaps to the screen.

"And there's baby's heartbeat. Strong and healthy." I reach for Linc's hand, lacing it with mine and tightening my grip. I'm fighting back tears as the mish-mash of blips on the screen take form. Legs, arms, hands, and feet.

"Is it okay?"

"Give me a few minutes to take some measurements." I look to Linc, worried that she hasn't given an immediate answer.

"Take a deep breath, southpaw. I counted. There are two arms, two legs, one head. It's going to be fine." A warm grin spreads across his face. "Better than fine. It's going to be beautiful, just like its mother."

"Be still my heart. Where did you find him, Dee? I'm in search of a good man."

"He just sort of appeared at my door, and I haven't been able to shake him since." I try to make light of the subject, waiting for Linc to interject, to tell her that we're not a couple. That we're only in this room together because we couldn't stop fucking even though we had no desire to get to know each other as human beings in the beginning.

He's transfixed by the squirming tiny baby on the screen, swimming around, becoming a fully formed person. It's—*breathtaking*.

"I'm her barnacle, doc. She keeps trying to shake me off, but she's stuck with me. I don't scare easy."

"Would you like me to show you your baby?"

"Yes." Linc's voice is like a bucket of ice water, shocking me back to reality. His eyes are filled with childish wonder, and that's what scares me more than anything. He's being swept up in the everyday miracle of pregnancy without thinking of what our version of co-parenting is going to look like.

My OB traces the lines on the screen. "There's a little head and a hand waving." Her southern drawl is oddly comforting like smooth, velvety hot chocolate on a cold winter night, warming me from the inside out.

"Holy crap, she's waving at us, Diana. Look. She's waving."

She.

"Is it healthy? That's all I care about."

"Yes. All measurements are on track. How's the hyperemesis?"

"I don't want to speak for her, mainly because she'll kick my ass, but I know she'll say she's fine. This woman doesn't like to admit anything but one whiff of the wrong thing, and it's still a race to the trashcan." His features are different somehow as I search his expression for a hint of what he's feeling.

"You can look forward to some new pregnancy symptoms as your pregnancy progresses."

"Like what?" My heart sinks. What's the next hurdle to get over?

"A lot of women report a significantly increased libido later in pregnancy."

An ache swells between my legs that kicked in the moment I first felt Linc's kiss between my legs, and it's never gone away. "Already there."

Linc's face grows somber, and he drops my hand. "Doc, will it damage the baby in some way if we get jiggy wit' it?"

"Did you just quote Big Willy Style?" We both erupt into an easy laugh, sidestepping everything he just said.

The OB interjects. "No, I hate to be the bearer of bad news, Mr. Nash, but no matter how blessed you may be between your legs, you're not going to reach the baby."

"Even if it's huge?" He gestures a length before shifting his hands a further few inches apart.

"Even then."

I stare at him in disbelief. "Did you really feel the need to ask that question?"

"I like to cover all my bases, southpaw. If you jump me the second we get you home, I need to know it's not going to cause any damage." He wiggles his eyebrows at me, and it ticks me off that a thrill courses through me. If I thought he was going to ravish me, then by all means, ask the embarrassing questions. But the fact that I'd be flying solo with my vibrator negates the need for this awkward moment.

Linc's attention quickly goes back to the ultrasound and the baby. "Wow. Just incredible."

"I'll print some pictures for you. Do you want to know the sex?"

"Hell, yeah!" he blurts out before turning to me like a kid in a candy store, eyes wide and filled with excitement. "If you want to know."

"I guess it's good to be prepared."

"Exactly." He's grinning ear to ear as he looks back at the screen with an innocence that comes from honest, uncomplicated, heartfelt joy. "How can you tell? I get the basic anatomy is visible, but surely, it's difficult to be certain of finer details unless it's a boy, and he's hung like a donkey."

"*Linc!*" I can't believe he just said that. Thankfully, my OB has a sense of humor and finds it funny.

"Well, that certainly makes my job easier, but once you've done a good number of these scans and you know what you're looking for, it's like anything else... you get better at identifying the markers. There does need to be an element of baby cooperation. If they don't open their legs during the scan, then I may not get a look at the necessary body parts."

"Ugh, isn't it a nightmare when they won't spread their legs?" He says it with such a straight face I can't contain my laughter.

"Oh my God. You can turn anything into a dirty conversation." A snort slips out, and I descend into an uncontrollable kink.

"It's a gift, and you secretly love it."

Seconds span out for eons as we wait with bated breath. I reach out and clutch his hand, my knuckles turning white, suddenly so aware that this is something we'll share for the rest of our lives. No matter what happens or whether we find a way to be an *us*—we're having a baby together.

"You're going to be proud parents of a beautiful baby girl."

"Oh my God." With his other hand, Linc runs his fingers over my stomach in the same swirling pattern of the ultrasound doppler. "That's our baby girl in there, Diana." I've never seen him emotional, but his eyes are glassy with unshed tears.

"A girl." I'm in shock.

"Damn." Linc lifts his fingers which are now covered in ultrasound gel. "Didn't think that through."

"So, pretty much like everything else you do," I jest.

"And yet amazing things come from my questionable judgment." His gaze burns into me, unlike any man before him, and just for a moment, I wish I could see myself through his eyes. I wish I knew how he sees me now in the midst of all this.

"I can't argue with you there." This is as close to a tender moment with Linc as I've let myself have. Anything more is too overwhelming.

"Everything looks great. Make an appointment to see me in three weeks. If you have any concerns in the meantime, feel free to call." The OB busies herself printing our pictures.

"Thank you."

"I'll leave you to get organized, and see you both again soon." The second she leaves the room, I set about cleaning the gel off my stomach. When I'm done, Linc reaches over and pulls my top down for me before caressing his hand over the small swell of my belly.

"There's really a baby in there. Our daughter."

"Yep. Does it weird you out?"

His eyes widen as he drags his gaze from my stomach to my face. "No. I'm in awe of you right now."

"Really?"

"You're growing a human. The most amazing thing I'll manage today is jaywalking in Manhattan without being run over by an irate taxi driver."

"True. I guess I'm pretty kickass. I deserve a three-course lunch for sure."

"Anywhere you want, beautiful."

"Can I ask you something?"

"Shoot." He offers his hand to steady me as I get up.

"Why didn't you correct the doctor when she assumed we're together?"

"Because it's none of her business. And I figured if you wanted her to know, you'd tell her."

"I should have. Sorry." My stomach bottoms out, dropping into my boots. It was wrong of me to let her think Linc is my boyfriend. It's strange that with all my accomplishments and my career flying in the face of social expectations for women, I still don't want to be seen as an easy lay or labeled a Jezebel.

"You don't have to apologize, Diana. I'm here for you, and you don't owe anyone an explanation of our relationship... whatever this is we're doing."

"All the same, you didn't have to play it up by asking about the safety of us having sex."

"Who said I was playing up?" I wait for a sly wink or mischievous grin, but his expression remains serious.

"What?"

"You said you're really horny."

"We're not dating, Linc. Just because you're the father, I don't expect you to be my sex slave while I turn into the Goodyear blimp."

"I know you don't *expect* anything from me, but that doesn't mean I can't give you what you need. Think about it. It's not like we haven't kicked the tires before." He takes a step closer. "Friends with benefits isn't the worst idea in the world, is it?"

"Yes. You don't want to sleep with a pregnant woman."

"You're not some random preggo chick, Diana, you're having my baby. We're choosing to be friends, but I can help. You know I can make you feel good. I've already made you come countless times before. Tell me the sex isn't great between us."

"It was, but I don't want to complicate things."

"Orgasms don't have to be complicated. They can be simple... earth-shattering... and plentiful."

"We're going to be in each other's lives forever now that we're planning to co-parent. Our friendship is based on a few drunken nights of amazing chemistry and the fact my IUD was a dud. Maybe for you, the lines won't get muddied, but I'm not sure I can do the friends-with-benefits thing with you, Linc."

"Why?"

"Because I'm hormonal, alone, and I don't want to get too attached."

"You're not alone. And no offense, Diana, but you're the least attachment-prone woman I've ever met. I'm pretty sure you'd kick me out of bed before my jizz had time to cool."

"Gross. We definitely wouldn't need to worry about romance."

"Just think about it. The offer is there. If you want me, I'm yours." His eyes drift to my lips. "While you're up the duff and craving the D."

"When you put it so eloquently..."

"Do you want me to get down on one knee?"

"Of course not. Look, I appreciate you offering to take the hit to help a girl out, but I wouldn't do that to you. You're hot and single. There are a million young, hot, *not* pregnant women in Manhattan who are desperate to warm your sheets. You shouldn't have to slum it with me for months because we accidentally made a baby."

I grab my purse and head for the door without meeting his gaze, but as I reach for the door handle, he spins me around, cupping my face in his hands. "Don't ever talk about yourself like that again. Any man would be lucky to have you, Diana, me included. Whatever damage you have from your ex that makes you say things like that... I'm sorry. If you're not having sex, then neither am I."

"Who said I'm not having sex?"

"What? You did. Are you joking?" His brow furrows at the notion.

"We're not together, so technically I can have sex with anyone, same as you can." I wouldn't because the thought of it makes me want to vomit, but he doesn't need to know that.

Without warning, he captures my mouth in an all-consuming

kiss, firm and sensual with an urgency that makes my pulse race.

"If another man so much as lays a finger on you while you're carrying my child, I'll rip his fucking throat out."

"I'm not yours to own, Linc." My body defies my words, giving itself freely, begging to be claimed as his. It must be the pregnancy hormones.

"Then consider mine yours to own while you're pregnant. My cock, my mouth." He ghosts his lips down my neck. "My tongue."

I fight back tears for the tenderness in the low growl of his voice but also because this isn't how I pictured this time in my life. I wanted love, trust, and forever. My baby is from a broken home before she's born. Although I'm not sure you can break what has never been. I've screwed this up, and we haven't even started yet. What kind of mother am I going to be if I can't get this part right?

"Linc, what are we going to do?"

"Whatever you want, Diana. If you need to hate me, I'll let you. If friendship is what you want, you have it. If you crave passion, I'll gladly oblige." He hesitates, staring deep into my eyes as he cups my face in his hands. "If you want my heart, I'll give it to you."

"I... I don't know what to say."

He presses a gentle kiss to my lips. "You don't have to decide now. Think about it." He wraps his arm around my shoulder and pulls me close to his side, pressing a kiss to the top of my head.

"Thanks for coming with me today."

"You're welcome. Thanks for growing my immaculate DNA in your uterus. It's kind of spectacular."

My brain has no scathing remark or witty retort. Instead, I'm trying to dampen the desire sparking to life in my core, an ache that's been building with every day that passes. The more time we spend together, the more I want to be around him. I'm not sure when I stopped hating Linc or if I ever felt anything close to hate in the first place. There's a fine line between love and hate, and our strange, combative friendship is quickly becoming the most important relationship in my life.

CHAPTER FIFTEEN
LINC

"WE'RE GOING OUT TONIGHT." Anders and I hit the batting cages this morning. I've been waiting weeks for Diana to tell Brooke about the baby so that I can have a conversation with Anders, but she's backed out every time. I suggested we tell them together, but she wants to tell Brooke alone, and I need to respect that.

"I can't. I'm having dinner with Diana."

"What the fuck are you doing, bro? You're clearly into her, and this whole we're-just- friends thing is going to blow up in your face." He grabs a few bottles of water from the cooler and chucks one in my direction.

"I'm not having this conversation with you. You and Brooke were the ones who wanted us to get along. We're getting along. Is it such a big deal that we're spending time together?"

"Depends. You don't generally hang out with women to be their friend. It was fine when I thought you wanted a relationship, but I don't want you and her hooking up 'as friends' and then Brooke and I have to pick up the pieces later. What are you getting out of this?"

"For a start, it's none of your fucking business..."

"She's my sister-in-law."

"I know! You've pointed it out every time I've been in the same room with her since the day we met. Brooke tells me every time she opens her mouth. Diana and I are fine with the way things are right now, so I suggest the two of you get over yourselves and stop judging the rest of us from up on your fucking pedestal of perfect marital bliss."

"If you're really just friends, then it's not a big deal for you to switch your plans and come to Viper with me tonight."

"The ball and chain okay letting you out of her sight and into a club?"

"Don't act like you don't love the crap out of Brooke. She's amazing, and you know it."

"Yeah, I do. I'm happy for you, bro, but you throwing my inadequacies in my face every two minutes is getting old. Once upon a time, you were my wingman, and my moves had nothing on yours."

"That's fair. Brooke is worried. She says Dee isn't herself, and they're not talking the way they used to. It comes from a place of love. Dee's been through a lot. She had a breakup before the fight that ended up being postponed. Brooke is concerned she might be a little fragile right now."

"Maybe you both need to take a step back and really look at Diana. She's anything but fragile. I promise you I have nothing but the best intentions when it comes to her. We have a good time together. We hang out, eat takeout, and watch crap TV together." As much as I want more, she asked me not to flirt, and I'm abiding by her wishes ninety-five percent of the time. If she's honest, the other five percent comes on the back of her initiation.

"Come out with me tonight. Brooke can hang with Dee, and we can grab a few drinks, have a few laughs." This is our chance to tell them. Plus, if I tell him in a public place, I might get out of it alive.

"I'll make you a deal. You shut the fuck up about my friendship with Diana, and I'll come out with you. If you mention it again, I get a free punch."

"Deal. Not in the face, though. I'm too pretty to take a hit to the face."

"Wow, your estrogen levels must be sky-high right now."

"Fuck off."

"I wouldn't waste a free hit on your face anyway. I'd nut-punch you for sure."

"You'd seriously go to any lengths to get a grope on all this good stuff. Are you sure you and Dee aren't gal-pals? Is she your beard?"

"I'm gonna nut-punch you right now if you don't shut up."

"Grab your bat. Another thirty minutes, and we're done. Now, call your bestie and tell her painting each other's toenails will have to wait another night."

"You realize if I told her you said that, *she'd* come down here herself and beat the shit out of you."

"Yeah. Please don't tell her." I let out a belly laugh as I pick up my bat and put some distance between us.

"That's what I thought." I quickly pull out my phone and tap a quick message.

Me: *Brooke wants to hang with you tonight. Anders is pestering me to go out with him and give you some sister time. This is the night. You tell her, and I'll tell him. No backing out.*

After a few minutes, my phone vibrates in my pocket, distracting me as a pitch heads right for my face. I manage to duck at the last second, but it's a close call.

Diana: *Oh. I was looking forward to snuggling with Tink.*

Diana: *Brooke is going to freak out.*

Me: *I think she'll surprise you.*

Diana: *You sure you should be the one to tell Anders? We could let Brooke tell him. ;o)*

Me: *It has to come from me.*

Diana: *Okay.*

Me: *So... you're only going to miss Tink?*

Diana: *She's my snuggle buddy.*

Me: *She'll miss you too.*

She's been avoiding any mention of us since the ultrasound. I gave her a plethora of options when it comes to our relationship moving forward, and I know which path I want her to choose, but I'm hesitant. I don't know if I can trust her. She didn't want a relationship when I put myself out there to begin with. If she changed her mind now, how will I know if we're together because of the baby or because she actually has feelings for me?

VIPER IS PACKED TONIGHT, but thankfully, the VIP room is a little more sedate—plenty of whiskey, a sprinkling of hot girls on the prowl for a roll in the hay with a VIP, and a dark corner for Anders and me to sit and nurse a few drinks with Carter.

"All right, all right. I haven't seen you guys in months. I was hoping to catch up with you in the Hamptons, but I had a babysitter and an empty house with my naked, very hot wife in it. You're never going to win that one."

"No brainer on the Hamptons. Get your freak on, bro. To be fair about this place, you rarely grace it with your presence." He's too busy living his amazing life with his wife and kids.

"True, but have you gentlemen been here in my absence?"

"No."

He startles at my admission. "Did you break your dick, my friend?"

"May as well have. He's mooning over my sister-in-law. They're 'friends,' according to him," Anders interjects.

"Cazzo fi Madonna." Carter is prone to dipping in and out of Italian during conversations. "Do I have to create a fucking paint by numbers for you two?"

"I'm married. I'm fine." Anders has that smug grin on his face, and I want to slap it right off him.

"And I remember when you were in here 'mooning' over Brooke and letting her slip through your fingers. If it weren't for Linc and my CCTV cameras, you'd be shagging everything that moves, and Brooke would've moved on long ago."

"When did this become about me? He's the one who's pining."

"I'm not pining, for fuck's sake. What do I have to do to get you off my back? Fuck a woman right here on the bar?"

"That sounds more like you."

"Jesus, Anders, you're like a broken record." I grab my drink and leave him and Carter to discuss my inadequacies. I may as well talk to the bartender. He doesn't give a shit if I'm fucking or friending Diana. How the hell am I supposed to tell Anders about the baby?

The minute I sit down, a VIP chaser is pulling up a barstool at my side.

"You're Lincoln Nash, right?"

"Yeah. And you are?" Hot. She's hot and available, and I feel nothing.

"Becky. Want to buy me a drink?"

I take a moment to look around me. This isn't where I want to be or who I want to be with. "No, actually. I really don't want to buy you a drink. Or any other woman."

"What?" Her annoyance is clear, and I can't blame her, but I don't have time for pleasantries.

"Sorry, Becky. You seem like a nice person, but there's something I've got to do. Have a good night."

I don't wait for a reply. With renewed purpose, I stride across to where Anders and Carter are deep in conversation.

"Struck out already? You're losing your touch, bro." Anders lifts his glass to his lips.

"Diana's pregnant. And it's mine."

A mist of whiskey and saliva coat my shirt when Anders chokes on a mouthful. "You better be fucking joking."

"I'm not. She didn't want to tell anyone before now."

He's up in my face in a heartbeat. "One fucking pussy. Stay away from one fucking pussy. That's all I asked of you! Don't fuck my sister-in-law unless you're serious about her. And you couldn't even manage that. What the fuck is wrong with you?"

"It's not like that. It started as a bit of fun, but I really like her."

"Fan-fucking-tastic. You've ruined her life because you couldn't keep your cock to yourself. I know you can be selfish, but this, I expected better."

Carter steps between us. "I think you both need to step off right now."

"Yeah, step the fuck off, Anders. I haven't *ruined* anything. This is the best thing that's ever happened to me. I'm going to have a family. Yeah, it wasn't planned, but we're happy about it."

"So the 'we're just friends' has been a lie this whole time?"

"No. We're not together."

"You just said you knocked her up."

"Yeah, and I want more, but she's not there yet."

"How could you be so fucking stupid?"

"I'm going to stop you before you say something you can't take back. I haven't *ruined* anything. You're going to be an uncle. I'm going to be a dad, and I'm fucking terrified but also so damn happy I could burst. Rather than bawling me out, some support might be helpful."

"I'm going to be an uncle."

"Yeah, so if you use the words *ruin, mistake, knocked up, pussy,* or *stupid* concerning my kid or Diana, I'll beat the shit out of you."

Realization dawns as the harsh set of his brow softens. "You really like her."

"I'm in love with her!" Saying it out loud, I acknowledge the truth of my words. I've been feeling this way for a while, but now that I just admitted it to Anders, I know what I have to do.

I have to tell Diana. Now.

"Are you sure?"

"I've never been *more* sure of anything in my life. I have to go."

Maybe I can't trust her one hundred percent and she's not in love with me, yet, but it's better to take the risk—right? I have to tell her.

"Where? We're not done talking about this."

"I have to tell her. It can't wait." Before he gets a chance to reply, I'm already making my way to the exit to hail a cab. I pull out my phone and dial.

"Hey, you. Having fun with the boys?"

"It was fine. How's your night of sister bonding? Have you told Brooke yet?"

"Yes."

"Wow. I'm proud of you. How'd she take the news?"

"She wants your nuts in a vice."

"Expected."

"She was actually pretty great, and stayed with me while I called my mom and broke the news."

"Fuck. How did that go?"

"Are you kidding? My mom freaking loves you. She's so excited."

"Really?"

"Yeah. I think she loves you more than she loves me. Did you tell Anders?"

"Yeah, and he just wants to rip my nuts clear off. There's a running theme here of my balls not being attached to my body for much longer. I left the club with all my teeth, so I figure it went pretty well."

"I told Brooke that I don't want her or Anders giving you a hard time about it. We're consenting adults, we made a baby, and we're friends now. I spent the first two hours being a twitchy mess. It was like every time I opened my mouth, the cat got my tongue. It was horrible."

"Really? I happen to love it when a pussy's got my tongue."

"You're so gross."

"That's not what you said when your pussy…"

"Stop! Don't finish that sentence," she screams down the phone.

"Why?"

"Because if you talk about us, it makes it harder."

"What does it make harder for you, Diana? It just makes me plain hard as a fucking rock."

"I know Anders took you out to get laid. Brooke told me."

"Yeah, that was his plan until I told him you're pregnant. I don't think that's where his head's at now. Listen, Diana, I wanted to talk to you about tonight. About me getting laid..."

She cuts me off mid-sentence. "We're friends who are having a baby. You're entitled to..."

"I'm in a cab."

"Oh."

"Alone."

"*Oh.*" Silence hangs on the line between us.

"Can I come over?" I wait what feels like hours for her reply.

"Yes."

"I'll see you in ten."

"See you then. Could you stop at Duane Reade and pick up some rocky road?"

"Of course. Anything else? Pickles? Peanut butter?"

"Very funny. Bye. Rocky road. Love you..." What the fuck? "... friend."

She hangs up the phone before I can respond. Did she just say what I think she said? She wants rocky road? That's a travesty against ice cream. I'm flipping the fuck out as the cab makes its way to Diana's block. Do I mention her call sign-off? Probably not. It's an easy slip-up. There's no way she meant it.

I grab two tubs of Ben and Jerry's before heading up to her apartment. Knocking on the door, my stomach is in knots. All night she was on my mind every moment. I just wanted to come here, stand in this exact spot, have her open the door, and greet me with a kiss.

The lock turns, and the jangle of the chain being slid open makes me impatient to set eyes on her. When she appears at the door, she's in sweats and a cute figure-hugging top, and I can't pull my stare from her stomach. Her baby bump is growing by the day, and hoodies won't be able to hide it any longer. It's gorgeous.

"What? Do I have food on my shirt again?" She starts swiping at the fabric for invisible crumbs. "I don't see it."

"I know you don't." I pull her into my arms, willing myself not to kiss her. The smell of her shampoo is so subtle but enticing. She wraps her hands around my waist, holding me tight as she rests her head on my chest.

"Are you okay?"

"Better now." I hug her a little too hard.

"Easy, my bladder has been reduced to the size of a grape. I'll pee myself if you squeeze too tight."

"Sorry." I step back before absentmindedly reaching my hand out to cradle the soft swell of her stomach. "Are you okay?" As her eyes meet mine, time stands still, my gaze fixed on hers, my heart hammering in my chest.

"I..."

"What? Tell me." My voice is barely recognizable, a whisper in the midnight air.

"I need to go to the restroom. Come in. Make yourself at home, and I'll be right back." She quickly scurries off down the hallway to her bedroom. I want to go after her, but the moment has passed. I forage in her kitchen for a clean spoon so she can devour her rocky road, but the girl is a one-woman shitshow when it comes to domestic matters. The sink is piled high with the remnants of her dinner with Brooke, and yet the dishwasher is sitting empty. How does anyone living alone manage to use every spoon they own making one dinner?

When Diana reappears, her cheeks are flushed, her demeanor almost shy.

"Here's your ice cream." I hand her a tub and set about cleaning up her kitchen.

"You don't need to do that."

"No offense, but your place gives me hives. How hard is it to put a dirty dish directly into the dishwasher? They don't have to make a stop in the sink for three days."

"Those have only been there for a few hours."

"Yeah, because I was here yesterday and left this place spotless."

"You're so domesticated, Linc. After your baseball career is over, maybe you can be the next Martha Stewart."

"What, end up in prison? No thanks. I'm thinking more of the Pioneer Woman vibe." That diffuses the tension, and I'm rewarded with her radiant smile.

"So, hotshot, how was your night? You smell like whiskey... and a hint of some cheap perfume. It made me gag when you hugged me." Do I see a hint of jealousy in her eyes?

"That would be Becky."

"Becky?"

"Yeah, the piranha at Viper who wanted to make the beast with two backs the minute she clocked who I was."

She turns on her heels and heads for the living room, dumping down on the couch with her ice cream. I take a moment to finish cleaning up her sink before grabbing a beer from the refrigerator and taking a seat beside her.

"Was she good?" She can't even look at me.

"What are you talking about?" I set my drink down on the coffee table and grab her ankles, lifting her feet into my lap.

"Your bathroom-stall hookup. *Becky.*" Her snide voice makes me laugh. She can't hide her distaste.

"Why do you care? You keep telling me we're just friends. I've offered you more, and you haven't even broached the subject since then."

She opens her mouth to protest but instead fills her mouth with a heaped spoonful of rocky road. I pull off her socks and start massaging her feet. "You don't need to do that. My feet are gross."

"They're cute. If you want to see troll feet, you should see mine."

"Don't even. I bet even your feet are sexy."

"You think I'm sexy?"

"I didn't say that." She shuts herself up with another spoonful.

"You said *even*. That implies everything else about me is sexy also."

"Can you not tease me when the smell of another woman is wafting up my nose?"

"Does it bother you? The thought of me kissing another woman?"

"We're just friends. I don't have the right to be bothered."

"That's not what I asked." I continue to caress my hands over her feet, applying just enough pressure to make her groan.

"How are you so good at that?"

"You know I'm good with my hands, southpaw."

"Why do you call me that?"

"Because it sounds cute and playful, like you."

"No one has ever described me as either of those things."

"Then I guess they didn't take the time to get to know you very well, did they? You still haven't answered my question."

"You just didn't like my answer. I think I gave you a reasonable one. We're not together. End of." Her gaze is fixed on the floor.

"So it really doesn't bother you? The thought of my lips trailing down a woman's throat, my hands cupping her breasts as my erection strains against her thigh."

"No." Her voice is a breathy whisper. She tries to pull her foot away, but I hold on tight.

"You don't care about my hands spreading her legs, my teeth grazing the apex of her thighs, tugging her panties out of the way before flicking my tongue over her swollen flesh. It doesn't bristle that she'd be screaming *my* name as she crashes over the edge, coming against my tongue... the same way you did."

"Stop." There's no conviction in her voice.

"That's what *you* told me, but not her. She wanted every hard inch of me. Filling her, straining her to the point of painful pleasure until I hit that sweet spot that made her growl."

She rips her foot from my grasp, storming down the hallway. "Get out, Linc."

I quickly follow, bracing my hands on either side of her, gently pressing her back against the wall. Leaning in, I whisper in her ear, "Say it."

"What? What do you want from me?"

"E-v-e-r-y-t-h-i-n-g."

"Then why did you come over here smelling like cheap perfume? To throw it in my face?"

"Why would I want to throw something like that in your face? Do you have that low of an opinion of me? I didn't lay a hand on another woman. I haven't since the first night I tasted you on my lips, but you already know that."

"I..." Her breath is labored as she struggles against the electricity sparking between us. The chemistry that's been there since the day we met. "I don't believe you."

"Because you don't trust me or because you can't let yourself want me?"

"Both."

I graze my hand down her side before guiding her hand to my crotch. "If you need evidence of what you do to me, this is it." She gasps, turning her head to avoid my gaze. "Say it, Diana. Tell me it doesn't make you angry to think of another woman finding pleasure in this."

Her fingers trace the length and girth of my erection. "It won't change anything."

"Say it. Once. I need to know."

"It makes me physically sick to think of you with another woman. There. I said it. Now, can you leave?"

"Not yet." I lift my hand from hers, but she continues to press against my straining cock. I ghost my lips up her neck, so close I can feel her pulse racing. "Do you know why I *know* it bothers you?"

"Because I'm sad and pathetic."

"Wrong. I know because I feel nothing but rage when I think of another man putting his hands on you. Of him claiming you, tasting your arousal, and having everything I want and can't have."

"You don't mean that. I'm not your charity case or your chance for a do-over of your childhood." Fucking hell. I opened myself up to her in a way I've never done with anyone else, and she uses it to push me away.

I drop my forehead against my arm before forcing myself to walk away. If I don't, I'll say something I regret or kiss her with wild abandon until she forgets everything and everyone except us.

"I can't believe you threw that in my face. I trusted you with something honest and raw, and you twisted it, using it against me because you're scared you might actually want me. Or that I, in return, might crave you with every breath I take."

"Linc."

"Diana, I'm going to go home, and I'll call you in the morning."

"You don't have to do that."

"What? Leave or talk to you tomorrow?"

"Both."

"If I don't leave now, I'm going to kiss you, strip you, and fuck you. Are you ready for that, Diana? Because once I sink balls deep inside you and make love to you until you don't remember your own name, there's no going back. Friendship won't be enough, and our pretense of 'it was only fucking' will crumble."

I wait an eternity for her to say the word. Give me the green light. Tell me she wants me too.

"I can't lose you. You're my best friend."

"*Friend?*" The word is a dagger to my heart. I'm the bladesmith of my own destruction. I handed her the knife with friendship emblazoned on the sheath, and tonight, I put the point of the blade over my heart. I never expected her to push it into my chest.

"Yes."

"Okay. Then I'll see you around... friend. Let's just call tonight a drunken mistake." I lean in, pressing my lips to hers in a gentle, chaste kiss, the taste of her lip balm lingering as I savor the moment. I don't push my luck, but it takes everything inside me not to deepen the kiss. In the end, I pull away and head for the door, the way I did

179

that first night in Vegas. She didn't want me then, and she doesn't want me now.

When will I stop torturing myself?

I have to walk away tonight, knowing that the only thing more painful than leaving would be staying.

CHAPTER SIXTEEN
DIANA

WHAT AM I so afraid of? I let Linc walk out of here an hour ago, and I've been staring at my bedroom ceiling this entire time, replaying our conversation over and over in my mind. I can't believe I was so careless with his heart. It makes me physically sick to know that I used what he told me about his childhood to put a wall between us again.

I have to apologize. I need to tell him that I can't stand the thought of losing him, not just as a friend or the father to our unborn child, but as—I'm afraid to even think it or let myself dream.

The one day I need to leave the house quickly, and I can't find my damn keys. I search high and low. Fucking pregnancy brain! They're nowhere to be found. Not in my purse or the bedroom. I pull apart my closet, wondering if I laid them down while I was trying on every outfit I own or at the least the ones that still fit me. I strip the bed and shake out the pillowcases. If there's a harebrained possibility of some-where I've misplaced them, I'm checking it. By the time I scour the living room and toss all the cushions on the floor, I give up.

There's a concierge in the building—how bad could it be to leave the door unlocked for an hour? I need to see Linc, and I'm afraid if I wait, I'll talk myself out of it. Telling Brooke that I'm pregnant was nothing compared to the anguish of imagining Linc with another woman. If I don't go to him now, I might be too late. I've been in this place once before with him, and last time, I ran. I made the wrong decision, and I've regretted it every day since. Why can't I let myself be happy?

In my haste and apparent loss of spatial awareness due to growing a human, I stub my toe on one of the barstools at my kitchen island on my way to the door. "*Son of a mother!*" Hopping on one foot, holding the other, I let fly a string of expletives, quickly followed by a terrified scream when my front door bursts open.

"Diana! Are you okay?"

"What are you doing here? You scared the crap out of me."

"I heard you swearing."

"From across town?"

"No. I couldn't leave. I didn't say what I came here to say. I've just been pacing up and down out here like a pussy. Then I heard you swear at the top of your lungs, and here we are."

"Oh." I try to calm my breathing, my adrenaline in fight or flight after that scare. The throbbing pain in my foot fades away as he stands before me.

"It sounds really creepy when I hear it out loud. Sorry. I didn't even realize how late it was getting. Where were you going at this time?"

It's now or never. With a deep, steadying breath, I launch into a babbling stream of incoherent thought. "I was coming to see you."

"Me?"

"Yes, you. Can you just not say anything until I get through this?"

His body stiffens as he closes the door to my apartment, hesitating before turning to face me, his expression schooled in a blank stare. "Say your piece."

"I was coming to see you because there were things I should've said earlier. And things I shouldn't have said at all. I'm sorry I used your childhood against you. If I could take it back, I would. It makes me sick to my stomach that I was so cruel when all you've been is kind since you found out about the baby."

"Apology accepted." His quick response is unnerving.

"No talking, or I'll chicken out again."

"Sorry."

I start pacing the length of the living room, my hands drifting to my growing baby bump. It's not huge, but I'm starting to love it.

"We were never supposed to happen. Us... the baby... a relationship... of any kind. But then no matter how hard I fight it, you've become my best friend."

"You said that earlier. I don't need a recap. Trust me, it's burned into my brain."

Oh my God, he seriously can't keep his mouth shut. I close the distance between us, grabbing his face with my hands and planting a hard kiss on his lips.

"*Shut up!* I'm trying to tell you that I'm in love with you, and you won't stay quiet long enough for me to get it out. I'm terrified to want more from you. I don't want to lose your friendship, and I don't want to make it more difficult for us to co-parent, but here's the thing..."

He sweeps an errant strand of hair off my face, tucking it behind my ear as he leans in with the softest caress of my lips. "What's the thing?"

"I don't want us to co-parent. We should be a team. A family, if that's what you want too. Somewhere along the way, I've started depending on you and missing you when you're not around. Friends with benefits wouldn't be enough for me, Linc, because I want it all. Everything. With you. I'm stupidly, annoyingly, head over heels in love with you, and the thought of you with anyone else doesn't make me angry... it breaks my heart. I've never felt this way before, and I don't enjoy feeling like I'm on a rollercoaster without a safety harness. It's uncomfortable and horrifying, but I want you more than my next breath."

He doesn't respond or kiss me. Instead, he remains frozen in place, his eyes searching mine for answers.

"Aren't you going to say anything? I just poured my heart out."

"I wanted to make sure you were done. Are you done?"

"Yes." My voice is barely a whisper at this point.

"Good. Now, I can say what I came here to tell you tonight, and you're going to listen."

I drop my gaze to the floor, my chest sagging under the weight of his impending rejection. "Okay."

He slides his index finger under my chin, coaxing me to look up at him. "You're a mess, Diana. Brash, even cruel at times, and yet when I look at you, I see nothing but beauty, strength, and a softness you don't like to admit is there. You can go from being a UFC powerhouse to a vulnerable, feminine beauty in the blink of an eye. You're breathtaking. When you let your guard down, you're stunning, and that's the woman I've fallen for. Your heart and soul."

"Really?"

"You've had me by the balls since our first kiss. What do you think? Can we make a go of this even though we drive each other nuts?"

"I'd rather be driven nuts by you than have some boring cookie-cutter life with anyone else."

"I'm in love with you, Diana. The crazy, stupid kind that would leave me standing outside my apartment, naked with my cock in my hand. I left my heart in the hallway that night. I'm scared to love you because you have the capacity to break me, Diana Lexington, and from that, I'd *never* recover."

"I'll do whatever it takes to earn your trust, and hopefully, in time, it won't be so scary. I'm scared too." Tears trickle down my cheeks. "I don't want to lose myself again, and that's what I let him do to me."

"Your ex?"

"Yes."

"I'll never let that happen. Why would I want you to lose yourself? I fell in love with you. You're all I'll ever want." He seizes my mouth in a soul-shattering kiss, his tongue teasing at the seam of my lips, begging entrance, which I freely give. His hands slide into my hair, holding me in place as he makes love to my mouth with slow, sensual strokes, filled with a longing I recognize all too well.

"I'm going to take control now, Diana, just for tonight. Let me."

"I..." I can't concentrate, his proximity pulling me down into the depths of desire.

"I'm going to take great delight in stripping you naked and kissing every last inch of your body."

"Mmm." I'm an incoherent fool.

"Then, and only then, will I make love to you. You'll take every hard inch of me until you're groaning my name while you come, over... and over... and over... again. You *own* me, Diana. I'm yours. Let me love you."

I push myself up onto my tiptoes, my lips capturing his as every fiber of my being cries out for him. For once in my life, I give over control, willingly and without reservation. "Take me to bed, Linc."

Without another word, he scoops me up into his arms and heads for the bedroom, stopping every few steps to kiss me with a reverence that sends shivers throughout my body, my nipples tightly budding, arousal thick in the air between us.

Linc and I have always been about hot, rough, sex—*fucking*. As he lays me gently on the bed, I know this is different. This *means* so much more.

His eyes are dark with desire, transfixed on mine as he reaches for the waistband of my jeans. "What the fuck is this?" Expecting to find buttons or a zipper, he's caught off guard by my new belly band, stretchy maternity leggings.

"Maternity clothes. Not sexy at all."

"Are you fucking kidding me?" He slips his fingers under the waistband and pulls them off in one fluid motion. "Easy access is the best kind of sexy, especially on you."

"You have to say that, you really want to get laid right now."

"Diana..." He lifts one leg to his lips, kissing his way from my ankle to my knee. "I say it because it's true. Now, take off your shirt." He moves to the other leg, teasing me, blazing a trail of fire from ankle to knee, but no higher until I'm left in nothing but my bra.

"I want to see all of you, Linc." He takes a step back, making sure I get a good view as he slowly unbuttons his shirt, shrugging it to the floor.

"Is this what you want?" His washboard abs are a glorious sight, the defined V dipping beneath his waistband.

"More." My voice is unrecognizable, so thick with arousal.

He scrubs his hand over the stubble on his jaw, giving me a sly wink as he lets his hand travel down his torso, and it's so damn hot. I'm wet for him without so much as a touch between my thighs.

I want to rip his pants off, but the show he's putting on right now is addictive. An ache builds as he unzips his fly and reaches under the waistband of his boxers, taking himself in hand before letting the heavy weight of his erection spring free. "Are you sure about this, Diana?" he asks as his pants and boxers drop to the floor.

"Yes." My breath is labored as I part my legs in invitation. "All... of... you."

He steps out of the pool of clothes around him, emerging like a goddamn sculpture of masculine perfection. My eyes are transfixed on where his fist wraps around the base of his cock, anticipation setting my world ablaze.

"That bra needs to come off."

"Then come and get it." There's nothing playful in my challenge tonight. I need him more than my next breath. The dark, dangerous yearning of his gaze transforms as a wicked grin tugs at the corner of his lip.

"There's no going back after this." He coils his hands around my ankles, slowly pushing them further apart before stalking the length of me. Bracing his arms on either side of my body, careful not to press down on my stomach, he begins to lick, kiss, and nip his way over the edge of my bra, sliding one finger inside, tugging it aside to expose my naked flesh.

"God, Linc, I need you." He grazes my nipple with his teeth before sucking it into the wet warmth of his mouth. I arch my back up off the bed, desperate for more, but he doesn't quicken his pace, instead savoring every flick of his tongue on my tightly budded skin.

"You're so beautiful, Diana. Do you have any idea how stunning you are?" He moves his attention to my other breast, reaching around to unhook my bra as I writhe under his ministrations.

As he works his way down my stomach, I shy away, self-conscious of my growing belly. I've always been lean, toned, and muscular. I don't recognize my ever-changing figure as the weeks go on. "You don't have to do that."

I move to cover my stomach with my hand, but he gently intertwines his fingers with mine before pinning my hands at my sides. "I don't *have* to, but I *want* to. It's so fucking sexy, it makes my cock twitch every time I see you." He lowers his lips to the soft swell of my bump, raining featherlight kisses over every inch. "This... is mine."

He continues lower. "Say it, Diana."

"I can't."

"You can." He captures my clit in a soft, open-mouthed kiss. "Let me show you how good it can feel to give your body over to the pleasure only I can elicit from you. I promise you'll enjoy it."

"Linc..." I moan his name as my brain wages war with my heart and this insatiable thirst for him.

"I'm yours, Diana. Let yourself be mine." He darts his tongue out, kissing the length of my pussy in one long, languorous lick.

"I'm yours, Linc. My heart, mind, and body are yours. My pleasure is yours alone. Please, don't break me."

My words are his undoing. Soft licks give way to firm kisses, and when he sucks my clit into his mouth, I can't contain the moans of pleasure that escape me—unrecognizable, primal, and saturated with the desire to be claimed as his.

"Oh God, Linc... yes... right there... don't stop."

His hands brace my thighs on either side, pushing them to their limit. "You taste so fucking good, Diana. I could kiss you for hours and never tire of your arousal on my tongue."

He laps at my entrance like a man lost in the desert, finding water for the first time. "Right there, please... oh God."

"I've got you, Diana, I always will." For the first time, I truly let go, giving myself completely to another person—to him. At this moment, I know he means it and trust that we can find a way to make this work.

Closing my eyes, I let my hands drift up my sides, cupping my heavy breasts as he continues to lavish me with his tongue. "Linc..."

"You're so beautiful." His eyes are pinned on me as I tease my nipples while he flicks my clit until I'm on the edge of orgasm.

"I'm close."

"I know." He pushes one finger inside me, setting the same slow rhythm as his mouth. "You're so responsive right now, as if you were made for me. *For us.* I want to hear you come, Diana. Can you do that? Come for me."

It's not a command. *It's a plea.*

He continues to coax my body higher, closer to the earth-shattering release I know is building deep in my core. "Come for me, Diana."

"I want you to come *with* me, Linc."

"I'd make a mess right now, southpaw. Don't worry, when I come, you'll be right there with me, screaming my name. This is just a warmup. An appetizer." He nuzzles between my thighs, his tongue relentless as sensation takes over, and my body sets me free. I take flight, spreading my wings as I soar to new heights, breath labored as if taking in a lungful of clean air for the first time. My head is swimming with nothing and everything at once. Every word spoken between us, stolen moments of passion, and angered words simply fall away.

"Linc..."

"It's okay to let go, Diana. I've got you. I always will. I love you."

Those are the three words that unlock the key to passion without fear. Fisting my hands in the deep blue of my bedsheets, I crash over the edge, headlong into an abyss of infinite pleasure—surrounding me —coursing through me—weaving itself into the very fibers of my being.

"Oh my God... Linc..." His name becomes my litany of worship as I'm overcome, riding the aftershocks of release, my body slick with a sheen of sweat.

Trailing featherlight kisses up and down the inside of my thighs, his fingers graze my stomach in a tender caress before he moves his mouth to take their place. His touch is soft and sweet, yet animalistic in the way he stalks my body, full of carnal desire.

"You're so exquisite, Diana." He continues to brush his lips over my curves, straddling my hips, ever so protective of the bump. He draws my nipple into his mouth, circling his tongue over the tip. My body is changing, and my breasts are no exception. They're full and heavy, more sensitive to touch and *pleasure.*

When we're eye to eye, there's fire in his ice-blue gaze, and a love I never knew was there before, and yet seeing it now, it's familiar. It reflects my own, even before I understood the aching push and pull I felt every time we've been together.

It's always been him. It was always meant to be him.

My fingers dance along the planes of his broad shoulders, his muscles taut as he supports his weight on either side of me. Everything about Linc is intoxicating. The remnants of his cologne soothe me as I breathe him in. His skin is like running your hand over the finest silk but just beneath the surface is a toned sculpture worthy of Greek mythology.

I slide one hand between us, my pulse quickening as I form a fist around the base of his cock, my fingers far from touching because of his size. Positioning him at my entrance, I press a sensual kiss to his lips. "Make love to me, Linc, because *I love you.*"

With a groan that makes my body tingle, he thrusts inside me, devastatingly slow and sensual until he's seated to the hilt, filling me, stretching me, claiming every part of me as his.

"*Diana.*" His breath is labored, almost anguished, as my name falls from his lips. "Jesus, you feel so good. I can't..."

"I need you."

He circles his hips, pulling back, a deep, shuddering breath running through him as he rears up, letting his head drop back as a roar escapes his chest. "Fuck." He thrusts deep inside, visibly restraining himself.

"I don't want you to hold back, Linc. I won't break." We begin to find a rhythm, our bodies moving as one, the passion between us transforming from the frenzied fuck that brought us together into a sensual, earth-shattering intimacy I've never had before.

Every kiss and touch are a gentle caress, a love letter between souls yet to be written. I'm lost to anything and everything around me. All I see is us—the way the muscles in his arms cord as he braces himself above me and where our bodies meet as he circles his hips. Gradually, he quickens the pace until the first vines of pleasure wrap themselves around me, their tendrils spreading like wildfire, the beginnings of my release taking hold.

"Oh God, Linc... I'm... oh God." My voice trembles as his thrusts become longer rather than harder. It's torturous and wicked, yet with such tenderness, my heart is full. I'll never get enough of this—of Lincoln Nash.

As my thighs begin to shake, Linc captures my lips, our tongues twisting and tangling in time with his long, sensual strokes. When I can't hold on any longer, I wrap my arms around his neck, deepening our kiss. "Linc..."

"Come with me, Diana." His words are my undoing, my orgasm crashing over me—through me—washing away my past, leaving only us.

"Linc... yes... oh God." He swallows my cries as he finds his release, kissing me as if it were his last. The warmth of his tongue, coupled with the power of our joint release ripping through us is an explosion—sensory overload in a perfect philharmonic symphony of indulgence and desire.

We ride the aftershocks together, lost in soft kisses and whispered words. I'm loathe to give him up when his arms can no longer hold him above me. As he rolls off me, he opens his arm, pulling me close to his side, and I try to catch my breath.

"Diana." He sweeps the hair off my face, pressing a soft kiss to the tip of my nose.

"Yes?"

"You have nothing to fear with me. I adore you, and I'm not going anywhere. I'm all in. The whole nine yards. I want everything with you. This is just the beginning for us."

"I think I'm going to be sick."

"Are you ever going to let me say romantic shit to you? That was top-quality boyfriend material."

"It was beautiful, and I love you so freaking much it's ridiculous, but I meant I'm literally going to hurl." I jump out the bed and run to the bathroom.

I can hear him shuffling around, so I offer a preemptive strike.

"Don't come in here."

"I've seen this a million times. I'll hold your hair."

"We just made love for the first time, and trust me, I'm about to gag at my word usage, but it's the truth."

"Exactly. I love you, so let me come in and look after you."

"No. I need this one thing. I promise tomorrow you can get all gung-ho about the boyfriend life, but tonight, I just want you to think about the me of two minutes ago, not this part. Okay?"

"Okay, southpaw. I'm going to look for your favorite sweats and leave them at the door. I'll go make you some of that peppermint tea. Holler if you need me."

"Thank you."

"You're welcome."

"Linc."

"Yeah?"

"I love you." I know he's already heard it tonight, but it feels really great to say it, like I want to shout it from rooftops.

"I was right about you all along. You're a fluffy pink unicorn, girly girl with glitter and tutus and a soft squishy center."

"Our little secret. Dee Lex isn't a girlie girl."

"You've never been Dee Lex to me, but you'll always be my Diana."

CHAPTER SEVENTEEN
LINC

IT WOULD SOUND ridiculous if I said it out loud—I'm nervous about tonight. After the insane path Diana and I have taken to find each other, tonight will be our first official date. I don't know whether to be excited or drop to my knees and say a hundred Hail Marys. I'm taking my girlfriend—it's still odd calling her that—on our first date, and she's currently six months pregnant with our baby girl.

We've exchanged the words 'I love you' and are a few months away from welcoming our name-yet-to-be-agreed-upon baby. Why am I so anxious? I've been on a million first dates, but none of them mattered, not like this. I want everything to be perfect for Diana. She deserves the quintessential romantic first date we never had. A drunken text message and going down on her in a Vegas hotel room was hot, but the version of her I have now is so much more.

I went all out with the fancy restaurant and a quiet table in the corner. I didn't book out the whole place because Anders said it was a dick move, and thinking about it now, she'd have hated it. If I'm honest, this isn't what I envisaged for a first date with Diana, but nothing about our relationship has been conventional, so I wanted her to have one night of being treated like the lady she is—a breathtaking beauty. Anders and Brooke will be meeting us at the restaurant at Diana's insistence. Now that everything's out in the open, they're making an effort not to kill me, and I'm letting them.

I arrive at her apartment with a bouquet of flowers and a box of chocolates, and as I wait for her to open the door, I know I must look like a big Hallmark card asshole. That's exactly how I feel right now. When the familiar clunk of her deadbolt echoes in the hallway, my insides cringe to the point of hiding my face with the flowers. I can sense the death blow before it's delivered.

"Oh, I'm sorry, sir, you must have the wrong apartment. You're looking for 1945 Cheesy Rom-Com Avenue, two blocks south of Have You Lost Your Mind Boulevard. If you end up at Cliché Road, you've gone too far."

I literally crumple against the doorjamb as side-splitting laughter overflows. "I knew it!"

"Lincoln Nash, what were you thinking?" I love her laugh—so melodic and infectious.

"I wanted to do one thing right. The first-date stuff."

"The flowers are beautiful."

I hand them over, completely unprepared for the sight of her tonight.

"Forget the date, we're staying home. You look good enough to eat. Wow... just... wow."

"You like?" she asks before leaning in for a soft, welcoming kiss.

"You look incredible." I throw the box of chocolates on the nearest surface and take her hand, encouraging her to give me a three-sixty angle on this dress. "Fuck me, I'm hard already. You only wear this dress from now on." My cock is straining against my pants, she looks so damn hot.

"I wasn't so sure about the figure-hugging maternity clothes, but I'm feeling pretty sexy in this one, even though my pantyhose are so big they cover my bra."

"Shut the fuck up. Are you serious? I need to see this."

"No, it'll ruin the sex appeal."

"Then you shouldn't have told me. And let's face it, the anaconda is stiff as a board right now. I don't care what those pantyhose look like on you, they'll be sexy as fuck."

Her dress is so tight it could've been sprayed on at the local body shop—black, sleeveless, and clinging to that gorgeous baby bump of hers that's really starting to pop now. The neckline slashes straight across, giving no eyes on cleavage, but those puppies are hugged so tight, I could cry. I've been reading *What to Expect When You're Expecting*, and it warned me to expect her breasts to 'enlarge.' They really need to change it up a little for us scared dads—give us the positives to take our mind off the responsibility coming our way. Something like:

AS PREGNANCY PROGRESSES, your partner will grow weapons of mass consumption and consumer world power. Don't try to fight any argument that may come your way, she will win. One glance at those perfectly plump breasts, and you'll sell a kidney for one squeeze of the fun bags.

Also, keep in mind when out in public, other men will look, but if you slaughter every one of them and dispose of the bodies, you'll have a landfill in an undisclosed location before she gives birth. Don't murder people. Always remember—she chose to make a baby with you. You are the only one who has permission to enjoy those watermelons of Aphrodite.

In conclusion, never forget the key element of pregnancy breasts for partners. Do not, under any circumstances, agree to any large purchases—minivans, new homes in the suburbs, an annex to your existing home for your in-laws to move in—during this crucial time. Your partner may seem sweet and ethereal as you gaze upon her radiant beauty, but she knows her superpower, and she's not afraid to take her top off after planting the seeds of kicking the tires on a few cars. Once the top is off, it's too late, you're buying a minivan.

· · ·

"EARTH TO LINC." She stretches the neckline of her dress forward to let me see the pantyhose, but I take a step back.

"We're not getting a minivan. *Ever.* You can't make me."

"What the hell are you talking about? Come and look at this, it's funny, and you're being weird."

"Not before you say it." I give her a panty-melting smile to recover from my odd behavior.

"No minivan. Or if we get one, I'll back over you in it to put you out your misery." Her nose scrunches up as she giggles to herself. It's so stinking cute.

"That's real love. Thanks, southpaw."

"You're welcome, baby."

I tentatively step forward, peeking down her front. "Holy shit! This dress is coming off."

"No. We'll be late for our reservation, and you don't need to see this."

"I beg to differ. I definitely do need to see them to assess why the hell you're wearing pantyhose. It's warm outside."

"They hold all my soft bits in."

"Those are all the best parts." I drop to my knees and slide her dress up her legs, over her hips, and up over her head. She wasn't wrong. The pantyhose are, in fact, covering her bra, and I was right—she makes it look sexy as fuck.

"Satisfied?" She's trying to be annoyed, but it's too funny to keep a straight face. Both of us descend into a fit of giggles, but I'm still dealing with a tent pole situation over here.

I bite down on my knuckle. "Will you hold it against me if I tell you, you look seriously hot in that get-up?"

"You're a perv, Lincoln Nash."

"Yeah, but I'm your perv." She snatches her dress back, but I have one alteration to make before she puts it back on. "You don't need these." I divest her of the pantyhose, kissing her stomach as I push them down over her hips. "Hi, princess. Don't worry, I won't let

Mommy roast you alive all night in these crazy girly things. She doesn't need them."

"Watching you talk to her like that might have exploded my ovaries, so make the most of her when she gets here. I think my ovaries are liquid right now."

"Put your dress on, Diana. If you don't, I'm going to start saying things to you that'll make other parts of your body explode."

"Would they really care if we didn't show up?" A wicked grin creeps in at the corner of her lips, a devious little minx coming out to play.

"You invited them! As much as it pains me, put your dress on. It'll be on my bedroom floor later."

"Now, this first date just got a whole lot better."

When she's ready, I cup her face in my hands, lowering my lips to hers in a firm but chaste kiss. "Let's go."

Diana's manager released a statement last month confirming rumors of her pregnancy, but she's kept a low profile, and my name wasn't part of the equation. I was surprised when she suggested we walk to the restaurant tonight. It's only a few blocks from her place, but she's not a PDA let's-show-everyone-we're-in-love kind of girl.

We stroll hand in hand through the streets of Manhattan, enjoying the beginnings of a summer breeze and possibilities in the air.

"I thought I might come to one of your games sometime soon if that's okay?"

"You're a Yankees fan, you can go to any game you like. You don't need my permission, southpaw."

"I know. I meant, maybe I'd sit in your seats, as your... person... plus-one type thing."

"You mean you want to come as my girlfriend?"

"Yes."

"Hell, yeah. I've been waiting for you to say the word."

"There's something else."

"O-kay, you look pale all of a sudden. Are you going to hurl?" She rolls her eyes as if that assumption is way out of left field. It's a daily occurrence. At any given time, if I'm in the same room as Diana, I know where all exits and trashcans are located. I'm like the secret service of vomit protocol. It's getting better, and there are foods she can keep down now, but it's a short grocery list.

"I'm not going to be sick. Not yet anyway. I wanted to know how you feel about releasing a statement that we're together, and you're the baby's dad? I know I don't owe the world an explanation or anything, but I'm proud of you, us, and our baby girl when she arrives, so I just wanted to put it out there. You can have a think about it and let me know."

"No thinking required. Fuck, yeah!" I drop her hand, pulling her into my arms and twirling her in the middle of the street.

"Really, you'd be okay with it?"

"Are you kidding me? Okay isn't the word. Over-the-fucking-moon is more like it. I haven't mentioned it because I want you to be comfortable throughout this whole process. I'll tell anyone and everyone who'll listen."

Her smile is bright, shining like the sun as I bask in its warm glow. We walk the rest of the way in our blissed-out bubble, all goofy grins and smartass conversation. It's not until I hold open the door to the restaurant for her that our bubble is well and truly burst.

"Anthony?" I follow her gaze to the weasel standing in the doorway, staring at her belly with disgust.

"You're pregnant? Is it mine?" Diana's face drains of color, her sunny demeanor of only moments ago has vanished.

Anthony—the douchebag from Anders' wedding. The married douchebag. Now, he has the audacity to look at her stomach with twisted distaste and ask if the life growing inside her is *his*. I step in front of Diana, reaching out my hand, trying to curb my rage.

"I'm Lincoln Nash. And who the fuck are you, you presumptuous prick?"

"None of your business." He brushes past me and grabs Diana's arm, pulling her aside. "What the hell are you doing here? Did you come to ambush me with *this?*" He gestures to her stomach.

I wrap my hand around his wrist, twisting at just the right angle for maximum pain, forcing him to relinquish his hold on her. "I strongly suggest you don't lay a fucking finger on her."

What an arrogant son of a bitch.

"This is none of your business, so why don't you get out of my way?" Diana is timid behind me, and so many pieces fall into place. Her reticence to open up with me, to trust me with her heart, and the walls she's built around herself because of this scumbag.

I'd like to see him try to move me out of his way. I've got seven inches and fifty pounds of muscle on him. I'm also fucking pissed because he just had his hands on the woman I'm in love with and the mother of my child.

"No can do, dickweed. Diana became my business the day I met her, and you gave up the right to touch her the second she found out what a two-faced, cheating piece of shit you really are. So, unless you want me to have a nice little chat with your wife and tell her about your late-night 'meetings,' I suggest you shut the fuck up and listen to whatever Diana may want to say to your pathetic ass. Then, and only then, can you leave with your limp dick hanging between your legs. Do you understand?"

He looks past me to Diana. "Is this guy for real? There's nothing pathetic about my dick, but you already know that, Dee. Maybe you should've been more selective about who you spread your legs for."

Rage takes root in my chest, spreading like fire, licking through my body until I'm consumed by it. My blood, replaced by molten lava, pumps hard through my veins. I turn to Diana. "Say the fucking word. Please."

"Go for it." It's all the encouragement I need.

Before he knows what hit him, my fist connects with his face— one calculated punch that sends him stumbling onto the sidewalk. "What the hell?"

"Consider that a warning shot. If you *ever* disrespect her like that again, *I will fucking end you.*"

I step over him and gesture to Diana as I hold the door of the restaurant open for her. "After you, beautiful."

"Thanks, Linc, but do you mind giving me a few minutes to talk to Anthony?" Her voice is small, nothing like the confident woman I know and love.

"Are you sure?"

"Yeah. I need to do this for me and for us. I have to let it go."

"I'll be at the bar. I can see Anders over there waiting for our table. If he so much as looks at you the wrong way, I'll knock his fucking teeth out."

"And I'll let you, baby." She locks her lips to mine, and I pour every ounce of strength I have into this one kiss, praying she'll find the closure she so desperately needs.

I stare down at Captain Fud Flaps. "You heard the woman. She wants to talk to you, so get moving and remember to play nice. If you don't, I'll come find you, or better still, I'll make good on finding your wife. You think you're the only one in your marriage with a roving eye? I'm known for turning happily married women into screaming fangirls. I'm sure she'd enjoy an orgasm in a bathroom stall. Tit for tat, Tony boy. Don't make me slum it with your wife to prove a point. I'll wait until after to tell her what a cheating sack of shit you are." I'd never look twice at his wife, but I know the threat of sleeping with her enrages him. I would be taking something of his. I hate that he knows Diana intimately, and revel in making him feel just a fraction of my anger.

It amuses me to see his seething rage building under the surface as his fists ball at his sides, but Limp Dick Harry knows he couldn't take me in a fight.

He picks himself up, dusts himself off, and makes a piss-poor attempt at a threat. "I could ruin your career with a few phone calls. I have friends in high places."

"So do I, *Tony,* but I don't need other people to fight for me. Let's not start a battle of wits. You came unarmed. And just for the record, that baby in her fucking glorious stomach isn't yours. It's mine. She's mine. And I *always* protect what's mine. Now, go and listen to Diana, then you can get the fuck out of my sight."

He's about to open his mouth with another snide remark but thinks better of it when he meets my steely glare. I watch every move he makes as he follows Diana to a discreet table in the corner. He's looking around, checking no one has clocked him with a woman other than his wife. I fucking hate him. It takes every ounce of self-restraint I have to walk over to the bar and a puzzled-looking best friend.

"Hey, bro. Is there a reason why your date just sat down with another guy?" He signals the bartender for a round of drinks, handing me his glass of whiskey, which I down like a cheap shot of tequila on spring break.

"You don't recognize him? He was at your wedding." I scrape my hand over my five o'clock shadow, tension rolling off me in waves.

"I remember him. He was her date," Brooke interjects as she slides under my arm for a hug. "Smarmy bastard. I didn't like him."

"I didn't think I couldn't love you more, Lexington, but it just happened. I do. I'm ready to become Anders' brother-husband just for you."

"What about my sister?"

"I'll buy us a big compound to live on or something." I can't take my eyes off Diana, even for a second, watching for any sign she might need me. Anders replaces my empty glass with a full one. That's what best friends are for.

She looks to be crying at one point, wiping tears from her cheeks. I'm ready to move, every muscle in my body tensed and ready to pounce, but Brooke rests her hand on my shoulder. "You need to let her do this alone. Whatever happened there obviously wasn't good."

"Has she told you anything about him?"

"No. She's private about relationships, as evidenced by her seeing you and being more than halfway through her pregnancy by the time she told me. How crap a sister am I?"

"I'm sorry. I wanted to tell you we were seeing each other. And I didn't even know I was going to be a dad for the first trimester. What does that say about me? Diana had her reasons, and everything worked out in the end."

Eventually, the douche canoe rises from the table, jutting the chair out so hard it falls backward. Being the dickhead he clearly is, he doesn't bother to pick it up, storming out of the restaurant without so much as a backward glance.

Diana rests her elbows on the table, her head in her hands. Brooke rushes over, and Anders asks me to give them a minute together.

"I need to check on her, man. That guy is bad news."

"And he was sporting a black eye when he left. Can I assume that was your doing on the way in?"

"Yes," I say proudly. "He deserved it."

"Well, all right then. Let's go have dinner with our girls."

We weave our way through the tables, everything an obstacle in my path to Diana. I drag my chair closer to her, wrapping my arm around her shoulder. "Are you okay?"

"Yeah. I said what I needed to say, and he had some choice words for me that I don't feel like repeating right now. Can we just order?"

"Of course."

A night out with Anders and Brooke is always a good time. They carry the conversation with some hilarious moments and talk about the future until Diana shakes off her encounter and joins in the fun.

"When are you guys going to have a baby? Our kids are going to grow up together. How weird is that?" She throws it out there so nonchalantly as she tucks into a Caesar salad.

"We already have children. Twins actually. Freddie and Mercury. We had them six months ago, and they live in our laundry room. Didn't we tell you? My bad." Brooke can't even get through her own jibe without amusing herself.

"Very funny. I get it. I'm the worst sister ever for depriving you of watching me spend months with my head down my toilet."

"She did you a favor, Brooke," I interject. "It's been so nasty. I'm thinking we'll just sell both our apartments after she gives birth and buy something new because we'll never be able to get those bathrooms clean enough to erase the atrocities that have happened in there."

"And that's just when you guys were having shower sex. What about where Dee's been sick?" I can always trust Anders to one-up me.

"It's like flashbacks to 'Nam every time I walk in there."

An idea forms as I polish off my steak, letting the rest of them talk amongst themselves. Diana rests her hand on my thigh, garnering my attention. "Are you okay? You've gone uncharacteristically quiet."

"I think we should move in together." I ready myself for battle with a list of pros and cons—mostly pros—knowing nothing with us is ever simple. "Just hear me out..."

"Yes."

"What?" Brooke and Anders echo my surprise, which I find mildly offensive, but now's not the time for it.

"Yes, I'll move in with you. I was going to ask you to move in with me, but I like your apartment better."

I'm dumbfounded. This isn't how I expected this conversation to go. I had a million answers for 'no,' or 'I'll have to think about it.' I have no words for an unequivocal 'yes.'

"Are you fucking with me right now because that would be cruel?"

She cups my face in her hands, pulling my lips to hers. "I'm not fucking with you. I'm in love with you, and we're about to have a baby together. We spend every night together already. Yes, I want to live with you. We're a team now, right? All baggage... punched in the face at the door. Thanks for that, by the way. I couldn't do it myself. It's a bad pregnancy look for a UFC fighter."

"My pleasure, southpaw. It was my absolute-fucking-pleasure."

"Congratulations!" Brooke raises her glass to us. "To you guys."

We all lift our glasses—Diana's is a glass of water—and toast to the future.

The rest of our evening is perfect. Even though it started out with an unwelcome intrusion, we're ending it on a high note. Anders and Brooke want to continue celebrating at Viper, but my girl needs to crawl into bed with me. She may not be on strict bed rest at this point, but she also doesn't have boundless energy.

"I'm going to take Diana home." She doesn't even try to protest, so I know I'm right. "You guys go ahead. Have fun and don't do anything I wouldn't do."

Anders slings his arm over Brooke's shoulder "Damn, baby, the world is our oyster tonight."

"You're a fuckwit, bro."

"Back at ya, bell-end. See you at practice on Monday." He holds the door open for Brooke, but in the blink of an eye, they're back inside, Anders shaking his head in my direction.

"Fuck." We quickly make our way over to them, but I keep Diana tucked in at my side, instinctively protective of her and the baby.

"There's paparazzi lining the street. Is there a back entrance to this place?"

"No," the concierge inserts himself into our conversation. "Should I call the police?"

"Not yet." Diana never backs away from a fight, and tonight, she faced her fears and came out on top, and my guess is she's ready to rumble.

"You're not going out there for them to swarm and paw at you. No fucking way."

"I have an idea. Do you trust me?" She stares up at me with such warmth and love, knowing this question means so much more than this one moment.

"Yes."

Turning to face the entire restaurant, Diana cups her hands at her mouth and hollers at the top of her lungs. "Hey! Can I have everyone's attention?"

That did it. Every eye in the place is on her.

"Hi. Sorry to interrupt your evening. I'm Diana Lexington, and you may know my friends here." She points to Anders and me as phones start being lifted from the table. "As you can see, I'm very pregnant right now. What no one knows is that Lincoln Nash, our beloved Yankees legend and my favorite person in the world, is the father. We're very much in love, and it's all gooey and pink and glittery or whatever. Now, there are a lot of reporters outside who would love to barricade us in here for the evening, and Linc is about ready to pop a vein in his forehead if one of them so much as breathes near this baby bump. Isn't that right, baby?"

She looks to me with wide eyes and a stunning smile.

"She's right, people. I'm gonna Hulk out if any of those guys try to get in her personal space."

"So, I was wondering if you wouldn't mind helping a pregnant chick out and form a little tunnel to a waiting cab if that's possible? Not how you thought your night was going to go, but we're here, and Linc has graciously offered to pay for everyone's dinner and drinks tonight for your trouble."

"I did?"

"You did, baby."

"What can I say, I'm a generous guy."

CHAPTER EIGHTEEN
DIANA

A RIPPLE of laughter and camaraderie spreads throughout the room, and one by one, men and women stand from their tables, lining up to form a human cage around me. I may just have had a small moment of genius.

"Thank you, everyone. I really didn't want to bail Linc out of jail tonight. The smell alone would have me hugging the toilet for a week right now."

"She's not even kidding."

He signals to Anders to head out first. I know there's no way he's leaving my side, even for a second. It doesn't take a rocket scientist to work out who tipped the press off to our location. Anthony. He couldn't even give me this as a parting gift after everything he put me through. So much for a quiet press release this week.

Brooke shrugs out of her cardigan and stuffs it under her dress, much to Anders' horror. "What are you doing?"

"Giving them what they want. A pregnant Lexington." She sticks her tongue out at us with a sly wink before going to her husband's side. "This is going to be fun." I may be the brawler of the family, but my little sister has never backed away from a fight, especially if someone she loves is threatened in any way. She takes more of a sneak attack approach, so I can only imagine what she's cooking up.

"Okay, everyone, thirty seconds, and you can enjoy the rest of your night on us. Thanks again."

And with that, the door opens, and mayhem ensues. We shuffle out slowly, Linc protecting my stomach as we're jostled back and forth inside our little human cage. I don't know why but I'm grinning ear to ear right now. This is so silly, so fun, and so completely Linc and me. Then, I hear Brooke, and my smile grows wider.

"Yes, you can all have pictures. Anders and I are very excited." She's rubbing her belly, overexaggerating every move. "I thought I was hiding it pretty well and that maybe you guys would just think I'd had one too many Twinkies recently."

Anders has flagged down a cab, so we only need to get six feet forward and into the back seat.

I think Brooke is going for an Oscar performance. "There was a time when my devoted husband was concerned that I had betrayed him and was, in fact, carrying a Twinkie baby, but genetic testing confirmed that his tinkie-winkie is the culprit."

Our human cage arrives at the cab, laughing and joking as everyone listens to Brooke's insane ramblings.

"Oh my God, I think I'm going into labor." She starts groaning and caterwauling as I slide into the back seat of the yellow cab.

We're not leaving them in the lurch, waiting as Anders weaves through the crowd to Brooke, grabbing her hand to signal it's time to go. She screams and lets her cardigan drop between her legs. "I'm so sorry, Anders, it's not a Verbeck baby after all. It's a Versace." He swipes it off the ground and pulls her through the crowd. Linc jumps in next to me, followed quickly by Brooke.

Anders slams the door behind them and gets in up front, thanking our fellow diners for a job well done. "You guys are rock stars! Thank you. Enjoy your night."

Paparazzi swarm around the cab, but this driver is a New York cabbie, he's done this shit before, probably for us at some point in our checkered past of bad decisions and celebrations.

"Where to?"

"Let's go home." I rest my head on Linc's shoulder, giving the driver the address for *his* apartment.

"Do you really want to live in my apartment? We can get a new place."

"Why?" It's sweet that he'd be willing to move for me, but I honestly don't want to waste time looking for a new home just for the sake of a charade of equal footing. The balance in our relationship doesn't hinge on where we sleep at night.

"Women like to nest."

"You're my home, not the place. I'll nest just fine like this." I wrap my arm around his waist and settle in for some wall-to-wall traffic for the ten blocks to his place—*our* place now.

"Brooke, you're a goddess. What you did back there was amazing." The sultry rasp of Linc's voice almost lulls me to sleep, I'm so tired.

"Hey, she might be your baby mamma, but she's my sister, and that's my niece in there. No one messes with a Lexington girl."

"Damn straight," Anders heralds from the front seat.

They drop us at Linc's place, seeing that I'm too drowsy for any continued celebrations, and I'm glad to have Linc to myself for a little while. The moment we're in the door, I drag him to the bedroom—not in a rip-off-your-clothes-hot-sweaty-sex way—but he follows all the same. After we strip out of our clothes and get under the covers, I shuffle around to position myself tight against his chest.

"Do you want to talk about it?" He sweeps a loose curl from my face, but I can barely look at him.

"About what?"

"Anything about the weirdest non-first first date in history."

"I loved it because I was with you." I lift his hand to my lips in a tender kiss, keeping my back to him. I've never been a cuddly sleeper, but pregnancy has changed everything about my sleep patterns. Apparently, that includes being the little spoon.

"Can we talk about your ex?" I'm so tired, but after what happened with Anthony tonight, Linc deserves answers.

"If we must."

"What did he say to you, southpaw? You were crying. I just want to make sure you're okay."

"I am now." It takes me a few moments before I continue, my heart beating so hard I'm certain Linc can feel it fighting to break free. "He called me a whore. Said that I saw what I wanted to see, and if I'd really looked, I'd have known he was married." He doesn't push or try to placate me, giving me the space to continue at my own pace. "He said you won't stick around." A lump forms in my throat, making it almost impossible to speak. "He said my bastard child will be left with a whore of a mother, and you'll move on... because I'm not the forever girl. I'm no one's forever."

I twist in his arms to face him, vulnerable as scared tears roll down my cheeks. "That's what he said."

He wipes my tears, caressing my face with his strong, callused hands. "You... are my everything, Diana. My yesterday, today, and all the tomorrows we have to look forward to. You're not my forever girl... you're my forever *woman*. Strong, bold, fierce, and so fucking beautiful inside and out. Someone like him will never understand what we have because he's not worthy of being loved by a woman as amazing as you."

I don't understand why he always sees the best in me, even when I've given him no reason. "Linc... what if you change your mind? What if you think you're in love with me now because we're having this baby together, but maybe if we weren't, I wouldn't be the kind of woman you could love?"

He gently lifts my chin, forcing me to meet his gaze, and as his ice-blue eyes see through all my bullshit, I can barely breathe. When Linc looks at me, he doesn't see what everyone else does. He sees me without judgment or expectation, accepting every part of me.

"Diana, I am so excited to meet our baby girl, but I'm not with you because you're pregnant. I don't love you because you're pregnant with my child. Think back for a moment, and it's staring you in the face."

"What?"

"You're pregnant *because* I'm in love with you. The night we conceived this little princess..." he says as he runs his hand down to my stomach, "... happened because I asked for more. I loved you even then when I barely knew you. My soul knew you were mine and that *I* wanted to be yours, forever. This baby was made with love, even if you hadn't caught up yet." My heart skips a beat.

"I want you to be my forever, Linc."

"Like I told the OB, I'm your barnacle. There's no getting rid of me now."

"I'm good with that."

"Then we'll get you moved in tomorrow. How does that sound? I don't know about you, but I'm ready for our forever to start now."

"Me too." Linc moves to reposition me with my back to his chest the way he knows I like to sleep, but I stop him in his tracks, overcome with the desire to be loved by him. "Make love to me, Linc. I want our forever to start the same way our love story did. A botched dinner and an earth-shattering orgasm."

I kiss him with every ounce of love and devotion coursing through my veins—in every beat of my heart, giving myself to him mind, body, and soul.

"SOUTHPAW, that's the last of your boxes. I can't believe it only took us two days to move you in."

I've been relegated to unpacking my clothes while everyone else has been doing the heavy lifting. I tried to explain that I'm pregnant, not incapable, but when Linc has Brooke and Anders in his corner, I lose the argument every time.

"Why are you surprised? You could've fit my entire apartment in your living room."

"Good point. Thank God you didn't ask me to live at your place." His playful smile makes me laugh.

"Would you have done it?"

"Fuck, yes! I'd live in a dumpster behind Applebee's if it meant being with you."

"Geez, you two are insufferable." Anders pipes up as he stacks the last of my training gear in the hallway.

Linc and I exchange glances, knowing exactly what the other is thinking.

"Are you fucking kidding me?" That's my man, always the height of diplomacy. I slink under his arm, relishing the warmth of his embrace. "We've had to play third wheel to you two since the moment you met. It's nauseating at best. You and your smug relationship goals perfection. Now it's time for you to get a taste of your own medicine."

"They aren't single anymore. How will we make either of them a third wheel exactly? Won't we just be a whole car now? Or a go-kart? Do we even know what the wheel refers to?" I hate to be the one to burst his bubble, but they all start laughing, and it's not at my observation.

Linc rubs my belly, his sly grin making his eyes sparkle in the twilight as it creeps in through the floor-to-ceiling windows. "Baby, a third wheel is an unwanted extra, therefore, a bicycle or something. If you're a third wheel on a car, you're a threesome in need of a fourth."

"Don't even think about saying it, Linc. I've assured my parents and my lovely knocked-up sister that you're a good guy. If you make a joke about sister threesomes, I'll have to retract those statements before kneeing you in the groin." Brooke and I definitely know how to pick them. When she looks to Anders, he's trying—and failing—to stifle his laughter.

"Oh God, my child isn't going to have any male role models in her life. All she'll have is you two goofballs. We're doomed."

Linc tilts my face upward, leaning in to brush his lips over mine in a ghost of a kiss. He knows exactly what that does to me. "You love me, goofball or not." He darts his tongue out to tease me, leaving me panting as he pulls back. "Admit it."

"I love your balls, you goof." As I chuckle to myself, an odd ripple travels the breadth of my stomach, and it stops me in my tracks. Panic grips me, worried that I've overdone it today and something's wrong with the baby.

It happens again.

And again.

"What's wrong, Diana?" Linc's voice is strained as he searches my face, the knit of his brow etched with worry.

As realization dawns, I grasp his hand in mine and press it tight to my stomach. "Just wait."

"Are you hurting?"

"No..." It happens again.

"Holy shit! Was that the baby? Did she just kick me?" His gaze is full of wonder, sparkling with love and adoration as he drops to his knees, cupping my stomach with both hands.

"Yes."

"Hi, princess." Another kick. His eyes shoot up to meet mine, his smile nothing short of awe-struck. "That's... incredible. You're incredible. Our baby girl just kicked." He turns to Brooke and Anders, his voice thick with emotion. "Come feel this."

"Are you going to invite everyone to touch my stomach now?"

"Sorry. Is it weird if they touch it? I'm just so incredibly in love with you right now, and I think you're the most amazing woman in the world with the most wonderful little life growing inside you. It's beautiful, Diana. You're stunning." He plants the softest kiss on my stomach.

"You're the only one who's allowed to kiss it, okay?"

His face sobers, the protective Linc I know and love getting territorial. "Anders, no touching for you. Southpaw just made it weird, and now I'm going to murder any man who puts his hand, or anything else, on this beautiful belly."

"Don't be silly, he's my brother-in-law. It's fine for him to feel the baby kick. It's not like he's going to try and mack my stomach like you do."

"Are you trying to rile me, woman?"

"Is it working?"

"Yes."

"Good, I like you riled up right before it's time to go to bed."

"Brooke, we're leaving. Boxes are done, and these two are creeping me out. I don't know if I even want to feel the baby kick now. They've sullied it for me, turning it into some weird foreplay."

"Shut up and come over here. It's amazing." Brooke doesn't need to be told twice, rushing over to rub her hand on my basketball-size belly.

"How will I know?" The baby kicks at the sound of her voice. "*Oh my God!* She knows Auntie Brooke already. Anders, get over here and feel this."

"Did I just hear your womb skip a beat?" If I didn't know any better, I'd think the mighty Anders Verbeck is a little afraid of that possibility.

"Oh, hush. Come here." As soon as he's within grabbing distance, she thrusts his hand onto my stomach.

He meets my gaze. "Sorry about this, Dee. It's a bit of an invasion of your personal spa..." He snatches his hand back as soon as the baby kicks as if he's just been scalded by a pot of boiling water. "What the fuck was that?"

"The baby!" Linc exclaims, giddy as a schoolboy. "It's phenomenal, right?"

"It's... like something out of *Aliens*. Am I the only one freaking out that there's an actual baby in there? Inside her body."

"Bro, did you just call my baby an alien?"

"No. I'm clearly not a baby person." He puts some distance between us like the baby's going to jump out and grab him at any moment. "I'm fine over here while you guys enjoy the miracle of pregnancy."

When the baby finally settles down, I'm ready to curl up in a ball and go to sleep, but they're all having some laughs at the end of a long day, so I opt for the couch. Closing my eyes for a few minutes, I listen to them chatting excitedly about their upcoming games and planning a baseball career for my daughter before she even enters the world. It's cute hearing Linc talk about her, and I'm certain he's going to be the most amazing dad.

Eventually, the threads of conversation are hard to hold onto, but it's okay because I'm surrounded by family as I let myself drift off—my sister, my brother-in-law, and Linc. Linc is my family now, and this is our home, together.

———

"COME ON, SOUTHPAW, TIME FOR BED." My eyes flutter open as Linc hoists me into his arms. I'm disorientated. The apartment is quiet, and all the lights are off.

"Where are Brooke and Anders?"

"They went home. You can go back to sleep, I've got you."

"I only shut my eyes for a few minutes. Ten, max." I nuzzle against his chest as he carries me down the hall to our bedroom.

"That was four hours ago. I tried to bring you to bed earlier, but you kept swatting my hand away any time I tried. Then you mumbled something about the anaconda, and that's when Brooke and Anders decided it was time to make a sharp exit."

"I did?" I'm still dazed, my limbs heavy as they hang over Linc's arms.

"I'm only kidding. You asked me to marry you."

"Did you say yes?"

"On the proviso that I get to wear the veil."

"No." I mumble—obstinate—still in the space between sleep and wakefulness. "I get to be the girl with you. No one else ever noticed I'm a girl. I want the dress and cake and all that good stuff."

"I'll remember that, southpaw. Only the best for you."

He lowers me into bed, tugs off my pants, and strips to his boxers, climbing in behind me, wrapping his arm over my stomach.

"Did I really propose?"

"I'm afraid not. I guess we'll need to save that for another day."

"Good. I don't want to ask you."

He presses featherlight kisses on my shoulder. "Ever the romantic, southpaw. Can we get through move-in day before you dash my hopes and dreams?"

"I just mean... I want to be asked... not be the one asking."

"I know."

"You do?"

"I do." He continues to trail his lips up my neck, nuzzling me with sensual kisses.

"I love you, Linc." Desire unfurls deep in my core, brushing sleep aside as an ache is awoken. A need that only he can sate.

"I love you too, Diana. Welcome home, baby."

I reach my hand behind me, letting it trace the length of his cock. "We need to christen the bed."

"You're tired." His words defy his actions, his tongue darting to the back of my ear, knowing it makes me squirm as he grinds against me. "Besides, we've slept in this bed together a million times."

"But now it's ours. I want you to fuck me in *our* bed, Linc."

Pushing my panties over my hips, he slides them down my legs, shrugging them to the bottom of the bed along with his boxers. His erection grinds against my ass as his fingers dig into my hip, anchoring me in place.

"I could fuck you every day for the rest of my life and never tire of the way your body comes alive at my touch, Diana." His fingers blaze a trail of fire between my legs, positioning himself at my entrance before thrusting inside me, taking it slow, savoring every kiss of my flesh. Even with Linc at my back, there's an intimacy that surpasses anything physical.

As we rock together, perfectly in sync, I've never felt so connected to another person—so completely loved. Our bodies speak a language that transcends words, attuned to each other's pleasure, born of a passion so fierce it threatens to consume us.

He fucks me long into the night, groaning my name as we find release, my name a litany of worship on his lips, just as his will always be on mine.

CHAPTER NINETEEN
LINC

SINCE THE WORLD found out Diana and I are an item and we're expecting, the media attention has been insane. With baseball season in full swing, we're in the limelight a lot, and the Yankees are having another killer year. Anders and I are at the top of our game with everything to play for. Winning three years in a row would cement our places in the Hall of Fame for sure. There have been rumors circulating, but nothing is a done deal until you get that phone call.

"I want to come to the game tonight." Diana appears at the doorway of our closet in her belly-hugging raglan shirt stretched to within an inch of its life. She's growing every day at this stage and gets more beautiful by the hour. With tight little braids in her hair today, she couldn't look any cuter if she tried.

I stride over, kissing her before dropping to kiss the bump. "It's a big crowd. The place will be packed. It makes me nervous with you this far along. You've only got a few weeks left to go." I already know she's coming—I asked Brooke to bring her. I want to do a little something sweet for her and the baby tonight. I have to play dumb and put her off the scent.

"Exactly! I might not make it to another game for a while. Brooke will be with me, and we can come with you guys, so we don't arrive with the fans. I'll even let you have one of the security guys in the stands with us, but only one."

"Two. And you let me come get you in the stand at the end of the game."

"You just want your face up on the screen looking all doting-father-to-be." The baby kicks against my hand as I rub Diana's stomach. "See, baby girl agrees with me."

"This is my life from here on out, isn't it? Outnumbered by women who gang up on me and have me wrapped around their little fingers."

"You know it. So, I'm coming, and you can't say no. I already told Mom and Dad they could come too." She widens her smile, batting her eyelashes like butter wouldn't melt in her mouth.

"That's good. I know your dad will take out anyone who comes within a six-foot radius of you."

"I can do that myself. You forget, I'm still a UFC fighter, even if I can't fight right now."

"When do you think you'll be back in the ring after the peanut princess arrives?" I'm being supportive of Diana as she continues to gently train throughout her pregnancy while keeping my fears to myself. It's easier right now when there's no fighting, only body conditioning. And with her hyperemesis, even that's had to be curtailed significantly. The thought of watching her fight in the future scares me. I hate when she gets a papercut, so seeing some woman trying to beat her half to death isn't high on my list of favorite things.

"Realistically, it'll be a while. Even if the birth goes smoothly, I want some time with you and the baby before I really need to hit training hard again. At least six months, maybe longer."

"I'll be here, cheering you on, changing diapers and all that good stuff. You'll get back where you want to be. You're the most deter-mined woman I've ever met in my life."

"I know, and I love you for being so supportive, but tonight is about you and your game."

"We're having a great season. I think tonight's going to be a crowd-pleaser."

"Yeah?"

"Yes. Now, you need to leave so I can do all my weird pregame rituals you make fun of. I want tonight to go off without a hitch."

"Wait until you see my pre-fight bullshit. You'll have plenty of opportunity to get your own back." She giggles as she turns to leave.

"Like what? You can't throw something like that out there and leave me hanging. I didn't have you pegged for the superstitious type."

Shrugging her shoulders, she throws her hands up. "Athletes... we're a superstitious bunch. With greatness comes at least a small amount of crazy."

"Never a truer word spoken." As she disappears down the hall, I can't believe my luck. I snagged the most amazing woman in the world, and she hasn't realized yet that I'm punching way above my weight with her.

I set about putting my kit bag together, triple-checking I have everything I need. I've always been a man of routine during playing season, but this one is unlike any other, full of the biggest upheavals, huge risks, and awesome rewards, and we're not even done yet.

I went into the first game of the season with my life in shambles, having no clue which way was up. If you'd asked me then if I thought Diana and I would figure our shit out and have moved her shit in, I never would've believed it. As I look around, I love the sight of her belongings mingled in with mine, but I can't find a damn thing in here.

When I've got everything I need, I grab my keys, and it's time to go.

Let's do this!

STEPPING out onto the field tonight, the roar of the crowd is electric. My eyes go straight for Diana to where I know she'll be sitting with her family and one security guard that she knows about. She's flanked on either side by Brooke and her dad, just the way I like it. Even from here, I can tell she's smiling, her hands resting on that big, beautiful bump of hers.

"You need to focus on the game first, bro."

"I know. I'm laser-focused."

"On your girlfriend."

"Says the guy ogling his wife."

"Touché. I can't believe you're the guy who's going to make me an uncle. That's so disturbing on so many levels and simultaneously fucking awesome."

"It's the magic sperm, bro."

"Can you two stop staring at them for a few hours and play the game. We only have all of New York counting on us." Coach is being a little dramatic, and I can't pass up the chance to correct him.

"Technically, only half of New York. The rest are praying we crap out, or are we no longer counting Mets fans as New Yorkers anymore?"

"Always with the smart mouth. You're lucky you have a good swing, Nash, and even luckier that woman agreed to go on a date with you, never mind spawning your young. What the hell is it about the Lexington women that has you both so strung out? Let's play ball, fellas."

As he walks away, we look at each other, then up at the stands.

"We're attracted to women who have a propensity to vomit." I cross my arms over my chest, puffed up like I've just solved a Rubik's cube in under five seconds.

"Holy shit, you're right. Brooke blew chunks on me the night I met her, and Dee does nothing *but* puke on you. Fuck, there's something seriously wrong with us."

"And yet, those two women up there are fucking perfect."

"We must have done something right."

"Are you guys here for decoration or what? Take off your bras and get to work." Coach shouts from the dugout.

With the first swing of my bat tonight, I knock it out of the park, jogging an easy home run to warm me up. There's nothing like the crack of a new ball against my bat—when I catch that sweet spot, guaranteeing a phenomenal hit—to make my cock feel as big as the bat itself. The Astros know I'm coming for them tonight.

Anders is on fire, throwing some of the best pitches of his career. I've been watching the screens from the dugout, my pulse racing every time Diana's face appears, clapping and cheering. I've assumed the role of protective baby daddy with ease, and even in the middle of a game, I'm thinking to myself—she needs to stop bouncing around. Her bladder's the size of a walnut now, and I really don't want to explain to the media that she peed herself on the Jumbotron.

We take a few knocks, but as the innings come and go, we're in the stronger position coming into the bottom of the ninth. We only need one run to break a tie and take the game, but I never count my chickens when it comes to baseball. I'm the last one up with *no* bases loaded. I shouldn't feel this confident, but tonight, there's something in the air. The atmosphere's sizzling, Diana's in the crowd, and I can taste the impending victory as I step up to the plate.

I look to where she's sitting as my fingers flex the bat, finding a comfortable grip, hoping for one last beaming smile, but what I see is something else entirely. Diana is hunched over, clutching her stomach.

If I drop the bat and run out on the game, a rookie is going to be pulled off the bench and thrown to the wolves. It's as good as ensuring a tie. *But this is Diana.*

I turn to Anders, who's already getting on the phone and pointing up at the screens. Brooke is standing at Diana's side, signally between her legs like a maniac. *Fuck!* Her water just broke. This can't be happening right now.

The Astros pitcher is a friend of mine, and he steps back, giving me a moment to compose myself as the crowd becomes focused on what's happening in the stands rather than on the field. I need to go to her. It's one game. *She's everything.*

Anders comes sprinting up to the plate.

"I've got to go, Anders. She's in fucking labor."

"I called her mom from the phone in the dugout. Her water broke."

"I'm out. Tell the team I'll make it up to them. I'll buy them all Lamborghinis for Christmas."

"Wait. Diana grabbed the phone out of Martha's hand and screamed at me. Verbatim. *Tell Lincoln Nash that if he even thinks about coming up here before winning this game, I will personally kick his fucking ass. I'm pushing a human out of my vagina tonight, so he better knock it out of the damn park.* Then she hung up."

"She'll literally kick my ass."

"I know. You can do this, Linc."

"The run part or the dad part?"

"Both. Now hurry up, you have a girlfriend to get to the hospital. The team doctor is already on his way up to the stands, and an ambulance is on its way." He pulls me in for a hug, slapping my back so hard it hurts. "We're having a baby today."

"Holy fuck. I'm going to be a dad today." I swing the bat in my right hand, grounding myself with the one constant I've had my whole life—baseball. I can do this. "Anders," I shout, as he jogs off the field, "I have to run the bases for it to count. You need to go now! Get to Diana for me. I can't do this without you."

"I've got you, bro!" He takes off at a sprint, the crowd going insane as I step back up to the plate. It's louder than any World Series game in here right now, tens of thousands of fans cheering for us. Not the Yankees. For Diana and me. For her when she needs it most, and for me until I can get to her.

There's no time for messing around. No room for error. It's balls to the wall. Let's see how big mine really are when it matters. The World Series was a schoolboy game compared to this. I take one last glance at Diana before readying myself, correcting my stance, letting my fingers find their grip. I swing at the air a few times, closing my eyes, shutting everything else out. It's just me, the bat, and the soft scent of Diana's perfume lingering on my shirt from earlier tonight.

I can do this.

Everything stops, the cacophony of sound drowned out by my heartbeat thundering in my chest, creating a vacuum. A moment suspended in time. I take a deep breath, filling my lungs, calming my mind as if every hit since the first time I picked up a bat at the age of four was leading to this. To her. To the beginning of our family.

When my eyelids flutter open, I'm bombarded with a screaming stadium, waiting with bated breath to see if I walk it off and take the draw or man up and do what Diana asked of me.

The pitcher pulls back, and I watch in slow motion, the ball hurtling toward me at ninety miles an hour. It's a split-second decision, knowing where the strike zone is going to be and committing to the hit.

There's no second swing tonight, no second chances.

My bat connects, smashing the ball sky-high with every ounce of force I have left in me. All I can do now is run and pray it doesn't come down in the hands of an Astros outfielder.

I take off at a sprint, tossing the bat aside as I run hell for leather, the crowd erupting in a collective roar as I speed toward first base.

I round second.

There's no stopping now. Even if I did, there's no one left to bat. I keep running, glancing up at the screen as the ball comes barreling down, every Astros outfielder in the vicinity trying to get to it.

It hits the deck as my foot connects with third base. I dig deep, knowing it's a race between them and me. Can they get the ball back to home plate before I get there?

My lungs are burning as I push myself, thinking of Diana and the world of pain she's in right now. She's all that matters. I'll outrun every fucker on this field for one reason, and one reason only, because she wants to see me win before she brings our daughter into the world.

With home plate in sight, I gauge my slide, the difference between victory and defeat.

The familiar thud of my foot slamming against the plate sends a vibration ricocheting through every bone in my body, and I have no idea if it was enough. Did I get to it before the ball landed in the catcher's mitt?

I don't even wait to find out, scrambling to my feet and taking off toward the stands, tracking Diana as the medics help her down to the tunnel.

The fans are going wild as my teammates rush the field, following hot on my heels. I glance at the screen just as *HOME RUN* flashes in bold letters before the camera pans back to me, sprinting across the field and into the stands, to Diana.

I have the biggest fucking smile on my face right now and tears in my eyes as I reach her.

"Diana!"

She grabs my face, her lips crashing down on mine in a soul-shattering kiss. "You're so lucky you hit that. If you made me wait while I'm in labor, I was going to be so pissed."

"I hit that eight and a half months ago, that's what got you here in the first place." I couldn't resist, knowing it would make her laugh.

"Now is the time you're going to make that joke? Really?"

"Sorry, it was too obvious to pass up."

"That hit was incredible."

My mind is exploding. "Why are we still talking about baseball? You're in labor. Let's go have a baby."

"Good idea. I need the OB and the good drugs now."

"I'm on it, but let's ride in the ambulance." I gesture to her pants which are soaking wet with amniotic fluid. I know that because I've read every pregnancy book available and yet feel completely unprepared. "We're not ruining the leather interior of my car with all this."

"I swear to God, Lincoln Nash, I'll sucker punch you in the nuts."

"Duly noted."

As promised, an ambulance is ready and waiting at the team exit. Once they have Diana safely loaded, Brooke hands me her purse. "We're going to follow right behind you. Anders will go and grab your stuff from the locker room. Phone, keys, and whatever else you keep in there. Hopefully, a clean change of clothes."

"Yeah, I don't want to meet my daughter for the first time in an ash-stained, funky-smelling uniform."

"Trust me, she doesn't want to meet you that way either," Diana quips from the rig. "Can we get going? I'm kind of in the middle of something here. You can coordinate by text. My phone's in my purse."

Brooke practically shoves me up into the ambulance. "Godspeed, Linc. I hope you survive the ride to the hospital with her. She's not the nicest right now."

"She's shoving a human out. Let's see how pleasant you are when it's your turn." I grab the doors and haul them shut. "We'll just catch up with them at the hospital."

I perch on the bench across from Diana, clasping her hand in mine. "How are you feeling, southpaw?"

"Better now that it's just us."

"I'm so sorry I couldn't get to you right away."

Her face contorts, her sweet smile replaced with an agonized grimace as she crushes my hand in a vice-like grip. "Contraction."

"Holy fuck, southpaw. You're hurting me." She tightens her grip.

"You didn't just complain to me about pain. You and your hand can go fuck yourself!"

"I'm sorry. If it were any other woman in labor, I'd agree, but you're a UFC champion, Diana. You're genuinely capable of snapping my bones like a twig." As her contraction subsides, she restores blood flow to my hand and starts laughing. "Should I be really scared now? Laughing is worse than shouting at me in this scenario, right?"

"I love you, Linc. Only you could make me laugh at a time like this. There's a human trying to fight her way out of me at this moment, and you still make me smile."

"I can't believe your water broke in Yankee Stadium."

"Did Anders give you my message?"

"He did. I told him we were taking the draw, and I'd buy the team flashy cars for Christmas to make up for it. Then he came at me with the fact that you were planning to come and kick my ass even though you were in labor, so I figured I better do as I was told."

"I knew you were going to hit it first time."

"Is it big-headed if I say, so did I?"

"Yes, but why change now? I fell in love with an ego maniac, and let's be honest, what you just did out there on the field was hot. You earned your anaconda-swinging moment."

"You thought it was hot?" I give her my best come-hither look as another contraction hits.

I'm a lesser man for it, but there was a slight hesitation before I took her hand on this one.

"Oh my God. Having my face punched *with* a broken nose was less painful than this. What the fucking... fuck!"

"I wish I could take the pain for your, baby."

"So do I, but you wouldn't be able to hack it."

"What?" Her grip tightens, and it's all I can do to swallow a yelp.

"Who are you kidding? You're ready to ask for a morphine drip right now."

One of the EMTs starts checking his watch and flips the switch on the sirens.

"Is everything okay?"

"I just need to monitor a few stats." The deep-set furrow of his brow is ringing alarm bells as he checks her over. "Ms. Lexington, were you feeling any discomfort before your water broke?"

"On and off. I just thought it was Braxton Hicks. I get them all the time. And please, call me Dee."

"Did you notice them happening more regularly in the past twenty-four hours?"

She chances a glance in my direction before answering, which can only mean one thing.

"In hindsight, I've probably been having contractions for at least six hours."

"*Six hours!*"

"I don't need a lecture, Linc."

"Your contractions are two minutes apart. I'm going to need to examine you and see how far along you are."

"Okay." I help Diana out of her pants and pull the blanket they provided over her to give her as much modesty as she can have under the circumstances.

"Why didn't you tell me you were hurting? You shouldn't have even been at that game."

"Because I knew you'd worry, and I wanted tonight to be special."

Why would she say that? *Brooke.*

"I am going to wring your sister's neck when I see her."

"Don't be mad. She didn't tell me anything. I guessed something was going on when my mom and dad were hinting for an invite, and Brooke only said that you had a small surprise planned for me and the baby. I don't know anything other than that. It doesn't really matter now, does it?"

Another contraction hits, and the EMT reaches for a bag on one of the shelves. "Can you give her something to help with the pain until we get to the hospital?"

"Dee, are you feeling the urge to push?"

"Oh my God, make it stop."

"Diana, look at me, baby." I sweep her hair off her face, trying to focus her attention on the sound of my voice. "Do you feel like you need to push?"

"Yes! Isn't that the whole fucking point? Every fiber of my being wants to push."

The EMT looks to me, his face stern, a conversation passing between us without a word spoken. This baby is coming now.

I start stripping off my uniform caked in red ash. "Just breathe, Diana. Everything's going to be fine."

"Jesus, Linc, you can't fix everything with the anaconda, for crying out loud. Why are you taking off your clothes?"

"Because we're about to have this baby, and I'm going to get up behind you and sit at your back the way we practiced, okay? I don't want you or the baby getting covered in baseball dirt off my ass."

"I am not having this baby in the back of an ambulance on a random street, sitting in traffic in New York. I'll hold it in until we get to the hospital."

I get up behind her, pulling her back to my chest, propping her up into an almost sitting position. "You can't hold it in, southpaw. You're as strong-willed as they come, but this is one time nature will take its course. You can do this."

"I can't." Tears fill her eyes as the overwhelming desire to push takes over.

"You're already doing it."

"The baby's crowning. You're doing great, Dee. Next contraction, bear down and give me a big push, okay."

She drops her head back against my chest. "It wasn't supposed to be like this."

"Whatever way it happens, we're going to meet our daughter today, Diana. The *where* doesn't matter."

"It matters to me! I wanted one thing to happen the right way for us. This was supposed to go according to plan for us, Linc."

"As long as you and the baby are healthy, it's going to plan."

"You know what I mean. Stop trying to make it okay. I'm about to give birth in a moving vehicle. Nothing about this is the way it was supposed to happen."

"But everything about *us* works, Diana. Maybe we got here in an unorthodox way, but we're here, and we're together, and I love you."

"I love you too." I hold her tight as she gives an almighty push.

"You're doing great, Dee. The baby's head is out. Same again on the next contraction, and you'll be meeting your little one." The EMT gives us a reassuring nod as we speed through the streets of Manhattan.

"Linc, I'm scared."

"You've done all the hard work, and I'm in awe of you. You can do this. One more big push, and you get to meet your daughter."

"That's what I'm afraid of. I'm not ready. What if I'm a terrible mom?"

"You'll be a wonderful mom. You're strong and tough when you need to be, but you're also incredibly sweet and kind and..."

"Holy son of a motherfucker!"

CHAPTER TWENTY
DIANA

EVERY FIBER of my being contracts, a force of nature so intense, ripping my body apart as I bear down for one last push. A white-hot fire consumes me, searing pain followed by the sound of our baby girl crying as she enters the world.

The EMT immediately places her on my chest and covers her with a blanket, my heart filled with love the second I lay eyes on her.

"Oh my God. She's so tiny." I lean my head back against Linc's chest, more exhausted than I've ever been in my life. He showers my face with kisses as he sweeps my sweat-slicked hair off my cheek. "You're amazing. I love you so much."

"I love you too, Daddy."

"Holy shit. Oops. Sorry, princess." He reaches forward, tracing his finger down her cheek with tears in his eyes. "She's so beautiful. Look at her little hands." As he runs the pad of his thumb over the back of her tiny fist, I notice there's something in her fist.

"Linc, she's holding onto something."

"What? She literally went from your womb to here. There's nothing to hold onto."

"Can you just check?" Her fingers are so cute, but she's definitely clutching something.

Linc tries to coax her hand open, scared she's too fragile, but she's got a tight fist on her—a little fighter in the making.

Her fingers uncurl, releasing whatever it is into her daddy's hand. "What the hell is this?" He holds it out to me, and I can't believe my eyes.

"It's my IUD." He drops it like a hot potato.

"You're messing with me, right?"

"I couldn't make it up even if I tried." I'm trying not to laugh, but Linc's face is a picture right now.

"She's your daughter. Who else would give birth to a baby who comes out clutching her victor's scepter? One night of unprotected sex... no problem. IUD... hold my breast milk. Only a Lexington girl would keep a hold of the damn thing to prove everyone else wrong."

"That's my girl."

"You're going to be a real ball-buster, aren't you, baby?"

"She's perfect." I can't believe she's finally here, covered in goop and the spitting image of her daddy. "I think she looks like you."

"Poor baby. Don't listen to Mommy. I think you look like her for sure."

"Really?"

"She has cute dark hair."

"We both have dark hair, Linc."

"Does it matter who she looks like? She's all the good parts of you and me."

I marvel at every tiny detail of her face, wondering if the name we agreed on is right for her.

"Do you think she looks like a Lilah?" I tear my gaze away from my beautiful daughter just long enough to watch Linc grin ear to ear at the mention of it.

"Yeah, she's definitely our Lilah."

I delicately caress her tufty little hair with my finger. "Welcome to the world, Lilah Lexington Nash."

"We're parents." Linc seems a little shellshocked as the words come out of his mouth.

"Would you like to hold your daughter... Daddy?"

"Are you sure? I have no idea what I'm doing."

"Me either, but we'll figure it out together."

He gently works his way out from behind me, terrified he's going to hurt us. I make sure Lilah is snug in the blanket before Linc lifts her off my chest, and I already miss the warmth of her teeny, little body against my skin. I didn't know it was possible to have such a capacity for love in an instant.

Seeing Linc hold our daughter for the first time makes me fall in love with him all over again. Rocking her gently in his muscular arms, he melts under her spell in seconds. "Hey, Lilah, I'm your daddy. You sure know how to make an entrance, little one. We're going to have quite the story to tell you about the day you were born when you're old enough."

The ambulance comes to a halt. We're finally at the hospital— better late than never. The EMT who was driving tells us to wait for him to open the rig, and I wonder where he thinks I plan on going right now? I just gave birth, my legs are spread eagle, and there's a stranger staring at my vagina to deliver the placenta. Throw in the fact that Linc is rocking Lilah in his underwear, and rest assured, we're staying put.

As the doors swing open, there's a collective gasp before a familiar voice bellows from the ambulance bay. "What the fuck, bro? Why the hell are you naked? It finally happened. You grew a uterus and gave birth." Anders.

Under normal circumstances, I'd be horrified, but I find myself laughing uncontrollably, imaging the sight of us in this particular snapshot moment. "Could you all go ahead and avert your eyes until my legs are closed?"

Brooke and my mom are already crying tears of joy and thank God my dad has his back turned. My sister ignores my plea for privacy, jumping up into the ambulance to catch a glimpse of her niece.

"You gave birth on the way here. Honestly, Dee, are we ever going to be around for the major moments of your lives?"

"My water broke all over your shoes. What more do you want from me, sis?" She's not even listening to me as she sets eyes on Lilah for the first time, mesmerized by her in an instant.

"I can't believe you guys made her. She's incredible."

"She's amazing, isn't she?" Linc is every bit the proud peacock. I'd say he's fanning his feathers, but he's currently wearing nothing but a pair of boxer shorts, and Brooke is quick to point it out.

"I can't listen to a word you're saying right now, Linc. Your nipples are marring my enjoyment of my brand-new baby niece. Do I even want to know why you're not wearing any clothes?"

"You know what he's like, sis. He saw my legs open and thought it was an invitation."

"Laugh all you like, but I didn't want Diana, or this little munchkin, covered in my home run cruddy uniform." He nuzzles Lilah's nose. "Isn't that right, princess? I didn't want you and Mommy getting some nasty infection from my funky clothes. They can all laugh, but I don't care. I'll walk around this hospital all day long in my boxers if it means I get to snuggle with you."

Brooke's all doe-eyed and broody as she watches Linc with the baby.

"Anders, I think your wife's ovaries just imploded! You better come get her before she gets any big ideas."

"We're ready to get you inside. If everyone could give us some room, that would be great." The EMTs shoo Brooke out of the rig, and I catch sight of my mom waiting patiently, excited to meet her first granddaughter.

"Linc, maybe my mom could hold Lilah while you put some pants on. I think Anders has your bag with him." There's a sadness in his eyes, but it's fleeting, replaced with wonder when Lilah wriggles in his arms.

"Of course." He carefully steps down from the back of the ambulance, unfazed that he's naked but for a pair of boxers. I love him so much. "Martha, I'd like you to meet your granddaughter, Lilah Lexington Nash."

My mom clasps her hand over her mouth when she sees Lilah for the first time, a little bundle of blanket and a shock of black hair. "She's so precious."

"Would you like to hold her?"

"I'd like that very much."

Linc places our daughter gently into my mom's arms, tearing himself away just long enough to slip into a pair of jeans and a hoodie from the bag Anders brought with him. I watch as they hug it out, Anders being the closest thing to family Linc's had for so many years. It warms my heart to know he has his brother—in every way that counts—here with him today. When they're done with their bromance, everyone congratulates him, including my dad, which truly warms my heart.

I've always taken my family for granted. I'm the first to admit it, but Linc has made me appreciate what I have. Parents who've loved and supported me throughout my life, championing my dreams. A sister who's willing to give birth to a cardigan to protect me. And now, I have Linc and Lilah. We've started our own little family, and he's already an amazing dad.

Linc is back at my side as they lift me out on the gurney. "How are you feeling?"

"Ready for a hospital bed and some pain meds."

"You did amazing, southpaw. If I weren't already head over heels in love with you, this would've clinched the deal for sure."

"Can you bring me Lilah? I don't want her way from us, and everyone's going to have to wait for a while until we get settled inside."

"I'm on it."

My mom is besotted with Lilah, already humming a lullaby she used to sing to me when I was a kid. Linc tells everyone what's happening and that they'll have to wait for some snuggle time.

It's an odd feeling as my mom places Lilah in my arms. We have this shared experience that didn't exist a few hours ago. Suddenly, I see her in a different light, a lifetime of love viewed through a kaleidoscope.

"I'm so proud of you, sweetheart."

"Thanks, Mom. She's kind of great, right?" All is well in the world with Lilah back in my arms.

"Just like her momma." She leans in, wrapping her arms around me the way only a mother can, pressing a kiss to my cheek. "I love you, darling. You, Linc, and this little one are going to be such a beautiful family." She follows my gaze to Linc. "You picked a good man, Dee. That boy would go to the ends of the earth and back for you."

"I know."

My heart is full as we get settled in our room, having some quiet time, just the three of us before we're inundated with visitors.

"Are you sure you're okay with my family swarming around the hospital?"

"Of course. I love that they're all here."

We haven't really spoken about it before now, but I want to put it out there so he knows I'm okay with it. "Have you thought about calling your mom to see if she wants to visit?"

"I love you for asking, but my mom has no interest in my life." That same pained expression comes and goes in a flash as Linc stares down at our newborn daughter. "It's her loss, Diana. You and Lilah are my family now."

"If you ever change your mind, we can reach out to her together. We're a team, the three of us."

Linc's lips find mine, tender, firm, and earth-shatteringly beautiful, our fledgling family sealed with a kiss.

"THIS WAS A BAD IDEA. We should just go."

Lilah turned three weeks old today and is changing by the hour. We're sleep-deprived, and our house looks like a tornado hit it, but we've never been happier.

We haven't heard a peep from Linc's mom since Lilah was born, but this morning he decided he wanted to take us to meet her, so we jumped in the car, and here we are. "If that's what you really want, then we can get back in the car and go home, but you came here for a reason."

"It seemed like a good idea in theory, but now that we're here, I'm embarrassed."

"Why?"

"I didn't have the same kind of childhood as you, Diana. That trailer park in front of us is where I grew up. My mom doesn't give a shit that I got out and made something of myself. She hasn't even responded to the messages I left her, letting her know she's a grand-mother. I've been beating my head against a brick wall my whole life, and she's never going to change."

"Then why did you want to come today?" I suspect this visit has more to do with him than it does his mom.

"Because we're a family now. You, me, and Lilah. I asked you to have faith, build a life and a family with me. I feel like you need to see where I came from before I can move on. Before we can move forward. Does that make sense?"

"Yes, but I need you to know, nothing that happens here will change how I feel about you."

"I can't explain it. I need you to know everything before..." Lilah starts fussing, so I lift her out of her stroller and into my arms. "Let's just get this over and done with."

As we're walking toward the entrance to the trailer park, someone shout's Linc's name from the gas station across the street. "Lincoln Nash, as I live and breathe."

There's immediate recognition in Linc's eyes as he turns toward the familiar voice. "Kellan?"

"The one and only."

Even I recognize this guy. "Is that Kellan McKenzie? As in NASCAR Kellan McKenzie?"

"Sure is." They hug like brothers, slapping each other on the back with genuine affection.

"Kellan, I'd like you to meet my girlfriend, Diana."

"The whole world knows about you two. I was watching the game a few weeks back. This must be the little one who was causing all that ruckus."

Kellan McKenzie is the bad boy of NASCAR. He's devilishly handsome, and notorious for fast cars and fast women. I had no idea he and Linc knew each other.

"This is our daughter, Lilah." I love seeing him beam with pride whenever he gets the chance to introduce our little princess to someone new.

"She's a cutie. How long has it been since we last saw each other?"

"Five years, maybe."

"Damn, brother. It's been way too long."

"You should look us up sometime when you're in our neck of the woods."

"I may just take you up on that offer."

"What are you doing back here?"

"Family drama. Nothing worth talking about. You?"

"Thought I'd see if my mom wanted to meet Lilah."

"Things between you two still dysfunctional as ever?"

"Would you expect anything else?"

"No." He looks back toward his car. It sticks out like a sore thumb next to the relics that are kicking about this part of town. "I'm sorry, man, I need to get going, but it was really great seeing you. I'd like to get together with you sometime soon."

"Anytime, brother. My door is always open for you, you know that."

"Still at the same address?"

"Yeah." Linc pulls him in for another hug. "It was really good to see you, Kel."

"It was lovely to meet you, Diana."

"You too, Kellan."

He jogs back across the street, sliding into his car and peeling out of the gas station at break-neck speed.

"How do you two know each other?"

"He was a few years above me at school. We grew up together but sort of lost touch after he moved away. We've seen each other a few times over the years but not enough."

"Hopefully, he'll take you up on your offer and come see us."

"That would be great. He and Anders would be a riot to have in the same room."

"I bet. You and Anders cause enough trouble on your own."

"You love it." He slings his arm over my shoulder.

"I do."

Now that Lilah has stopped fussing, I snuggle her back in her stroller, ready to face the task we came here to fulfill. It's a short walk to the trailer park where Linc grew up, and when he stops outside his mom's place, I imagine Linc as a kid, running around here with a baseball in one hand and a bat in the other. No matter how he feels about it, his experiences here shaped him into the amazing man I know and love with all my heart.

"Sure you don't want to cut and run?"

"I tell you what, if it goes badly, I'll give you a really great blow job when we get home. Will that cheer you up?" There's that playful grin I love so much.

"Fuck this, let's skip to the good part."

The door to the trailer opens, a small, gaunt woman with the same coloring as Linc stands before me, and I can't for the life of me understand why she doesn't want to be a part of her son's life.

"Hey, Mom."

"Lincoln."

"Can we come in? I have some people I'd like you to meet." He shrinks before my eyes.

"I know who they are. I saw you on the TV, making a fool of yourself. Everything's always a big show with you. You were never content to be normal. It had to be flashy. You were too good for working a trade. Too big and fancy to stay here. And then you go and knock up this poor girl and have to make a big song and dance about having a baby."

My heart breaks for him, for the boy he once was.

"Come on, Diana. This was a mistake."

"Can you take Lilah for a moment? I want to talk to your mother real quick."

"It's not worth it. She doesn't care."

"*You're* worth it, goddammit." I turn my attention to his mother. "I'm Diana Lexington, and the sweet little baby in the stroller is your granddaughter, Lilah. Your son is an amazing man. A partner and a father I'm proud to call family. From what I can tell, Linc has grown into a successful, kind-hearted, wonderful man, *despite* your indifference to him. We came here today to offer you the chance to know him and to get to know his daughter, but the truth is, he *is* too good for this place. Not because it's a trailer park or he had aspirations that were outside the norm, but because he's too good for *you*. You don't deserve his love, but he gives it anyway. He owes you nothing, and yet you continue to take pieces of him with your vitriol."

She doesn't bat an eyelid. Linc was right, this was a mistake. My hands ball into fists at my side, the fighter in me ready to knock her the fuck out.

"Our door will always be open to you, Ms. Nash, simply because you gave birth to the love of my life. It's up to you if you chose to walk through it or fester here in your resentment and hate. Linc is a fucking legend, lady!" I turn on my heels and walk away, Linc following close behind.

"Wow. You unleashed Dee Lex on her. I'm impressed."

"I'm sorry. I just don't understand why she's so horrible to you. You're amazing."

"And as long as you think that, I'm a happy man. You and Lilah are what matter. As long as I'm being the guy you both need me to be, then I'm a success."

"I shouldn't have gone off on her like that."

"Five-year-old me was jumping for joy that she got a taste of her own medicine. I particularly liked how eloquent you were until the very end. Shouting 'he's a fucking legend, lady' was *epic*. I thought you were about to throw down."

"Oh God."

"Don't do that. You stood up for me, and that's everything. Protective is sexy on you, Diana."

"I'm always going to be protective of you. Remember what you told me. I'm yours, and you're mine. I've got your back, and I always will."

"I love you."

"I love you too."

"I have one more place I want to take you today. You up for it?"

"Sure. Do I get to punch things? My adrenaline's pumping, and I'm spoiling for a fight."

"No punching today. Save that for when we get you back into training for Vegas."

"Do you really think I can get back to where I need to be?"

"After what I just witnessed, I'd say, hell, yeah."

"I'm so sorry this didn't go the way you wanted it to."

"I had zero expectations of my mother. Today was for you and me. I wanted to share this part of my life with you before closing this chapter and moving on."

"Are you going to tell me where we're going?"

"Nope." He flashes me that panty-melting smile of his, and I know he's up to something.

"YOUR BIG SURPRISE IS YANKEE STADIUM?" We pull up at the player's entrance, but it's like a ghost town. There's no game tonight or training session, so I guess Lilah is getting a private tour of Daddy's work.

"Trust me."

We head inside, the stands empty, the hallways eerie without the hustle and bustle of game day. "What are we doing?"

"You'll see." He seems a little on edge as we make our way to the tunnel and out onto the field.

I'm not prepared for what I find when we emerge onto the iconic diamond of Yankee Stadium. I haven't been back here since the day I very publicly went into labor. Now, I'm cradling Lilah in my arms with tears welling in my eyes as I take in my surroundings.

There are candles everywhere with a path mapped out around all the bases. "What's all this?"

"I had a big flashy plan the day you went into labor." We come to a stop on home plate. "I was going to do this huge grand gesture after the game and before our little peanut princess arrived, but she had other ideas. I was standing right here when I saw you in labor, ready to bring our daughter into the world."

"You and everyone else in here. I was mortified." He lifts Lilah from my chest, cradling her in one arm, taking my hand and walking me to first base.

"You let me get a bit further than first base the night we kissed in Vegas. I knew then that you were going to change my life for the better. To be fair, I thought it was going to be with some mind-blowing sex that night, but you tossed me out on my ear."

We continue on, leisurely strolling to second base. "The night I tried to go all old fashion on you, cook dinner, and beg to be more than your booty call, we conceived Lilah. There will never be enough words to tell you how lucky I consider myself every day to have both of you in my life."

By the time we reach third base, tears are streaming down my face. "The day we moved in together, I knew you were the person I wanted to spend the rest of my life with. We may not always get along, but there will never be a day I don't love you with every fiber of my being."

Stepping back onto home plate, Linc drops to one knee with Lilah still nestled in the crook of his arm. "The day I watched you give birth to Lilah, I knew beyond a shadow of a doubt that I punched way above my weight with you, and I'm the luckiest guy in the world to be loved by you, Diana. I loved you before I knew what loving you really meant. You're the most beautiful, kind, loving, ball-busting, phenomenal woman I've ever known. I love you, and I want to keep loving you every day for the rest of our lives."

He reaches into his pocket, pulling out a small red *Cartier* box. "Diana Lexington, will you marry me?"

"Yes!" I drop to my knees, cupping his face in my hands as my lips crash down on his.

"Careful not to smush, Lilah."

I hold him for the longest time. "You asked."

"You doubted me? You'd have had the ring on your finger when Lilah was born if you hadn't gone into labor."

"You were going to propose that day?"

"Yep. I had a whole thing planned with the team and a human cage. It was going to be super cute."

"This is perfect. Just you, me, and Lilah."

"I couldn't agree more."

"I have one condition for setting a wedding date."

"Name it."

"I get my title back first."

"That was a given. You don't think I'm planning on marrying an ex-UFC fighter, do you? I know you, Diana. This is something you need to do for you, and you alone. Me and Lilah... we're here for it, ready to cheer you on all the way."

"What did I do to deserve you?"

"I'm not sure, but it must have been pretty awesome. How romantic is this?"

"It's amazing, and so are you."

We lie under the night sky in a field of candlelight, just the three of us, and I thank my lucky stars for the amazing man by my side and our beautiful daughter laying asleep on my chest. We talk and laugh for hours, making plans for the future. Tonight was perfect. Everything about it was stunning, elegant, and more than I ever could have dreamed of.

As Linc pulls me to my feet, he envelops me in his arms.

"I'm still getting that blow job you promised when we get home, right?"

CHAPTER TWENTY-ONE
DIANA

ONE YEAR LATER

USUALLY, I'm pumped and ready, adrenaline coursing through my veins as I stand in the wings, listening to the crowd chanting my name when they start playing my song. Tonight is different. I haven't fought in almost two years now, and as I begin the walk to the cage, there's a churning in the pit of my stomach as Katy Perry's "Roar" blares through the speakers of the MGM Grand's arena.

Every fight of my life until now has been about me. I had nothing to lose when I stepped into the arena, no one to answer to, and no responsibility to anyone other than myself. This is the first time I feel like I've got something to lose. It's not about the title anymore or even my opponent. Tonight is about me and my journey.

In the past two years, I've challenged myself in ways I never thought possible. The last time I was here, my life looked completely different than it does now. I'd just found out my ex was married, and I was pissed off at the entire male species. I let him take my self-confidence and sense of self-worth and crush it underfoot. Then, bam,

Linc came crashing into my life with all the subtlety and nuance of a bull in a china shop.

Tonight, he's ringside, waiting to cheer me on the way he has been all throughout training, working out and jogging Central Park at ungodly hours with me, pushing Lilah in her stroller.

We brought her with us to Vegas because I couldn't bear to be away from her, so we asked my mom and dad to fly out and babysit during the fight. Brooke and Anders are here, and if I'm not mistaken, Brooke has a slight curve to her stomach that I know all too well. I hid it long enough myself. I figure she'll tell me when she's ready.

Gray is at my side, talking me up with his thick New Jersey brogue, telling me I'm going to crush my opposition and walk away the victor. He's predicting a third-round knockout, but his optimism is doing nothing to calm my nerves. Gray still tries to motivate me the same way he did before I became a mother, and the problem with that is, I am forever changed by the birth of my daughter.

I take a deep breath and remember what Linc kept telling me last night. *Forget about the crowd. Forget about everything else around you. Your biggest fight is with yourself. Tune out the doubts and focus on your body. The natural ebb and flow of movement.*

He was right. If I overthink this, the jabs will be off by a fraction and my footwork clunky, but it's hard not to psych myself out. I close my eyes and try to tune it all out, shaking my arms and legs, letting go of the tension that's been building all day. Nerves are healthy, but fear is not. I've never been afraid of getting hurt before, but there's an unease in the pit of my stomach tonight—not for myself, but for Lilah. She needs me in one piece, not beaten to a pulp.

As I wait for them to announce my entrance, my stomach is on a spin cycle, threatening to make me heave at any moment.

"Get your head in the game, Dee. Where the fuck are you at right now?" Gray braces his hands on my shoulders, snapping me out of my thoughts. "This is the biggest fight of your career. It's your big comeback."

"Don't you think I know that? You pointing it out to me every five seconds for the past two months isn't helpful. I can hear sixteen thousand people screaming, and I've seen the odds on me winning, getting a knockout, or losing. I've studied all of Kayla's fights and moves. Just back the fuck off and give me a minute." I shrug out of his grasp and blow out a few deep breaths.

"We're all out of minutes, Dee. It's time to get back in there and make good on all these months of training. I know you're all sunshine and rainbows of happiness these days, but right now, you need to forget about the fact that you're a mom and go out there with the proper attitude. You're not a mom in the ring, Dee." That's where he's wrong.

"*Shut the fuck up, Gray!* I swear to God I'll pound you into the ground if you don't back the fuck off," I scream in his face.

"That's the Dee Lex I've been looking for. Go get her, killer."

I crack my knuckles one last time—a stupid superstitious ritual—before stepping out of the tunnel to the roar of the crowd, camera flashes blinding me from every angle.

"*Dee Lex. Dee Lex. Dee Lex.*" Thousands of voices band together to create a collective boom that reverberates through every cell of my body, shaking me to my core. This is it. It's now or never.

As I approach the cage, I search the crowd for Linc, knowing that he's the lone voice in the crowd, truly chanting my name—*Diana*. I know he's ringside—cage side—whatever you want to call it, and the moment I spot him, we lock eyes, and I hold his gaze in a desperate attempt to block everyone else out. He knows me better than anyone, but that's a double-edged sword. He's more worried about my safety than anyone in this arena. I can see it in his face as much as he's trying to hide it behind a big smile and puffed-up chest.

Shrugging out of my robe with *Diana* emblazoned on the back in large, bold black lettering instead of my customary 'Dee Lex,' I wonder if anyone but Linc will notice. Brooke and Anders are by Linc's side, cheering me on, all three of them clapping and whooping for me.

The closer I get, the more my nerves take hold, and it's written all over my face as I look to them for strength, but Linc, being the man that he is, only sees it as a challenge. Throwing his hands in the air, he starts a freaking Mexican wave that ripples through the crowd.

The camera crew catches on, following the wave as it moves back and forth through the sea of eager spectators, Linc appearing on the Jumbotron. He doesn't notice with his gaze still firmly fixed on me, and when I chance a glance back at him, I can't help but smile, his wry grin and a sly wink taking the edge off my nerves if only for a moment.

Once Kayla makes her entrance and her fans go wild, the announcer gives his little speech, and we step into the cage. This fight has now been two years in the making, the hype so much more than either of us ever planned. The familiar tension of the mat beneath my feet is comforting as we stand face to face. We're roughly the same height, so neither of us towers over the other.

The scents of blood, sweat, and disinfectant hang in the air from the warm-up fights that took place earlier this evening, getting the crowd ready for the headliner—me. I've fought here before and won every time, but never as the main attraction and never as a comeback kid. I became the best in other big venues, but everyone in UFC, male and female, wants to fight at the MGM Grand. This is a defining moment, and I want to savor every second without losing my nerve.

As soon as the bell rings and the first round begins, Kayla comes at me with everything she's got, body slamming me with brute strength over skill, knocking the wind right out of me. There's a collective gasp in the crowd, but I'm quick to extricate myself from underneath her and shake it off. I do *not* get pinned in the first round. I never have, and I'm not about to start now.

The next time she comes for me, I'm ready with a quick dodge and a fast blow to her side, ensuring a sharp pain in her kidney, her groan—all the confirmation I need that I hit the target. We trade blows until round one is under my belt.

The second I retreat to my corner, Gray is in my face with only the cage separating us. "What the fuck? She took you to the ground in the first five seconds." I get that he's pissed, so am I, but I'm just finding my feet. I haven't taken a hit that hard in a very long time, and my body knows it.

"And she didn't do it again. Trust me, she's hurting more than I am after round one."

"You need to pick up your feet. If you miss a single dodge, her fists are like The Hulk."

"I know, Gray. I'm the one taking the fucking hits. I'll move faster in the next round."

"She's slow, and she leaves herself wide open when she swings with her left. She doesn't guard herself at all. Try to take advantage of that where you can."

"Understood." One of my team squirts water into my mouth and another offers a bucket for me to spit. The metallic taste of blood isn't something I'm used to after the first round.

Time to head back in.

Brooke, Anders, and Linc are screaming for me in the front row, but I know they can't do anything for me now. It's all on me as the bell rings for round two.

This time I'm on the offensive. I swing the first punch, giving Kayla no time to block, throw a punch, or attempt a kick. I land a direct blow to her jaw, the sweet sound of bone connecting with bone bringing me enough satisfaction to outweigh the pain it causes my hand.

Next, I head in for a combination of kicks to her side before sweeping the leg, years of muscle memory flooding back in a rush of adrenaline. She's solid muscle, so it requires a lot to take her down, but I do it, and once she's down, I try to pin her, but she manages to throw me off and land a knee to my right side in the process.

Fuck!

The pain of taking a knee to the ribs is intense, like having someone crush you from the inside out. I've definitely cracked a rib, maybe two, but not enough to stop me. This is too big a fight to forfeit. Now, we're both scrambling to stand as this round comes to an end. It's a matter of pride to push myself into an upright position and stride to my corner with confidence.

Before I make it to my corner, Linc is at Gray's side, looking even more concerned than the day I gave birth to Lilah. While Gray barks at me, Linc crouches down at the side, his fingers holding onto the cage as he leans in so I can hear him.

"How many?"

"What?"

"How many ribs do you think you just broke?" His expression is as pained as my side.

"I'm okay, baby. I need you to trust me."

"Stop talking and breathe. You're injured, Diana. How many ribs?"

"At least two, but I'm not stopping." How the hell does he know, just from looking at me? He's a baseball player, not a fighter or a doctor.

"I know. I'm cheering for you." He says nothing else—although he wants to—letting Gray shout a few orders at me before the bell rings for round three. I can't think about him right now or how hard it is for him to see me fight. If I'm going to win, I have to be ruthless. *I have to be Dee Lex.*

Kayla is a fierce opponent, merciless and willing to exploit the injuries she suspects I'm carrying as we move through this round. I respect her for that. I do the same thing but being on the receiving end of it isn't so great. I want to crumple to the ground every time her fist connects with my right side, but I'm trained to fight through the pain. I know I've broken her nose, and I try to make sure she takes as many hits as I can land.

Gray's prediction of a knockout in round three vanishes with the bell, and if I'm honest, I'm just glad I didn't go down with a knockout in this round. We're both fighting hard, each a little slower, our punches and kicks having less impact, but neither of us is ready to give up. With two rounds to go, it's anyone's title.

Every muscle aches, and I know my face must look like a half-chewed caramel already. My left eyelid is swollen and tight, and my lips are split, bottom and top. I haven't taken a beating this hard in a long time. If I can just hold on a little longer and land a winning shot, the title is mine. It doesn't sound like much, but right now, at this moment, it feels like standing at the bottom of Mount Everest and being asked to climb with a broken—I was thinking leg, but I guess ribs are as good a choice as any.

My ribs are in agony with every breath I take, and it's little solace to see my opponent in her corner, bracing herself against the cage as we await the bell for the beginning of round four, struggling to breathe through her bloodied, messed-up nose. That's going to require some plastic surgery to make it right after tonight.

When the bell rings, it takes everything I have to push myself up off my haunches and onto my feet. The crowd is cheering, trying to give us that last boost we need to clinch the win, and I dig deep, finding what little burst of adrenaline I have left in the tank and tackle Kayla with everything I've got.

Grabbing her arm, I twist it in a lock behind her back, and she drops to her knees to avoid a break. This could be it. I can put us both out of our misery and claim my title. Kayla and I are both in desperate need of medical attention, but there's one more round and a minute left in this one, standing between one of us and victory—between both of us and a doctor.

She manages to catch me unaware with her free arm, thrusting her elbow upward, connecting with my ribs, forcing me to loosen my grip. I stumble backward, bile rising in my throat, but I choke it down and let the cage hold me up for just a fraction of a second, my vision swimming as I attempt to keep going until the bell.

One more round.

You can do it.

Just ring the fucking bell already!

I've never been so relieved in my life when the bell rings, and I slump to the floor. Thankfully, I'm already in my corner, and Gray is at my side in a flash.

"Do you have five minutes left in you, or do we need to call it?"

"You need to call it! Look at her." Linc's voice seems distant, even though I know he's less than three feet from me. "She needs a doctor, now. I don't care about the fight."

"I do." Shit. My voice is unrecognizable, I'm so exhausted. "I'm not giving up now, Linc. It's five minutes. I can hold on. We've been working toward this for close to a year."

"I hate to say it, Dee, but I think he's right. You're in agony. One more hit to the gut and your broken ribs puncture a lung."

"*No!* If you stop this fight, Gray, you're fired. Got it?"

"Got it. And if you puncture a lung, I quit. Got it?" He stares me down, ensuring I know he's as serious as a heart attack.

Linc drops to his knees. "Diana, can you hear me?" I nod my head, unable to look him in the eye. "Look at me."

"I can't. If I do, I won't be able to keep going, Linc. You can't get me through this."

"Look at me, Diana, right now, or I swear to fuck, I'm coming in there and stopping this shit. Fucking look at me." He slams his hand against the cage, sending shockwaves rippling through it.

When I meet his gaze, his eyes are thick with unshed tears. "Linc... I can't win. I'm not Dee Lex anymore. I'm not the person everyone came to watch tonight."

"Fucking right you're not. You're Diana-fucking-Lexington. Listen to me. You can do this, Diana. I've watched you battle more than this chick can ever take from you. You're the strongest woman I've ever met. You're right, I can't get you through this, I never could. This is all you, southpaw. Every hard-fought point. All the blood, sweat, and tears, it's all you. You've done this. You got yourself here. I was just standing on the sidelines with our baby girl, loving you, and believing you're a stronger woman for being her mother."

"I'm not when I'm in the ring."

"Bullshit! I watched you give birth, Diana. You stood in a stadium of thousands, in labor, and cheered me to victory. You brought our daughter into the world in a fucking speeding ambulance. You've got this, baby. If you ever listen to anything I say, let it be this. You're strong enough to do this, Diana. Not us, not Gray, and not this crowd. You and you alone. Don't do it for anyone else. I'll love you no matter what. If you want to stop, I'll carry you out of here right now. If you want to fight, then I will cheer the fuck out of this entire stadium for you. Say the fucking word."

The bell rings, and my heart sinks.

"What's it going to be, southpaw. It's your call."

"I'm fighting."

"Then go and win this thing because I'm really turned on by you right now."

"Has anyone ever told you, you're fucked up?"

"You do on a weekly basis."

"I love you."

"I fucking love you, Diana. Now go and show them the woman I fell in love with. Let them see the fucking glitter, southpaw."

As I step back up, I can tell the referee is watching us like a hawk, ready to stop the fight at any moment. In truth, there are a number of refs who would have already called it, but this arena is standing room only, and stopping a championship fight for an injury, unless it's bone protruding visibly through flesh, is a sure-fire way to get yourself blacklisted from refereeing another fight at the MGM Grand.

My ears are ringing long after the bell, my head swimming as I try to focus. The cheers of the crowd seem distant, as if they're miles away, down a tunnel, off in a land far from here, but I dig deep, focusing in on Kayla, throwing everything I have into one final swing of my fist, connecting with her jaw at just the right time for maximum impact.

She crumples like a house of cards, and at this moment, I know she's not coming back from it. The pain in my side as I drop to my knees, pinning her to the mat, is nothing compared to the obliteration of my pride if I don't win this fight. I have no fight left, so it doesn't take much for her to set me off-kilter.

Linc's word echo in my mind. *You're a stronger woman for being her mother*. Lilah. I reach inside myself, unlocking the part of me I thought would hinder me tonight. My daughter is the reason I came back to fighting, why I've pushed myself to the limits tonight. I want her to know she's capable of anything in this life. That no man defines you, but letting yourself be loved by one takes nothing away from the woman you can become.

Lilah gives me the final burst of strength I need to keep Kayla pinned until the referee counts her out.

The crowd erupts as the referee calls it and declares me the winner. *I did it*. I won! As soon as he lifts my hand in the air, tears stream down my face, cameras flashing from all sides, lighting up the arena like the Fourth of July.

Linc comes striding into the cage like he owns the place, large and imposing. For some reason, I thought he'd seem smaller some-how, being on my turf, and yet he stands, towering over me, his stance protective, blocking everyone around us as he envelops me in his warm embrace.

"You did it, Diana. You did it! I'm so fucking proud of you."

My legs go out from under me, but it's okay because Linc takes my weight with ease, my teammate in life, and the only person I want by my side in his moment.

When they present me with my belt, it's the moment I've been waiting for, working toward, and fighting tooth and nail for tonight. This isn't the first time I've won the title, but it means so much more having Linc with me and knowing Lilah is asleep upstairs.

When the interviews are over and my team is done patching me up, I'm too exhausted to even walk. "Linc."

"Yes, champ?" he says with tender adoration.

"Take me to bed."

"Are you trying to get laid right now? Don't get me wrong, baby, what you did out there tonight was hot, but at this very moment, even after them cleaning you up a little, you smell like my jockstrap after a three-day workout in the Mojave Desert, and your face is the color and texture of a bag of rocks, but I still love you. Maybe tomorrow with the lights out." Even a ghost of a kiss is painful in my current state.

"Ouch. You're not allowed to make me laugh right now."

"Sorry, baby." He scoops me into his arms, careful of every bump and bruise, the scent of his cologne soothing my soul. "I think you've done enough for one night. I've got you from here." As he navigates his way through the hotel, every step he takes with me nestled close to his chest hurts, but I have a strange sense of déjà vu, as if we've done this before.

We've done this before.

"It was you. The night my fight got canceled, I fell asleep in the gym but woke up in my hotel suite. *It was you.*"

"Not so much of a white knight back then. More like a horse's ass."

"You carried me up to my room. It was you."

"It was me."

It's always been him, and it will always be him.

Our love story began in the most unconventional of ways. Not a love story at all really, or so I used to think. It was supposed to be simple—no-strings-attached sex—but life had a different plan for us, and I'm so happy it did.

In two years, we've come full circle, finding ourselves back where it all began, right here in Vegas in this very hotel. Linc saw me for who I really am, even when I tried like hell to prove him wrong. I thought being a fighter meant keeping everyone at arm's length, making the first strike to avoid getting hurt. I thought love was a weakness.

Life with Linc and Lilah has taught me that loving someone, and letting them love you back, takes a strength I wasn't sure I had at times. Being vulnerable to another human being, giving your heart to them and trusting they won't break it, is harder than any cage fight.

You can heal from physical wounds, but it's the emotional ones that hold us back. Those are the wars we wage with ourselves, and choosing to let someone in who understands and supports you through the bad times and the good, takes courage.

It took me a long time to overcome my demons and realize that what Linc and I have is worth fighting for. Looking back now, I wouldn't change a thing because my journey gave me Lilah. It brought me to Linc. In him, I found the love of my life, and what a beautiful life it is.

EPILOGUE
LINC

THE VENUE IS STUNNING, the guests have arrived, and I'm standing sweating it out at the altar waiting on my two favorite women in the world to hurry up and walk down the aisle to me.

"Why are you nervous?" Anders is enjoying this. "It's not like Dee's going to be the runaway bride."

"Let's not tempt fate. And stop being so smug. I remember your wedding day, and you were shitting a brick."

"Your daughter is the flower girl. I think it's safe to say Dee's coming." He's right, but there's something about standing here with all our friends and family staring at me that has me on edge. I usually love being the center of attention, but I've been waiting for this day since our first kiss.

When soft strings begin to play and Brooke appears—her floor-length red gown hugging a now visible baby bump—I know it's only a matter of minutes until I set eyes on my bride. My pulse is racing, and all I want to do is marry the woman of my dreams.

There's a collective gasp from our guests as Lilah comes teetering through the doors, looking like the princess we all know her to be—

red on top to match Auntie Brooke, and ivory and 'pumphy' on the bottom, as Lilah would say. We've been practicing for weeks, teaching her to sprinkle rose petals for Mommy from her basket, only a couple at a time. She was doing great, but the moment she spies me, she tips the basket upside down, dumping all the petals in one spot before toddling toward me as fast as her little legs will take her.

"Daddy, Daddy, Daddy!" Why did we pick this church? The aisle is too damn long. I can't wait, so I jog down and sweep Lilah up into my arms.

"Hi, princess. You look so beautiful. Do you want to come with me and wait for Mommy?"

She buries her head against my chest, playing shy as I stride back to the altar, my nerves gone as I hold our daughter in my arms. But nothing prepares me for the sight of Diana when she appears at the other end of the aisle. She's stunning, ethereal in an ivory gown. Her smile lights up the room as she begins her walk, every step bringing her closer to the start of our forever.

By the time she reaches the altar, I'm fighting back tears. I can't cry in front of everyone I know. The entire Yankees team is on the guest list. If I break down, I'll be finding women's underwear and tampons in my locker until I retire.

Talk about a knockout. Corny, I know, but Diana leaves me dumbstruck as I take in every detail. Her dress is gorgeous, hugging every curve to perfection, sultry, sexy, and elegant. It fans out at the bottom—I have no idea what that's called—but it looks amazing on her.

"Hey. Looking hot today, Nash."

"Not looking so bad yourself, southpaw." I give her a sly wink before leaning in to kiss her cheek. "You look breathtaking. Are you ready to become Mrs. Nash?"

"I thought you were changing your name to Mr. Lexington."

"Are we ever going to have a conversation without some kind of jibe?"

"Where's the fun in that?"

It took Diana and me a long time to get here, and the road wasn't a simple A to B, but nothing in life that's worth having is ever easy. We've grown together, built our family on a foundation of love, respect, and above all else, friendship. When I fell in love with Diana, I didn't just find a lover and a partner, I found my best friend. She's the one—the person I want to celebrate the wins with and commiserate the losses. She's the love of my life.

When it comes time to say, 'I do,' true to form, Diana puts up a fight.

"I think you should say it first."

"That's not how we rehearsed it."

"I know, but I want to make sure you actually say it." Our guests chuckle at our playful banter, unable to get through our wedding ceremony without some kind of disagreement.

"Of course, I'm going to say it."

"Okay, why don't we say it together then? On three."

"Have at it, southpaw."

"Three..."

"I do." Her smile widens at the sound of those two little words.

"Two..."

I slide one hand into her cascading loose curls, pulling her to within an inch of my lips. "I do."

"One..."

"*I do*," we exclaim in unison, joining our lives together as one, cementing our future with a sensual kiss, the chemistry that brought us together, tangible in the air between us, dark with promise of a wedding night to remember.

Diana and I are proof that love can find you when you least expect it. Not everything in life has to be conventional or always go to plan—the right steps in the right order. There's a give and take in life, and love is no different. If you want it badly enough and strive to work and grow together, you can face whatever life throws your way.

Diana and I are a formidable team, and when it comes to *us* versus the world, love isn't a ball game... it's a cage fight.

THE END

ACKNOWLEDGMENTS

This book was a tough one for me. Our family endured a huge loss during the writing process, which made comedy feel like a distant memory at times. To my wonderful husband – even in the midst of your grief, you wrapped your arms around our family and reminded me why I choose you, every single day. You pushed me to find a way in the darkness, to connect with my writing and let it soothe my soul. You are the love of my life, and I will forever be grateful to the amazing woman who entrusted me with loving you.

Ria – Thank you for believing that I would find my way Linc and Diana. You never gave up on me, even when I wanted to. Your support and encouragement mean the world to me. I love you more.

Nicki – This was a difficult process for me, and your willingness to work alongside me and get me across the finish line with a book I am so proud of, means so much. I can't thank you enough.

To everyone who has given me words of encouragement along the way, and kept the faith that I could bring Linc and Dee to life, thank you from the bottom of my heart.

To my readers I want to say a huge thank you. Without your support I wouldn't get to wake up every morning and do my dream job. I knew I wanted to fly on the pages of the written word, but you gave me wings.